## "Maybe I should let it go at that. This, too."

He leaned away, his eyes somber on hers. He tilted her chin up with one finger. "Because all I have to offer you is this."

With tears trailing down her cheeks, he lowered his mouth to hers and kissed her. His lips felt firm yet soft, and she wanted to tell him he was wrong. He could care about someone other than his twins and his brother. He could care about her. She sensed it in his kiss.

But was he telling her goodbye? Was that the best thing for Jenna? She'd always known this time would come, that she shouldn't trust him.

For another brief moment it didn't seem to matter. She cared about him, and even with the words between them that should have made her leave now, as he would leave Clara's ranch, she stayed in Hadley's arms...

Dear Reader,

I'm so excited about this latest book in my Kansas Cowboys miniseries! This is Hadley Smith's story (he was the foreman in *The Rancher's Second Chance*), and this bad boy seriously needed reforming. That's now Jenna Moran's job, which she's not quite prepared to take on—along with Hadley's twins.

Twins have always fascinated me. When I was a teenager, my best friend and I used to babysit her cousin's twins. Although as toddlers they were a bit older than my fictional babies, they were equally adorable. Add their five-year-old sister, who was part of our babysitting assignment, too, and we really had our hands full. But the fun more than made up for the trouble!

It's the same way for Hadley in this book—even when he never expected to become a father and doesn't think he'd be very good at it. We all learn the hard way. At first, he doesn't welcome Jenna's involvement, and she's definitely not eager to risk her own heart again. But I hope you enjoy watching these two struggle as they develop a love, and a family, that neither of them dared to dream of.

As always, happy reading!

*Leigh*

# HEARTWARMING

# Twins Under the Tree

—

*Leigh Riker*

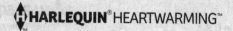
**HARLEQUIN** HEARTWARMING™

Recycling programs
for this product may
not exist in your area.

ISBN-13: 978-1-335-51088-4

Twins Under the Tree

Copyright © 2019 by Leigh Riker

This edition published by arrangement with Harlequin Books S.A.

For questions and comments about the quality of this book, please contact us at CustomerService@Harlequin.com.

® and TM are trademarks of Harlequin Enterprises Limited or its corporate affiliates. Trademarks indicated with ® are registered in the United States Patent and Trademark Office, the Canadian Intellectual Property Office and in other countries.

www.Harlequin.com

Printed in U.S.A.

**Leigh Riker**, like so many dedicated readers, grew up with her nose in a book, and weekly trips to the local library for a new stack of stories were a favorite thing to do. This award-winning *USA TODAY* bestselling author still can't imagine a better way to spend her time than to curl up with a good romance novel—unless it is to write one! She is a member of the Authors Guild, Novelists, Inc. and Romance Writers of America. When not at the computer, she's out on the patio tending flowers, watching hummingbirds, spending time with family and friends, or, perhaps, traveling (for research purposes, of course). She loves to hear from readers. You can find Leigh on her website, leighriker.com, on Facebook at leighrikerauthor and on Twitter, @lbrwriter.

### Books by Leigh Riker

### Harlequin Heartwarming

#### *Kansas Cowboys*

*The Reluctant Rancher*
*Last Chance Cowboy*
*Cowboy on Call*
*Her Cowboy Sheriff*
*The Rancher's Second Chance*

*A Heartwarming Thanksgiving*
"Her Thanksgiving Soldier"
*Lost and Found Family*
*Man of the Family*
*If I Loved You*

Visit the Author Profile page
at Harlequin.com for more titles.

For my family
Because that's what matters most

# CHAPTER ONE

*November*
*Near Barren, Kansas*

"WOULD YOU LIKE to hold your babies?"

The nurse's soft voice reached Hadley as if it had come down a long tunnel, the words echoing inside him. He stared through the big window of the nursery in Farrier General Hospital, where the two little infants wrapped in pink and blue blankets, looking for all the world to him like a pair of burritos, wriggled in their plastic isolette. One tiny hand waved in the air as if to say hello. Another set of china-blue eyes gazed straight at him. They were less than an hour old—and they had no mother.

Hadley couldn't seem to grasp the notion. Only this morning Amy had pressed his hand to her swollen abdomen. "I think it's today," she'd said with an angelic smile, not afraid at all of the painful process to come. She should have been.

Before she'd even turned thirty, Amy was no more. "Complications during delivery," the doctor had tried to explain, but nothing registered with Hadley. The words banged around in his skull like so much mumbo jumbo, and even Sawyer McCord's comforting hand on his shoulder couldn't make it real.

Hadley had stumbled from the waiting room down the brightly lit hallway in a daze, and he was still in it. Underneath the fog that had taken over his brain, though, something else kept demanding his attention, tapping at his memory and telling him to pay notice. Hadley just couldn't remember what that was.

The nurse repeated her question, then said, "We have a small lounge you can use." She gently took his arm and led him a short distance away to the open door of a room. "I'll bring them to you."

"No," he began, heart in his throat. Even after the long months of waiting, he wasn't ready; he'd told Amy often enough that he would never be ready, which had only led to yet another of their usual impasses.

But the nurse had already disappeared

through the door across the way where Hadley was able to pick out the low murmur of voices among the other nurses. He saw one of them swipe at her eyes.

This was not the happy occasion it should have been—most of all, for Amy—but Hadley didn't quite know how to grieve. They'd separated earlier in the year, but during one last night together they'd created two new lives. The news that she was pregnant had cut short their divorce proceedings.

He'd promised to stay with her until the babies were born, then they'd decide about the future.

The situation now seemed bizarre, and everything in Hadley's life had been temporary. His whole approach to things was what he called the finger-in-the-dike method, plugging up one hole as it sprang a leak, then the next. He didn't stay long anywhere he happened to land. He'd never had a home, a real family. What was he going to do now with the twins?

In the lounge, he sank onto the faux-leather couch, trembling inside. Trying to steady himself, Hadley looked down at his blue chambray shirt, faded jeans and scuffed boots. Even in their better moments, he was never the guy Amy had hoped he could become.

When the nurse stepped into the room again, he startled. "Baby Girl," she announced, carrying two bundles, one on each arm, "and Baby Boy. Have you chosen names for them, Mr. Smith?"

"No," he said, pulse stuttering in alarm. He'd left those choices, and most others, to Amy. He should have paid more attention.

He considered making another protest—what did he know about babies?—but the nurse transferred one twin, then the other, into his hastily outstretched arms. He could hardly have refused to take them; they would have ended up on the floor. Since the cover and the first mini cap were blue, he must be holding the boy. Next, in pink...the girl. "God, they're small," he muttered.

"Yes, but not preemies. They weighed in almost the same, remember, just over five pounds each. And healthy. Their Apgar scores were off the chart." She smiled, looking misty-eyed. "Go ahead, you can touch them. They won't break."

Hadley wasn't sure of that. He tried to

repress the image, but he couldn't help but note that the babies were no bigger than two sacks of potatoes, together maybe a quarter the weight of a good saddle.

He'd seen birth before…at least on the ranch. Give him a laboring cow to manage, let a newborn calf slide into his hands, and he knew exactly what to do. Its mama soon took over, and Hadley's job was done. He'd once reminded Amy's doctor of that, and Amy had chided him for comparing her to cattle. But he had no idea what to do with these two little babies.

He decided not to share this sum total of his experience with the nurse, who kept giving him weird looks anyway.

Saying, "I'll leave you with them," she vanished into the hall.

A fresh spurt of panic shot through him. What was he supposed to do? Even with his friends' kids, he'd only watched, never taking part in the childcare.

"Wait," he called after the nurse, but she didn't hear him. She'd promised to come back soon, but how long would that be? Minutes? An hour? He sat rigid on the sofa, his head throbbing. Already his right arm ached from the slight, warm weight resting against it, and something niggled at the edges of his mind again, then flitted off. In his numbed state, what was he missing? Then the boy snuffled, and Hadley's pulse lurched. Could he breathe all bound up like that?

With one finger Hadley nudged the blanket aside and saw a little face staring up at him, blue eyes wide and intent, the most focused look he'd ever seen. "Hey, pal," Hadley murmured. He blinked but his focus had somehow quit for the second time that day; the first had been when he learned Amy hadn't survived. The tiny girl's cover slipped, and there she was, too.

Like her brother, the baby had Amy's reddish-gold hair, and Hadley swore he could see Amy's face. Her nose, her lips, her chin. Well, maybe his ears, but that was all he could see of himself in the little girl. *Ah, Amy.* She would never experience this awesome sight. He noisily cleared his throat. "Look at you, sweetie pie."

She reached out her hand again, as she'd done earlier through the nursery window. A random motion or was she seeking *him*? When Hadley dared to touch her, she wound her impossibly small fingers around his and held on much tighter than he would expect from such a little mite, and his heart clenched. Her skin felt creamy and smooth. She smelled like…innocence. Her nails were perfect, translucent. An all-around miracle, as birth always was.

When Sawyer McCord suddenly appeared in the doorway in his white coat, Hadley couldn't speak.

Sawyer's dark blue gaze softened. "Nothing like it, is there?"

"Nothing," Hadley managed to say. He didn't suppose they meant the same thing.

Odd as it seemed, though, theirs was a shared experience. Sawyer and his wife, Olivia, had become the parents of a son only last spring. Hadley looked from one twin to the other, uncertain which seemed more vulnerable, sweeter.

Gazing at him, Sawyer had folded his arms as if he expected Hadley to try to shove the newborn twins at him, then run, the big tough cowboy who only wanted the open range and a horse of his own. He'd done bad stuff in his life, inherited bad genes, but… He gazed down at the squirming babies in his arms, and his whole being turned to mush. He hadn't been a good husband, at least not the one Amy had wished for. He sure hadn't wanted to have kids who might turn out like him. The one family member who'd relied on him years ago, Hadley had let down—to put it mildly.

If he wanted to live by the cowboy's code of honor, which Hadley did, he needed to accept the consequences of his own actions now. Never mind his rocky, on-again, mostly off-again relationship with Amy. That was, sadly, over.

In a few short moments, he'd morphed from a possibly divorced man into a widower, then a father. And finally he knew what to do. This would be different from his marriage. These were Amy's babies, always would be, but they were also his. What other choice was there? "Guess I'm a daddy now," he told Sawyer.

Because no way would he let anyone else have them. Once before, he'd given up someone he should have cared for, and it wouldn't happen again. Looked like he wasn't going anywhere. For now.

That was when he glanced up and saw the woman standing frozen in the doorway. And at last Hadley remembered the other problem that had been circling, half-formed yet unreachable, through his head. Jenna Moran would have been his easy way out.

Instead, he had a fight on his hands.

"I GOT HERE as soon as I could," Jenna said. "I can't believe this has happened. How terrible."

She'd been crying ever since her friend Olivia, who'd heard the news from her husband, Sawyer, called. During the drive from her apartment building to the hospital, Jenna had sobbed at the wheel. Poor Amy. The friendship they'd nurtured as neighbors over the past months of her pregnancy had just ended abruptly, and Jenna would never see Amy again. Which seemed impossible.

Sawyer touched her shoulder. "It's a sad day, Jenna. I'll leave you two to talk." He said a few low words to Hadley Smith, who forced a brief smile. Then Sawyer swept from the room in a blur of dark hair and broad shoulders that, unlike Hadley, she imagined would willingly carry the weight of the world. She was surprised Hadley was still here.

The consensus in town before Amy's loss was that Hadley would flee as soon as the twins arrived. Now he was an unlikely single dad. But from what Jenna knew, largely from Amy, she couldn't imagine this rough cowboy sticking around long enough to change diapers.

The cold look in Hadley's eyes, a penetrating steel blue, didn't change her mind about him, not that she was normally given to judging other people. But even physically—with his powerful, athletic build—Hadley seemed too tall, too big and, most of all, too remote to be a daddy. Those traits reminded Jenna of her own father, who had either neglected her or unleashed his anger on her. According to Amy, Hadley had a temper, too. She refused to meet his stare.

She knew what her friends in their Girls' Night Out group called him. The Bad Boy of Barren. There were others in town who were attracted to his rugged good looks and that brown, nearly black hair, but Jenna couldn't see past the picture Amy had painted of Hadley.

"Well," he said, "I know why you're here. And you're wasting your time." His mouth had tightened. "My kids don't need a stand-in mother."

"You mean a standby *guardian*," Jenna

corrected him. She'd never heard the term until a few months ago. "Amy asked me if I would be the twins' guardian, and I said yes." Because Jenna, who was unfailingly loyal, supported her friends. "But I never imagined anything terrible would actually happen to her."

"I didn't expect Amy to die, either."

Jenna blinked. "I wish with all my heart she hadn't. But you must have known about the court hearing to appoint me guardian." The judge would have made it official for Jenna to take over custodial duties for the twins in case something happened to Amy, and Hadley also left them and disappeared.

Heaven knew, Amy had wanted Hadley to love her as she loved him, a man who'd never wanted a family and claimed he couldn't love anyone. She'd never stopped trying to change him, but she'd also never trusted that he wouldn't abandon her, or in this case, their babies.

"That hearing," Jenna said, "was scheduled for next week."

"It won't take place now. Which means you're free and clear." He gazed at the babies he held. "Our marriage was always shaky.

By the time these little ones were born, I might have been somewhere else." He paused. "That's all changed now, though. To set your mind at ease, I mean to stay."

This wasn't at all what Jenna had expected. She wouldn't have to go through with the guardianship, which would have been difficult for her at best, and instead she could continue putting herself together again after her divorce. Nothing would ever again derail her the way her broken marriage had. No one, she told herself, including Hadley Smith.

"Amy ever mention what names she picked out?" he suddenly asked.

A couple of weeks ago, one night while Hadley was out, Amy had talked about her choices, and Jenna did recall several of them. "I remember Luke," she said, "and Grace. Didn't you know?"

"I'm not a very good listener," he admitted.

Jenna took a few more steps into the room. "I'm sure she left her baby name book on the shelf in her living room. There should be a list tucked inside with the names she liked most starred."

"Grace," he said, not looking at Jenna. "Luke. If you say that's what she wanted,

I don't see why not. Lucas Smith is a good name for a guy, don't you think?"

"Yes," she murmured, bending down and noting the babies' fine features. They didn't appear crumpled and wizened like many newborns' faces, probably because they'd been cesarean deliveries. "And Grace sounds soft but strong," she added.

Maybe the only thing they could agree on. Hadley raised his head to study her, and she forced herself to hold his gaze.

Jenna hesitated. She should turn away and go. Honoring her promise to Amy—not a legal issue now, but for Jenna, a moral one—would be equally difficult. Just as it was hard every time she walked into the Baby Things store on Main Street. The yearning she felt when she looked at the frilly miniature dresses and little shirts with adorable sports logos and cute short pants. They reminded her of her lifelong desire to have a family. Another of her shattered dreams.

She resisted the urge to stroke one finger along the babies' cheeks, to feel their soft skin, smooth and warm. In this town if someone she knew wasn't getting married, they were having a baby—like her own sister not long ago. It didn't seem fair that Hadley, who'd never wanted kids, now had two of them, these perfect little humans who had just been born. Jenna chided herself for the unkind thought.

She stared at the twins and felt her heart break twice over. Jenna hadn't forgotten her own childhood with a father who didn't care. She knew firsthand how devastating that could be. Her father had fractured their family, and Jenna would not let that happen to anyone else. Her legal responsibility for these newborn babies was, as Hadley had said, void now. Yet with Amy gone, the children had no protection. Jenna had to set aside her own sadness for the sake of the twins.

She mentally squared her shoulders. "Amy begged me to make sure the twins have a safe, stable environment—"

"Something you think I can't provide?"

"I didn't say that. But I made a promise to Amy, so this is what I'm going to do now. I'll visit the babies every week to see how they're doing. And if I think you're not taking good care of them, I will hold you accountable. I'll do everything in my power to bring the matter up with the court."

"So you could still become their standby guardian?" Hadley said. "I would never have signed off on that. I sure won't now. Besides, you'd have to get in line behind Amy's parents. I don't envy you that."

Jenna swallowed. "Do they know about her passing?"

He nodded. "We've never been on the best terms, but yeah, I called them. They're on their way now."

"And I will do whatever needs to be done." Brave words, when instead she felt torn, even frightened by her own decision. Still. It was necessary.

Regardless of whether Hadley wanted her to be involved, now the twins were all that counted.

*Luke and Grace*, she thought, aching to reach out and take them from Hadley, to hold them and feel their sweet weight in her embrace. No matter how painful this might prove for Jenna, whose arms would always be empty, she kept her promises.

# CHAPTER TWO

*Four months later*

"EVERYTHING ALL RIGHT TODAY?" After checking to make sure Jenna Moran's car wasn't parked out front, Hadley banged through the door at the McMann ranch. Jenna's weekly visits to the twins irritated him. He didn't like being under a microscope. Who was she to judge him? He was glad she wasn't there tonight because he needed to speak to Clara, the widowed owner of the ranch, about their living situation.

Clara rushed into the hall carrying both twins. "Couldn't be better," she said, but her eyes didn't meet his, and Hadley reminded himself, as he did most nights, that she wasn't a young woman anymore. With graying dark hair and light brown eyes, Clara was still slim, even thin, and she must be worn out after all day tending to his babies. Yet she'd taken over their care without a qualm. In fact, it had been Clara's suggestion for them to move in with her rather than return to the small apartment he'd shared with Amy. The only time Clara seemed flustered was when Jenna Moran came to the ranch, and only because Clara picked up on the tension between Jenna and Hadley.

"Got home soon as I could," he said. "Had a cow run through some wire and need stitches. Sorry I'm late."

"You aren't, dear. We've been fine." She glanced down at Gracie. "But she was a tad cranky this afternoon."

Teething already? Hadley started to slip a finger in Gracie's mouth to see if her gums were tender but thought better of it. He'd washed up at the NLS ranch, where he worked, but he doubted his hands were clean enough.

When he'd lived with Amy, Hadley used to take the long way home. Now and then he'd stop at Rowdy's, the only bar in town, for one beer before he continued on to the apartment. By the time he got there, Amy would have that look in her eyes that seemed to beg him to love her. "It's not in me," he'd told her a million times, yet she'd always chosen to believe he could change. Would it have killed him to let her think he really loved her before she died having his babies? They were his daily reminder of the wrong he'd done Amy.

He was also being unfair now to Clara, the kindest person he knew. Hadley owed her, not the other way around. In his teens the Mc-Manns had become his last foster parents, and he'd spent several years on their midsize ranch, learning to cowboy from Clara's husband, Cliff. He'd also learned to be a man— as much as he ever would be, considering his beginnings. By eighteen he'd been on his own, but no other place had ever felt the same, so finally Hadley had come back to Barren. A few years later he'd met Amy, married her, and he was still here, though he got twitchy whenever he stayed anywhere too long.

Hadley's talk with Clara had to wait until the twins finally fell asleep—at the same time, for once. He and Clara stood by their crib, which the babies shared, just gazing at them. Both twins had their thumbs in their mouths, and their eyes were closed with that expression of utter peace on their faces that always caught at his heart. Hadley laid a hand on each little chest.

"You don't have to check every night," Clara said with a knowing smile. "They're healthy as can be and ready to make more energy for tomorrow."

She often seemed to sense what he was thinking. Maybe it was neurotic of him to test their breathing, but he couldn't help himself. After Amy died, and he held them for the first time in that room across from the hospital nursery, he'd become a worrier. He supposed he'd carry that to his own grave.

He and Clara went downstairs where, by habit, they settled at the kitchen table. Darkness had fallen while they bathed the twins, then wrestled them into their sleepers for the night and said their prayers for them.

"Okay," he said, stirring his coffee, "let's talk. I've made a decision."

Clara straightened in her chair. "So have I."

Hadley stiffened. He'd sensed her earlier frown wasn't about Gracie being fussy. He'd been right. Clara was exhausted. He'd known this moment would come ever since he had moved in and filled her tidy house to the rafters with all the babies' gear. The twins seemed to outgrow their clothes every week, and he was now a regular customer at Baby Things. Apparently, so was Jenna Moran, who brought shirts and jeans and dresses and toys whenever she came to see them. Which, even once a week, was too often for Hadley. Fortunately, he was usually at work then.

"I should look for another place, Clara," he began, then held up a hand. "I know, you've told me you like having us here, and you're great with Luke and Gracie, but we're in your way."

Clara's eyes filled. "Move out now? How would you manage, having to work and care for those sweet babies with no one to help?"

Had he been wrong after all? Hadley tried to ignore a sudden mental image of Jenna. Why think of her? They were like oil and water. She had a sense of style that set off her auburn hair and blue eyes, liked antiques and probably other fancy stuff. Hadley preferred working in a barn. He was jeans and old boots. This was her hometown, but Hadley was already planning to move—on his terms, not like when he was a kid. "I can put the twins in day care. I know how tough this has been on you."

Her chin went up. "No, you do not. When I lost Cliff, I lost myself for a while. Then after you had those beautiful babies, I found out who I was again."

Hadley twirled his coffee cup. He'd never thought he was doing something for Clara. Quite the reverse.

"I understand about Cliff," he said. "But before you know it, the twins will be crawling around, then walking and running all over the place."

She frowned. "You're saying I'm too old to chase after them."

"I'm saying you deserve a rest. I can't ever thank you for everything you've already done, but Clara, we're imposing. I can't ask more of you."

"And where will you live?"

A good question. He wasn't foreman at the Sutherland ranch any longer and didn't have the house that came with the NLS job. Hadley was now an ordinary cowhand there, hoping he wouldn't be let go when winter came on again and the ranch hunkered down to wait out the snow. It was early spring now, and his job seemed safe; it was a busy season on any ranch except this one. He glanced out the window at the empty fields the McManns had worked for decades before Cliff died. "I'll get an apartment in town again," he said.

"You've got this all wrong, Hadley." Clara set her cup aside. "Does this have to do with Jenna Moran?"

"Partly, maybe. Sure." In his own place, she couldn't surprise him with a visit. She'd soon get discouraged, then stop coming to check on the twins—and Hadley.

"You'd let that sweet woman chase you off? When you're far more comfortable here than you would be in a tiny apartment?"

He blinked. He'd heard another note in Clara's tone. Sorrow? It had never occurred to him that Clara needed them as much as they needed her. He was never good with women, Amy being no exception. He could never figure out Jenna Moran, either, who got under his skin every time he saw her.

Clara struggled to continue. "I don't want you and the twins to leave…" Before she said the rest, Hadley knew he'd lost control of the situation. It wouldn't be his choice after all. "And I hate to do this, making matters worse, but with Cliff gone," Clara went on, "and our land sitting fallow, it has become too difficult—even with the money you contribute every month—for me to stay here. Nothing will happen right away, but—" She took a deep breath. "I've decided to sell the ranch, unless..." She paused. "Why don't you buy it?"

Her question didn't require an answer. They both knew Hadley had no money.

JENNA RARELY STEPPED into the Baby Things store on Main Street without buying something. And considering the fact that she would never have children of her own, she was running up quite a tab for her new nephew and Hadley Smith's twins. She seemed fated never to leave the shop without at least one package wrapped in colorful paper printed with elephants or lions, cupcakes or kittens.

From the rear of the store, Sherry, the owner, called out, "You're my first customer of the day. What brings you in this early?"

Jenna's gaze cut from the ever-tempting displays of children's clothes. "I promised my sister I'd pick up her order on my way to work—as if she doesn't have every possible item a baby might need."

"The order came in yesterday." With a

laugh, Sherry went back into the storeroom to find the box while Jenna stood stock-still in the center of the shop, determined not to notice the sweet yellow sundress on one table, or the pastel playsuit paired with the tiniest navy blue sneakers on another. When the bell jangled above the door, she turned to see... oh, no. Hadley I-don't-need-your-involvement Smith.

She'd actually run into him only a few times since that day in the hospital. Once she'd spotted him on the street here in town pushing a double stroller through the winter slush on the sidewalk. The twins had been bundled in adorable matching snowsuits covered with hoods so Jenna couldn't clearly see their faces. Instead of approaching, she'd hurried into Olivia McCord Antiques, telling herself she was late for work and couldn't stop even to coo over the babies.

Jenna shot a look at the storeroom, but Sherry didn't reappear from behind the curtain with its colorful pattern of sailboats and sand pails.

"Sherry here?" he asked.

"In the back. She'll be out in a minute." Now would be even better. "I don't work here," she added in case he'd thought she did.

"I know. You help at the store down the block."

"I used to manage it," she corrected him, surprised to think he'd been keeping tabs on her. Her friend and now former employer Olivia had two shops, one in Barren and the other in Farrier, the next town over in the county.

Jenna had enjoyed the job, but it wasn't what she wanted long-term. Having just completed her studies to become an interior designer, she'd served her notice to Olivia a couple of weeks ago and was starting her own business—Fantastic Designs—or trying to this first week. She had to support herself now. But she saw no need to share that with Hadley.

"Don't have much use for old furniture," he said, running a hand over the nape of his neck, "or new, for that matter."

Jenna didn't respond. She still missed her upscale house in Shawnee Mission, an afflu- ent suburb of Kansas City, where she'd lived with her ex-husband. Her apartment now in Barren was crammed with treasures she'd brought with her, although she and David still had a few things left to decide on.

"You waiting for something?" Hadley said.

She shrugged. "A quilt with sewn-on activities and noisemakers. For my sister's baby." Which was none of his business.

Hadley scowled. "I wasn't home the other day, but Clara says you came by."

Which sounded to Jenna like a challenge. When she did drive out to the McMann ranch to see the twins, she tried to schedule her visits so that Hadley would be at work. Sometimes she even passed by the NLS to make sure his truck was there. Silly, she supposed, but he made her uncomfortable. And she guessed, from the way he kept shifting from one foot to the other, she made him uneasy, too.

"I hope you don't have a problem with that," she said, although she knew he did.

His gaze lifted. "Amy may not have trusted me to see to the twins' welfare, but she was wrong."

"I'm not concerned about your relationship with Amy." Although she'd certainly heard an earful from her friend, Jenna knew better than to interfere. She'd done so once with her sister Shadow, and she wouldn't make that mistake again. "My only interest now is in the twins."

Hadley stared at her. "Clara tells me when you've been to the house. I've noticed the presents you brought. Gracie looks cute in those pink pajamas with the sheep on them." His tone was grudging. "And Luke looks ready to play football in the blue ones with the helmets all over."

"I couldn't resist," she admitted.

Sherry chose that moment to sweep through the curtain with the box Shadow had ordered, and Jenna could have kissed her for her perfect timing.

On impulse Jenna turned, plucked the yellow sundress and the multihued pastel playsuit she'd admired from the nearest table, then added the navy sneakers. Her cheeks flaming, she paid for them and made small talk with Sherry while she wrapped the gifts. The whole time Jenna could sense Hadley, still in the center of the room, staring at her back. Then, feeling too onstage with him watching, she carried her parcels toward the door.

Jenna had her hand on the latch when Hadley reached around her. The bell jingled as he opened the door for her. "Want me to take the presents home?"

How did he know they were for Luke and Grace? Oh, yes, why else would she buy double gifts in the same size? For a boy and girl? "Thank you, but I'll take them next time I visit the twins."

He'd been polite—at least he had manners— but Jenna didn't welcome his help any more than Hadley welcomed hers. Not that he would consider it help.

On his way to the NLS the next morning, bleary-eyed after a sleepless night, Hadley still felt shaken by his encounter with Jenna. And then he was startled by a different kind of encounter. As he drove through town, he braked hard at the only stoplight in Barren, certain that the dark-haired guy walking along the opposite side of the street might be the lone remnant of the broken family he'd been born into. But it couldn't be his brother, the one Hadley had betrayed. He hadn't seen him in years. Not that Dallas would want to see Hadley.

When he finally reached the ranch, the

foreman was waiting at the barn, his eyes the color of flint.

"You're late," Cooper Ransom said.

Hadley recognized the hard tone of voice. He climbed out of his truck. Once he'd have been ready for a fight, but he couldn't afford to lose his temper. He was a father now, and he and Cooper, who was married to the owner's granddaughter, had already shared some nasty moments. Still, he had the other man to thank for Hadley moving in with Amy last spring. He would never regret Cooper's advice to treat her more kindly. He hoped he'd given Amy a few happy moments—in between their quarrels—when she'd had so few of them left.

Hadley's mouth tightened. "My boy's got his days and nights mixed up," he told Cooper. "When he finally went to sleep, I crashed myself." Clara hadn't wakened him this morning. Either she'd thought he needed the rest, or she wasn't speaking to him. After their talk the other night, she'd made it plain he was welcome in her home until the ranch sold, but how could she show the place with toys and stacks of diapers scattered everywhere? "I got here as soon as I could."

"I appreciate that. I know it's hard to keep a schedule with two babies at once. But you left early yesterday. You were late once last week. Ranch work can't wait for you to show up."

He'd expected a stern lecture, but… "I'm being fired?" Again? He'd lost his job as foreman to Cooper last year.

The ranch owner, Ned, had always been good to Hadley and had rehired him, but as a ranch hand. Now he earned half of what he used to make as foreman.

He thought again about Clara's question. He'd give everything he had to run his own ranch, to be in full control of his life, but even buying a horse wasn't possible right now. Amy's outstanding hospital charges were eating him up, and the next payment was due. While he was glad her doctors had done everything humanly possible to save her, the ongoing expense was drowning Hadley. He needed this job.

"Listen," he said before Cooper could deliver the final blow. "I'm a hard worker. With calves being born every day here, you need me now," Hadley insisted.

Cooper said, "Sorry, I can't keep you. But let me make some calls. Maybe one of the other outfits can take you on and give you more flexible hours."

"Don't bother. I can find my own job," he said, his jaw tense. Hadley hated the notion of people doing him a favor, because sooner or later they'd want to collect on the debt.

Cooper shook his head, the sun glinting on his blond hair. "If that's the way you want it."

The other man started toward the house, muttering something about writing Hadley a check, which was nothing new, either. Minutes from now, with the money in his wallet, Hadley would feel tempted to leave rubber on the pavement as he turned onto the road, just as he had last year. But this time he forced himself to cool down. He didn't need a ticket for reckless driving from Finn Donovan, the sheriff. He had the babies to think of, not only himself. Responsibilities. It was just too bad the twins hadn't picked a father who, at this moment, could meet those responsibilities. He could save face, though.

"No, this isn't the way I want it," he called after Cooper, having made his decision. "Let's pretend you didn't let me go for staying up late with my baby. You don't have to fire me," he said, calling on the defiance that had helped him to survive any number of foster homes as a kid. "I quit."

Now, because of his stubborn pride, all he had to do was figure out how to feed the twins.

# CHAPTER THREE

AT LUNCHTIME THE NEXT DAY Jenna crossed the street, picked up some take-out food from the Bon Appetit, then went to see her sister. Shadow ran her own company called the Mother Comfort Home Health Care Agency, which was located in the same building as Jenna's new business. They often ate together when time permitted—which was more of an issue for Shadow, who was always on the run these days juggling her baby plus the agency. Meanwhile Fantastic Designs had yet to get off the ground. Jenna's rented space on the second floor above her sister's office seemed perfect, but she had no appointments for the afternoon, or any other time, really.

Shadow was at her desk, the phone tucked under one ear. "I appreciate your concern, Bertie," she said with an eye roll for Jenna. "I'm sure we can work something out. Let me get started. I'll call you back later. Yes, of course, you'll have final say over anyone we place in your home."

Jenna sank onto a chair in front of Shadow's cluttered desk. She laid out their lunch. "What's up?"

"Jack's uncle," she said with a pointed look. "He's not happy."

"Poor old guy."

But this wasn't only about Bertie, who was in frail health. His nephew, Jack Hancock, the owner and head chef at the Bon Appetit, had been seeing Jenna and Shadow's widowed mother, and two days ago they'd gotten engaged. Shadow thought that was great; Jenna was still trying to wrap her mind around the fact that their mother planned to tie the knot again. Hadn't Wanda learned anything during her miserable marriage to their dad?

Jenna swallowed a first delicious bite of her croque madame. When she'd returned to Barren, newly divorced, she'd had little appetite and lost weight, but Jack's restaurant deserved its rave reviews. "Jack's been taking care of Bertie with Mama's help. If they get married, what will happen to Bertie?"

"They're going to buy a house, which would leave Bertie to fend for himself. Jack and Mama want their own space, but Bertie didn't love my idea to look for another caregiver in his own home."

"I think Mom and Jack are being too hasty," Jenna said. She hadn't reacted well when their mother showed her the ring Jack had given her. "Shadow, she's been on her own for a while now, and you can see how much happier she is. All those years of putting up with Daddy, him losing one job, then finding another, only to get fired or quit that, too…" He'd always seemed to be between jobs when he wasn't sitting in his old recliner all day, channel surfing the TV or bullying one of the kids, especially Jenna. "Mama may be leaping at this chance with Jack when she should take time to really figure out what *she* wants."

Shadow started on her own lunch with a sigh of satisfaction. "I'm sure she hasn't forgotten how hard it was to put food on the table or buy all of us shoes—"

"Used sneakers from Goodwill or the church rummage sale," Jenna remembered. "Mama had a bad self-image then, and no wonder with the way Daddy treated her. I'd hate to see her give up her new independence only to get into another bad situation."

"She won't. I'll admit Jack's quirky," Shadow agreed, running a hand through her dark hair, "but so what if he pretends he's French when he's not? I find that endearing, especially in a town like Barren where cowboys rule. His restaurant's already a big hit, he's been good to Mama, and he's great with Bertie, who's not the easiest person to get along with. As I just learned all over again." Shadow's nearly black eyes held the hint of a smile. "I'll find Bertie a caregiver he feels comfortable with. Would you deprive Mama of her chance to be truly happy for once in her life?"

"Of course not. But what's wrong with a longer engagement that would give them both time to see if this is really the right thing to do?"

"Jack loves her. She loves him. What's to figure out?"

Jenna finished her sandwich, savoring the last bite of ham-and-cheese goodness, her gaze focused on a framed photograph of Shadow, her husband, Grey, and their ten-year-old daughter, Ava, on the desk. "This, from a woman who adores her husband, dotes on her new baby and has everything else she wanted in life? Including Wilson Cattle and everyone's favorite little cowgirl?" And Ava now had a baby brother, if not the sister she'd asked for. Being around their little family—or Hadley's twins—for Jenna was both a joy she couldn't resist and a sorrow she could never escape. She should worry instead about finding some clients.

Shadow saw her looking at the picture. "We have problems like anyone else, Jen." She tried a smile. "For instance, Grey's parents' house has taken forever to build. Everett's a great father-in-law, and I do love Liza, who's the best stepmother-in-law in the world, but really, they need their own quarters and so do we. Just like Mama and Jack. There's always something. Life's never perfect."

"I guess I still have to work through my own issues," Jenna admitted.

"Sure, and I get that—" Shadow had never liked David, Jenna's ex "—but Mama's wedding to Jack shouldn't be one of them. Your marriage didn't pan out. The divorce was hard. We all think David treated you terribly, but look at you now," she said. "You're better off, and you have a new business, which I *know* is going to be successful—"

"—if things ever pick up," Jenna said. She couldn't deny that, like their mother, she'd sacrificed a big part of herself to help further David's career and run the rest of his life so he wouldn't have to. "I thought getting certified as a designer would be hard. Compared to launching my business, it was a piece of cake—chocolate," she added, tapping one finger against the square white box Jack had packed for them with dessert.

"Even so, you're doing fine."

"Are you in Pollyanna mode today?" Jenna asked.

"No, but who needed that big house in Kansas City?" Shadow didn't point out that there'd been no babies there to fill the space. "Your apartment here is gorgeous and homey. All you need now is confidence." Her eyes brightened. "Why don't you call Liza? Now that their house is almost done, she'll want a designer. Maybe you can get the job."

"You're changing the subject. We were talking about Mama and Jack."

"I think the two are connected. Them and your divorce."

She glanced out the window. "I just don't want her to get hurt."

Shadow arched one eyebrow. "See what I mean?"

Jenna's hands twisted in her lap. "No. I don't. I care whether our mother makes another mistake, but that doesn't mean it's about me, too."

Shadow gazed at her. "I disagree." And Jenna could tell that what she'd dreaded was coming. "Mama's engagement, even your divorce, aren't the only issues. You're going to have to deal with the rest eventually too, Jenna."

She didn't pretend to misunderstand. "I can't believe you'd bring up my…infertility. Yes, I wanted kids—maybe too much—but that dream is over." She folded her sandwich wrapper, then dropped it in the trash can beside Shadow's desk. The closest she would ever come to a baby of her own was Shadow's three-month-old son, Zach.

Jenna opened the cake box and gave her sister a piece. Shadow sampled the slice set before her. "What's the best thing now for *you*? Maybe you should work on that." She hesitated. "And while we're in risky territory here, what's going on with Hadley Smith's twins?"

"I see them as much as I can—for Amy's sake."

"Jenna, if that's painful, you don't have to spend time with them. I think Amy would understand. Unless visiting the McMann ranch isn't just about the babies."

Jenna said, "I enjoy the twins, but I don't want to know Hadley any better than I already do."

Shadow blinked. "Now, that's interesting."

Yes, it was. Why had she assumed Shadow meant him? She couldn't deny he had a certain appeal with that dark hair and those steel-blue eyes. But he didn't want her around, and she didn't like to get near him, either. She went to the ranch for the twins, not Hadley. "I'm keeping tabs on him. That's all."

"Maybe you won't have to much longer. I hear Clara's going to sell her ranch."

That news surprised Jenna. "Then the problem will solve itself. Hadley won't stay in town."

Why hadn't she heard about Clara putting the ranch on the market? Jenna rose from her chair. Unfortunately, that also meant she'd no longer see the twins, hard as that might be, because Hadley would be out of sight before the sold sign was posted on the ranch. As expected. Jenna didn't want to examine her mixed emotions about that too closely, so she changed the subject. "I forgot to bring you the quilt you bought for Zach. I'll drop it off tomorrow. Would that make you happy?"

"Yes," Shadow said, "but I'd feel even more pleased if you'd help me with the plans for Mom's wedding."

Jenna didn't respond. That would be as hard for her as saying goodbye to the twins.

AFTER HE LEFT the NLS, Hadley had grabbed a quick lunch at the Sundown Café—he wasn't a big fan of the fancy French food served at the Bon Appetit—then ate his burger on the way to the Circle H.

Begging didn't come easily to him, but if that's what it took... Only Logan Hunter, Sawyer's brother and part owner of the ranch, quickly dashed his hopes. At the moment they were fully staffed.

After their brief conversation, Hadley left his cell number, then climbed back in his truck, disappointed. Still, he had to envy

Logan, who didn't have to worry about his family ever being kicked out of their house.

As he drove back to Clara's, he tried to appreciate what he had for now.

His mood softened, as usual, the minute he stepped into the kitchen at the house. When he lifted his girl from her baby seat, Gracie reached out her arms to him and giggled. Both twins had recently learned to laugh, which lit him up inside like a candle in a pumpkin. Trying to forget the past few hours, he scooped up Luke, too, but on his way in he'd ignored the stack of mail on the hall table—including a notice from the hospital, probably. "This wasn't exactly my day," he told Clara. "I'm not going to complain except to say that I almost got fired."

The last word made his stomach burn. For most of his life Hadley had been a loner, certainly since he was ten years old, the last time he'd seen his brother. And here he was with two tiny beings who depended on him for everything. Had he been out of his mind to quit his job at the NLS? Any severance pay was off the table now, because in the end, leaving had been his choice. Hadley had always believed he knew when it was time to go, but now he had second thoughts. He guessed he was getting his comeuppance. In the end his temper had gotten the best of him.

"Oh, Hadley. Fired. Why?"

"Being late for work, and instead I quit. But I'll find something else." He explained his brief visit with Logan, who'd been sympathetic, though in the end, he couldn't offer a job.

Maybe he should go back to the NLS tomorrow where he'd done some begging before the twins were born, see if Cooper might settle up after all.

Clara didn't look at him, but she kissed his cheek on her way to turn off the stove where the twins' bottles were heating in a pan of water.

When she faced him, he could see his story had affected her, too. And he remembered she was also facing a challenging and painful situation.

"You're sorry to be leaving here, aren't you?" he asked Clara, taking one of the bottles from her. Her skin felt cool under his warmer hand.

"Yes," she said. "I don't know how I'm ever going to sort through all the things Cliff and I accumulated in forty years. Well, me at least." Her husband had been gone almost a decade, years after Hadley left, and Hadley had never had a chance to say goodbye to the man who'd had such an influence on him. "Cliff and I never had children of our own, but my memories of the girls and boys we fostered—" Clara glanced at Hadley "—are in every nook and cranny of this house. When you left us, and you were the last, Cliff told me I'd made a shrine of your room."

A wave of loss ran through Hadley. That room for now was the twins' nursery. The McMann ranch was the closest he'd ever come to a home and a family in many years, until the twins were born. Clara sat at the table, and Hadley stood beside her.

He hadn't found another place in town that might suit him and the babies, and he recalled again Clara's entreaty to buy the ranch.

"I know what you asked me, Clara," he said, passing Luke to her. The baby latched onto the bottle, noisily sucking. Hadley sat down, too, and teased the other nipple into Gracie's mouth. Clara's challenge had been between them ever since. And here he was, out of a job… "If I could, I'd buy this ranch.

Then you could stay right where you are. But I can't," he finished, hating to let her down all over again as he had his brother Dallas in a different way.

"Stay, you mean?" she asked.

"No, I mean I don't have the money to buy you out."

"If you could, though, would you stay? With the babies?" Her gaze fixed on Luke nestled against her chest. "And before you say another word, I'm more than fine with that."

Hadley didn't know what to say. He couldn't afford the ranch, but maybe there was another option… "What if you didn't have to sell?" he asked Clara. "What if you kept the ranch—"

"It's not making any money. You're aware of that." She glanced out the kitchen window at the dry fields, the empty barn. "And I know, even when I've practically begged you to stay, that you're determined to leave again…" She trailed off.

Hadley gazed at the same outside view. "What if I didn't?"

Her gaze jerked up to meet his. And he swallowed hard. Four months ago he'd come here to her ranch for the twins. He'd been antsy for a change ever since, yet he realized his babies were too young for such a drastic upheaval, even the short move he'd planned from here to town. Just as important, where would Clara go?

"I understand things are tight, but if we could put enough money together, even borrow some to buy a few cattle, start a new herd for you—"

"Oh, Hadley," she said as she had before, one hand pressed to Luke's hair, the other to her heart.

"I'm a good foreman. I think I could get this ranch going again." Of course, if he stayed, he'd continue to have to deal with Jenna Moran nosing around in his business, making her weekly drive-bys. Still… Once Clara's place was making a profit, and the twins were old enough, Hadley could move on as he'd planned and get away from Jenna for good. Her eagle eye over his care of the twins made him nervous. In the meantime, whatever he had to do, he might be able to make this happen.

"I can't afford much, either," Clara said, and for an instant Hadley was mentally packing his bags, yet her tone had sounded hopeful.

If he and Clara did this, he wouldn't need another job as anyone's cowhand; he'd be his own boss again, his decisions, of course, subject to Clara's approval.

A streak of excitement zinged along his veins. Hadley almost didn't recognize the feeling. "We'll manage. Heck, I'd rather work for you than for anybody else."

# CHAPTER FOUR

THE NEXT MORNING Jenna drove out to the Mc-Mann ranch. *If that's painful, you don't have to spend time with them*, Shadow had said, and keeping her commitment to Amy was harder each time she saw the twins. She'd had a near panic attack on the way out here and had to pull over until her pulse settled. The bittersweet sorrow she felt whenever she held Amy's babies—part grief for her friend who would never see them grow up, part grief for herself that these sweet babies weren't hers—was something she had to manage. But these visits also filled her heart.

She was surprised to find Hadley at the ranch. On a weekday he should be working at the NLS. Too bad she hadn't driven by the ranch this time to check if his truck was there.

Jenna took a deep breath. She imagined he wasn't any happier to see her than she was to see him. Taking the bag from Sherry's shop off the seat, she got out of her car with a growing sense of dread, then started toward the house. She'd hoped he wouldn't follow, but Hadley fell into step beside her.

"I can take that," he said. "Luke and Gracie are napping."

"I'll wait for them to wake up. Maybe Clara has time for a cup of coffee. I like to watch her open my gifts for the twins."

"Maybe on your next visit," Hadley said. "If you turn around now, head back to town, I'll tell Clara you dropped off the presents."

Jenna groaned. First, he'd wanted to bring the package home from the store. Now he hoped to send her on her way without seeing the twins. But she was saved from having to respond. Clara appeared in the doorway with a broad smile and waved at her. "I have pecan coffee cake and a fresh pot. Hadley?" she said. "Will you join us?"

He stopped. "Thanks, but I was about to start cleaning out the barn. After that I'll mend the corral gate. Should keep me busy most of the day."

Jenna guessed he was helping Clara get ready to sell the ranch. She climbed the steps and went into the house, leaving him there on the walk. The door shut behind her, and Jenna followed Clara into the kitchen. The smells of brown sugar and butter and rich, dark coffee invited her in, and as Clara poured coffee, then set cream and sugar on the table beside the fragrant cake, Jenna cocked an ear for any sound from upstairs.

She handed Clara the gift bag. "Wait till you see these," she said, a soft ache starting in her heart. She stirred milk into her coffee while Clara tore open the first package wrapped in pink kitten paper. To Jenna's own surprise, it didn't contain the yellow sundress. "No," she murmured, "that's for Luke. Sherry must have gotten the outfits mixed up."

"Or she doesn't buy into the notion of pink for girls, blue for boys."

It didn't matter, of course. Clara oohed and ahhed over Luke's pastel playsuit and blue sneakers, then studied the label. "Dear me, this will be too small. Luke outgrew the three-month size. Could you exchange it, Jenna, for the next one up? Even nine months might be better. I hate to inconvenience you—"

"I'd be happy to exchange them." Why hadn't she thought of a bigger size? But Jenna had little experience with growing babies, and recently she'd bought mostly toys. "Grace's present, too," she said. "You don't even need to open it."

Clara did anyway. She took great pleasure in examining the yellow sundress that had been wrapped in blue paper, one finger tracing the satin ribbon trim that wound through the bottom hem. "She'll look adorable in this. Thank you." Her eyes grew moist. "I'm so pleased Hadley has decided to stay here with them."

Jenna straightened. "I heard you were going to sell."

"I was, but Hadley lost his job at the NLS and decided to get this place going again instead of leaving or finding another job. How could I say no? If he succeeds, I'll be able to keep my home, and the babies will have one, too. Next week he'll look into buying our first cows."

The announcement startled Jenna. Was this good or bad for her? On one hand, the twins would still be here, and Jenna could keep checking on them as well as on Hadley. On the other, she would have to put up with him. And vice versa. His attitude wouldn't make things easy.

Clara studied her over the rim of her coffee cup, raised halfway to her mouth. "I've noticed you and Hadley aren't exactly friends, but that man doesn't know what he needs."

"That doesn't sound like the Hadley Smith Amy described."

"You believe everything she told you?"

"That sounds naive, doesn't it?" But Jenna recalled the evenings she'd spent with Amy, hearing the other woman's complaints about Hadley, relating their quarrels—which might or might not have happened as she said. Amy's tears had been real, though, and not simply due to pregnancy hormones. Jenna had witnessed for herself how quickly Hadley's temper flared. Because of her father, she knew all about how harmful that could be to a young person, and she'd definitely keep her eye on Hadley.

Clara cocked her head to listen for a moment. "Ah, Luke's up. Grace will be, too. That little imp never lets his sister sleep once he's awake."

Wondering about her blind acceptance of Amy's stories, Jenna sat motionless in her chair at the table after Clara had left the room. The older woman returned a few minutes later carrying one twin on each bony hip.

Jenna couldn't seem to move. This wasn't the first time she'd become paralyzed at the sight of them, not the first time she'd wanted to pull back inside herself for protection, but Clara was having none of that.

"Here we are!" she said brightly. "Which little angel do you want first?"

Jenna thought of leaving before sorrow threatened to swamp her again. Then she remembered Hadley on the front walk obviously wanting her to go. And oh, how sweet they were! Grace with her fine features and rose-gold hair curling at her nape, Luke who was bigger with a sturdy frame and similar coloring, although his hair seemed to be getting darker. Being of different sexes, they were fraternal, not identical, twins, and so lovable just for being here that her heart turned over.

Her hands twitched with the urge to hold them. When Clara plunked Grace on her lap, Jenna's mouth went dry.

Grace wriggled in her embrace, then patted one tiny hand to Jenna's cheek, the baby's face bright as if she had no doubt she was welcome in Jenna's arms, and Jenna's throat closed. "She's smiling."

"They've been smiling since they were

born, if you ask me. People say that's only gas, but I don't believe it. They laugh now, too. And you should see how Grace fixates on Hadley as if he's the one person in the world she can rely on."

"Amy wasn't as sure about that," Jenna murmured, yet she couldn't deny that since Amy's death he'd stepped up to the plate. Hadley seemed to work hard and provide for them as best he could—in fact, she heard him hammering something down at the barn—yet the news that he intended to rebuild Clara's ranch stunned her. If he really meant to stay longer, Jenna's visits would be enough to fulfill her promise to Amy, yet he'd probably continue to object to Jenna's very presence.

"I know he's never been one to settle down," Clara went on, "but he has more reason now to sink a few roots." She shifted Luke, who was trying to grab the pan of coffee cake off the table. "Time will tell," she said with a meaningful look at Jenna.

HADLEY COULDN'T PUT it off any longer. Ever since that tragic day at the hospital he had been meaning to look through Amy's belongings and tonight seemed good enough. He admitted he'd been avoiding the task. If he and the babies were going to stay on the ranch for a while, he shouldn't keep stalling. He also wanted to take a look at the standby guardianship application Amy had filed. Even though the court hearing had never taken place, the situation with Jenna was still an issue. He didn't buy that her only reason for spending time with Luke and Gracie was some promise she'd made to Amy. He'd caught the melting look on her face more than once when she was with them. Now that their mother was gone, could she have some legal claim to his babies? And had she been biding her time, hoping to catch him in some misdeed with the twins?

"Clara, have you seen the bins with Amy's stuff in them?" he asked after dinner.

"I believe they're in the attic," she said.

Being careful not to wake the twins, Hadley went upstairs, then sat cross-legged on the wooden floor of the walk-up area under the roof beams. He forced himself to open the first bin and rummage through Amy's things. When he'd moved from their apartment, he hadn't taken time to sort out what to toss and what to keep for Luke and Gracie someday. Disoriented by Amy's shocking death, by his new obligations, he'd thrown everything into bins for later. From then on, he'd had his hands full just trying to be a good dad when good wasn't in his nature.

The first item he came across was the bifold program from Amy's funeral at the local church. It was the same place where, at her insistence, they'd been married, and where she'd sometimes attended services on Sundays. Without him. Hadley had resisted most of her attempts to change him from a bad boy into a solid citizen, something he now regretted, just as he regretted not trying harder to love her. She'd deserved better from him.

With a hard lump in his throat, Hadley skimmed the program, then the small picture of her at the top. "Way too soon," he murmured, tracing a finger over her image as if he could touch her again. "Never mind all those fights we had. As you told me, there were good times, too, in the beginning. Not sure what would have happened to us if you were still here," he said, "but we'll never know, will we?"

Now he was on his own, plowing through her belongings in Clara's attic.

"Hadley?" Her voice came from the bottom of the stairs.

"I'm here still. Come up if you want."

To be truthful, he didn't like doing this alone. Every piece of paper he touched, every sympathy card and article of clothing he'd saved, spoke to him. Amy's favorite green sweater, which he couldn't bring himself to touch, the one she'd knitted herself with the too-long sleeves that always made him smile for her effort. The baby books she'd bought because "I don't know any more about this than you do." The last birthday gift he'd given her, a certificate for a day at the spa in Farrier that she'd never gotten to use. Like the court order she'd never completed, which he wouldn't have signed off on. As Jenna well knew.

Clara laid a hand on his shoulder. "If this is too difficult for you, maybe I could find what you're looking for."

"No," he said, "I did my grieving." Hadley had cried himself to sleep that first horrid night, something he'd never admit to anyone. Until then he hadn't shed a tear since the first time his parents had dumped him and Dallas on child services and, later, when he'd watched his brother be taken away because of him. He'd cried about Amy, whose short life had been cut off so abruptly before she even saw their babies, cried for the mess he'd made of their relationship and for the twins he'd been left to care for—he, who would probably be the worst father any kid ever had, though he hadn't been able to leave them with anyone else. Including Jenna Moran. "One of the worst parts," he told Clara, "is Amy never knowing Luke and Gracie. Not watching them grow up, graduate from school, get married…"

"But *you* will, Hadley. For her. I'm sure wherever she is she appreciates that."

His voice sounded hoarse. "At least they have the names she chose for them."

Clara's hand gently stroked his shoulder, and he guessed she had trouble speaking, too.

"I need to find some papers," he told her. When Amy had mentioned the application for guardianship, Hadley had paid little attention except to give her a flat no. He wouldn't agree to that. Now he wished he'd read everything. "I don't understand all the double-talk legalese about standby guardianship, but I have to work out what all that means."

Clara hadn't responded before his fingers closed over the manila file in which he remembered Amy putting some papers. Then she'd shut the file away in a drawer. When Hadley had packed up after she was gone, he hadn't looked at it. Her death had still been too raw for him to face his own failure in that regard. He peered into the file now. It contained a few documents like their marriage license. "The guardianship stuff isn't here."

Clara examined the papers in the file, too, but also came up empty. "Maybe Amy had a safe-deposit box somewhere."

Was that possible? Then why not store *all* the important papers there? He supposed there might be layers to Amy that he knew nothing about. As a minor example, Hadley could never reconcile their bank and credit card statements with the purchases she'd made, and whenever he questioned her she'd told him not to worry.

Hadley rose, his knees popping from sitting

too long. "I'll check with Barney Caldwell at the bank tomorrow."

Hadley needed to find out what he was up against.

WAS IT JENNA'S bad luck, or some kind of weird karma? The very next morning when she walked up to the main entrance of the Barren Cattlemen's Bank, Hadley reached around her to open the door. Without glancing up, Jenna coolly thanked him. "Have a good day," she added, then went straight for Barney Caldwell's office. As vice president, he had a window that looked onto Main Street, and more than once she'd glimpsed him peering out to see what was going on in town and with whom.

Hadley was right behind her—again.

"You seeing Barney, too?" he asked, not taking a chair in the waiting area.

"I'm applying for a loan," she said, "to invest in Fantastic Designs." Jenna still had no clients. She needed capital to jump-start her business. And because of that, she would have to deal with Barney. Some women in town called him creepy, and he'd recently sent her several cryptic messages she'd never answered. What was Hadley saying…?

"That's not a bad idea. Clara and I should try that."

Which wasn't why he was here now then. Jenna tamped down her curiosity. Her only interest, she reminded herself, was in the twins. Remembering how she'd held them in her arms yesterday, she felt quivery and soft inside as she had all the way home.

Barney, who'd been at his desk poring over some papers, came to his doorway. "Who's first?"

"Go ahead," Hadley said with a motion toward Jenna. "I can wait."

"No, please. I'll probably have to fill out a dozen forms." And she wasn't eager to be alone with Barney. In school he'd had a crush on her, the memory of which still embarrassed Jenna.

"Well, I shouldn't be long," Hadley said. "Just have a question."

Barney, his short-cut hair the color of hazelnuts, clapped a hand on Hadley's shoulder, a gesture that seemed to make Hadley tense. "Have a seat. Ask away." The door shut behind them.

Jenna tried not to observe their interaction, but it wasn't long before Hadley's dark brows drew together over his piercing blue eyes. He juggled a brass paperweight from Barney's desk, then set it down again. They exchanged a few more words. Then Hadley abruptly rose from his slouch in the small barrel-shaped chair and stalked to the door. He jerked it open. "You'd better hear this," he said to her.

Following him into the office, Jenna took the chair Hadley had vacated. He stood next to her while Barney straightened the papers he'd been reading earlier. He studied her with his too-small eyes. "Hadley has asked me about his wife's relationship with this bank. It appears he didn't know she had an account—in addition to their joint checking—in her name alone."

That wasn't unusual; many women had their own accounts. So had Jenna during her marriage. "Yes, I remember that." She glanced at Hadley. "Amy once told me about a bank account, but that's all she said."

Barney said, "She opened the account some time ago." He checked the dates.

"Soon after we got married then," Hadley said.

"And Amy deposited money each month."

"Where did she get it? We never had extra."

"I believe, um, her parents sent the checks."

"It's like she was married to them, not me," Hadley muttered. "Why would she keep that secret? Because she worried that I might leave her high and dry?"

To Jenna, that didn't seem so unlikely.

Barney fidgeted in his chair. "Maybe her family wanted Amy to know she could use the money if she ever needed to—"

"Because she was married to a guy like me," Hadley said under his breath.

Jenna looked from him to Barney, whose gaze had fixed on his computer screen as if its contents were written in Sanskrit. "But what does all this have to do with me?"

Barney glanced up. "Not long before she gave birth, Amy amended the account to include a POD—payable on death provision. Which avoids probate. When the primary account holder dies, the money in the account goes straight to the named beneficiary. In this case to you, Jenna."

*How could that be?* "But if I'm the beneficiary, why wasn't I notified after her...death?"

Barney frowned. "I've been trying to get a hold of you for some time," he said, "but you didn't respond to any of my messages. Or the letters on official bank stationery."

"I thought those were merely forms to solicit investment." She'd thrown the letters away, unopened. The funds from her divorce settlement were earmarked for savings to buy a house, and Jenna didn't want to risk losing any of that.

"My next attempt was going to be knocking on your door," Barney said. "Which I intended to do until you came in this morning."

"Doesn't sound to me like you tried hard enough." Hadley glanced at him, taking in his dark suit and conservative tie. Barney might look the part of a vice president, but he wasn't known for his management skills or much else. He lived with his overbearing mother and was inclined to startle at his own shadow. "What do you do? Shuffle papers all day then go home at four o'clock? You've read those—" Hadley pointed at the stack of printouts on the desk "—three times since I walked in. Bet you couldn't tell me what a single line said."

"Are you calling me negligent? Pardon me, but I couldn't force Jenna to answer my messages."

"Pardon me," Hadley said, "if I call you a liar."

Surprised that he'd defended her, Jenna held up a hand. "Please. This isn't getting us anywhere. If I understand, Amy's accounts are now mine to control?"

"Yes. And the amount is substantial." Barney read a figure aloud that made Jenna's eyes widen. Amy had complained several times about her money woes with Hadley when all along she'd had access to these funds. Amy hadn't trusted him. As for Jenna, she had to admit she'd been avoiding Barney and couldn't blame him for this misunderstanding. An oversight on her part.

"But why me and not her parents?" she asked.

"I can't say. She made that change in the account with my assistant." Barney cleared his throat. He turned to Jenna and handed her a thin sheaf from the stack. "You're authorized, at your discretion, to use the account for the sole benefit of Lucas and Grace Smith."

In other words, Amy had again provided for her children's welfare in case Hadley disappeared when they were born. As she read, Jenna twisted her fingers together. She shot a look at Hadley. Their quasi-relationship wasn't friendly, as Clara had noted, not that she wanted it to be, but this new detail would make things worse. Now she wouldn't simply be paying a few visits to the twins; she'd be managing a rather large pot of money for them, overriding Hadley as their father. At least in his view.

His gaze bored through her, his eyes shards of blue glass.

Jenna stood. "This isn't my doing, Hadley."

"Like your agreement with Amy about the standby guardianship?"

"You can't think I put her up to that," Jenna said. Barney fidgeted at his desk, his face a dull red. A glance through the glass window into the bank revealed several people, including a teller, staring at them. "We're making a scene."

"I don't care. Obviously, Amy agreed with

everybody else in this town that I'm not to be trusted with my own children."

Hadley turned, yanked open the door, then stalked from the office. "Like it or not, which I'm sure you don't, Jenna, I'll have something to say about this money."

# CHAPTER FIVE

WHEN THE SUN went down, Hadley was still fuming. He imagined that the red ball of fire sliding toward the horizon, as if to define the western edge of Clara's ranch in the blaze of color, might draw him with it. Hadley would slip right over the boundary of her pancake-flat land like a man falling—or jumping—into an active volcano, then vanish from the twins' lives. That would probably suit Jenna.

The rare spurt of self-pity lasted just long enough to remind him that he didn't have the luxury of thinking about himself.

Before Barney had revealed the surprise bank account, he'd told Hadley that Amy did not have a safe-deposit box at the bank. So the location of the guardianship papers was still a mystery, and now he had a different problem. The threat Jenna posed as the beneficiary of Amy's account. He felt hamstrung. He didn't want anyone else in charge, especially a woman with no blood ties to the twins; he could take care of his own babies.

Hadley turned to the young cowhand he'd hired half an hour ago. "I'll be at a cattle auction tomorrow. While I'm gone, make sure the south fence is tight—and if there's a hole, fix it. With luck I'll bring back some stock." He planned to use the ranch's meager amount of cash to buy the cows. After those funds were gone, he'd have to see Barney again about the loan he hadn't applied for before he stomped out of the bank.

Cory Jennings grinned. Shorter than Hadley by an inch or two, he still stood over six feet. His dancing dark eyes met his. "Said I'll do a good job for you. That means taking the horse to ride fence."

A few days ago, Hadley and Clara had pooled enough money to buy the ranch's one horse, a rangy sorrel from a "dealer" who'd stopped in Barren on his way to Colorado. Hadley doubted the gelding was worth even the three hundred dollars they'd paid. In his view the horse had been on the road to the glue factory. Lucky for the horse, he'd found two people with soft hearts and desperate for any help the sorrel might provide in return for saving his life. "You sure you can ride him?"

Cory pointed at the big belt buckle he wore, a prize he'd won in some rodeo. "I can ride anything." Retired from competition, Cory was one of many mid-level players in the sport, Hadley supposed, but he didn't lack confidence. Cory could even be cocky. "Mean broncs, rank bulls... I'm an all-around cowboy."

Hadley tilted his head toward the nearby stall. "Yeah, well, this one has a tendency to buck so I guess that means you can handle him." He suppressed a brief flash of concern. Should he trust Cory? How capable was he? He knew very little about him. "Just in case, carry your cell. You get into trouble, call Clara at the house." Before the upcoming auction, Hadley hadn't found time to check the fence himself.

Cory's grin widened. "I'll not only secure your fence, I'll whip that nag into shape real quick. I've got the touch."

"But remember, the horse spooks at the slightest cause for alarm. A piece of white paper blowing across the yard. The hoot of a barn owl. A car coming up the drive." If that was Jenna, he could understand the reaction. The gelding took particular exception to the sound of Clara's dinner bell, rusty after years of disuse, being rung from the back porch. "Treat Mr. Robert like the gentleman he should be."

"He's no gentleman, all right." Cory ran a hand through his wheat-colored hair. "But then, neither am I."

"I wouldn't know," Hadley muttered. The ex–rodeo "star" had come with only vague references, but he and Clara weren't in any position to demand them. For now, they needed help—and Cory had been their only candidate. "Just do the job, keep your nose clean, and I'll pay you." Somehow.

Still, he had to admit, the guy was an enigma. He'd seemed to fall from the sky exactly when Hadley had needed him, and Hadley couldn't be choosy. In a way he reminded him of the kids he and his brother had been long ago, being abandoned here and there, which had turned Hadley into a drifter. He wondered if the same had happened to Dallas and where he might be now. On the road somewhere, as Cory had been? How long would he stay? Hadley blocked out the thought. If he was going to get Clara's ranch going again, he had to make it happen any way he could. For her, the twins and himself.

Cory started down the aisle toward the feed room, which was a mass of cobwebs at the moment, then stopped. When he turned around, his gaze faltered. "I left my gear in my truck. Where am I supposed to sleep?"

Hadley hadn't considered that. There was no room in Clara's house. The day after they'd hatched their plan to get the ranch on its feet again, he'd inspected the old foreman's bungalow. But the floor had nearly buckled under his feet, the boards were so rotten and warped. The front windows were broken, the toilet was missing, and there were mouse droppings everywhere. The bungalow made the foreman's house at the NLS seem like a palace. "If I were you, I'd lay some fresh straw in the loft tonight. You can eat your meals with me and Mrs. McMann. We'll figure something better out—but not today."

"I can sleep anywhere," Cory said with a shrug. He walked back to Hadley, then stuck out his hand. "Thanks for taking a chance on me."

As if not many people did. Hadley could understand that. They shook, and Hadley couldn't help but think of today's meeting with Barney Caldwell and Jenna at the bank. He sure could have used that account money—at *his* discretion—to put the McMann ranch on solid footing again, but Amy hadn't given him that power. Hadley had a new idea, though, which made him smile. He would definitely speak to Jenna again.

But all he said to Cory was, "Don't let me down."

AFTER A LONG DAY of beating the bushes for clients, Jenna let herself into the apartment she'd rented on the far edge of Barren. The sun had gone down half an hour ago, and although she'd enjoyed the mesmerizing sight of color splashed across the sky on the drive home, it hadn't raised her spirits.

She tried not to feel discouraged. Her ad in the local paper didn't seem to be working. Neither had the flyers she'd placed on the front counters at the library, the Bon Appetit or the Sundown Café. Oh, and every store in town. Sherry had taken some for the Baby Things shop, assuring Jenna that many of her clients were young marrieds and first-time homeowners who might welcome her advice on decor. None of her canvassing had worked so far, nor had her new website. Not a single person had liked the website or her Facebook page, and as of tonight Jenna had zero genuine followers. She wouldn't count her sister, her friends or her mom, who supported her but didn't need her services.

She certainly couldn't count Hadley. Their meeting in Barney's office preyed on her mind and soured her mood. Why blame her for Amy's decision about the bank account? She only wished she'd been more proactive instead of avoiding Barney for so long. They could have met without Hadley there and avoided the confrontation. Then she'd have been better prepared.

She set down her tote bag containing the leftover flyers just as someone knocked at her door.

"I've brought dinner," her mother said, breezing into the apartment, the aroma of pizza from the box she carried following her inside.

"I'm not hungry, Mama." Jenna turned on some lights.

"You have to eat. You're too thin. Do you have anything to drink?"

"Soda. Orange juice. Water," she said after mentally reviewing the contents of her fridge.

Wanda set the box on the kitchen table, the new diamond ring on her finger flashing as she moved, reminding Jenna of her talk with Shadow about their mother's engagement to Jack Hancock. Familiar with Jenna's kitchen, Wanda pulled out two glasses, then plates from the cupboard, and silverware from a drawer.

"Mama, really."

Her mother took a seat, then waved Jenna toward the opposite chair. Without warning, she said, "I hear there was an incident at the bank." As if she or Hadley Smith had robbed it. "Is that why you look so down in the mouth? Here." She pushed a slice of pizza across the table. "As I tell Jack's uncle Bertie, food cures everything."

Jenna merely raised an eyebrow. She and Clara should start a cooking school. Jenna wouldn't talk about the bank, or about Hadley. "Did you cut your hair?"

"I had it done at the salon," Wanda said, a lifelong do-it-herself-er. This was yet another change in her mother's life for the better. Wanda patted the sleek new style, her once-dull dark hair now shiny with coppery high-lights. "Jack likes it."

"I do, too," Jenna said. For a long time she had worried about her mom and the life she'd lived with Jenna's dad. Even now, she pushed food at Jenna as if to make up for the times when she hadn't been able to feed her family. But Jack? He'd drifted—like Hadley—in and out of his uncle's life over the years. "This is a good sign," she said. "You're taking care of yourself. I hope you'll keep that in mind."

Wanda's dark gaze sharpened. "Shadow told me you're not okay with our engage-ment. I decided to come by, get to the bot-tom of this."

Jenna groaned. "My sister doesn't know how to keep a confidence."

"No reason to," Wanda murmured. "We're family. If you don't like Jack for some rea-son—"

"I do like him. I'm not sure he's good for you, that's all." She paused. "What if he doesn't make a go of the Bon Appetit or gets bored after a year? He does that French thing, pretending he speaks the language, so maybe he's always thinking about somewhere else.

Barren isn't the most exciting place in the world."

"If Jack decides it's not interesting enough for him here, I'll move with him."

Assuming Jack would let her or, like David with Jenna, decide his new adventures didn't include her. "I'm sure the engagement is exciting, Mama, but what comes after that? When you're really married..."

"We already live together. We know each other." Wanda finished her pizza. "Jack would never hurt me the way—"

Jenna flinched. "David hurt me? Have you and Shadow talked about that, too? I'm not projecting my failures onto you. I only want to make sure you know what you're doing and what the risks may be."

Jenna had barely eaten at all, and when her mother held out another slice to her as if she were a baby bird that needed to be hand-fed, she drew back. Wanda nudged the pizza closer until, finally, Jenna took it. "All right, okay. Just this one." She took a bite, hardly tasting the melted cheese and oregano-laced tomato sauce.

"Honey, I'm fine. Please don't worry." As if to reassure Jenna—or herself?—her mother's engagement ring sparkled again, creating a rainbow on the far wall. Wanda studied the stone for a moment before a smile bloomed. "I've never been happier in my life, and I intend to stay that way. Shadow and I agree about where these concerns are truly coming from. Put that dreadful man behind you, Jenna." For a second, Jenna thought she was referring to Hadley. "If there was a more self-centered person than David Collins, I've never met one."

*Except Daddy*, Jenna thought. At least her ex had held a steady job, made decent money, and they'd shared a well-appointed home rather than a falling-down wreck. Finn and his wife, Annabelle, owned the Moran house now, and the renovations they were doing to it and the old farm buildings warmed her heart. Soon, there'd be few reminders of Jenna's childhood, her father's neglect or her parents' dysfunctional marriage. How could Mama want to change her name again? Jenna sure didn't intend to try another relationship.

So why did an unbidden image of Hadley run through her mind? Certainly, after today's meeting at the bank, it was even more evident that he was not relationship material. Like her father, he'd never held a job for long, as evidenced by his recently quitting at the NLS to take over Clara's ranch. How long would he stick with that? Or stay in Barren? Jenna would do better to remember the dark look on his face when he'd learned about Amy's account, putting yet another barrier between Jenna and Hadley.

CORY TOSSED HIS gear bag onto the fresh pile of straw in the barn loft and held his breath. This might not be the most luxurious of accommodations, but he needed work, and the McMann ranch—if he could term it that, since nothing was mooing in the nearby pasture or growing in the fields—seemed better than most ideas he'd had. Besides, what other option was there?

He rummaged through his bag, yanked out the pillow he traveled with, then the plaid woolen blanket he favored.

From the house the dinner bell clanged, but Cory didn't answer the summons. He'd eaten a fast-food burger in Farrier before he drove out to meet Hadley Smith, having heard about the job from another rancher. More to the point, he didn't want Clara Mc-

Mann in his face. The old woman had already pumped him for information Cory wouldn't share. He knew how to ride horses and rope cows—had the wins to prove it—but he had no experience with mothers or grandmothers. He patted his gaudy prize buckle, silently insisting he wasn't missing anything.

He rearranged his bedding, set down the Disney alarm clock he carried with him everywhere, then started to settle down in the straw.

"Mr. Jennings?" The McMann woman's soft voice called to him from below.

Tempted to ignore her, Cory dragged a hand through his hair. "Yeah?"

"Please join us for dinner. I hope you like enchiladas."

His stomach growled. "Ate my share of Tex-Mex on the circuit," he said, but his mouth watered. "No, thanks. I'll pass."

She didn't take the hint. "Let me fix you a sandwich, then, or I have leftover pot roast to reheat." Another rumble rolled through his gut. Apparently the burger had worked its way through his system and he was hungry after all. Then she threw in the ultimate temptation. "Do you like apple pie? With vanilla ice cream?"

"Yes, ma'am." Before he thought better of it, he'd climbed down the ladder to the barn floor and was walking with Clara McMann across the yard to the kitchen door. As soon as it opened, the scents of fruit and cinnamon, jalapeños and corn wrapped him in a cocoon of hunger. The warmth in the room felt like a too-cozy blanket.

At the table Hadley Smith was already dripping hot sauce all over an enchilada. He looked up at Cory with a grin that transformed his normally stern face. "I could have told you. Clara doesn't let anyone go without a good meal."

"Sit down, Mr. Jennings." She pointed at a chair and the place already set with sturdy stoneware and silver. She took her seat, unfolded her napkin with a nod at the one he hadn't touched, then said, "Now. We'll eat—and get to know you."

Cory bit back a groan. He should have guessed. The true reason for this invitation was to weasel more details out of him. That wouldn't happen. In his experience the more lies he spun, the more he had to remember so he didn't trip himself up later.

Cory took the platter of enchiladas from her, dished up a pair of them and slathered on some salsa verde. He grabbed a square of corn bread, still hot and moist from the oven, then hunched over his plate.

Hadley tapped his shoulder. He held out a beer.

Cory shook his head. "Not a drinker," he said. *At least not here.* Alcohol loosened his tongue. "I'd rather have a glass of milk." He sent Mrs. McMann a smile. "Kills the heat I created on my enchilada."

Hadley brought the glass to him, then returned to his chair. For a few minutes, silence reigned while everyone ate. Then the woman spoke again.

"Where are you from, Mr. Jennings?"

"Call me Cory, ma'am." He coated the corn bread with another layer of butter, the real stuff. "Here and there," he finally said, causing one of Hadley's eyebrows to rise. "I was born in Texas."

Cory avoided Hadley's gaze, and Mrs. McMann's. *Note to self.* He'd used the state before, not that hard to remember. It went with his past rodeo career, even with the job he'd be doing here for her and Smith.

"Your father was a rancher?" she pressed him.

"No." The one-word answer was his friend. He pushed a piece of corn bread into the sauce on his plate. "Don't rightly recall what he did for a living. He and my mom split before I was born." True enough, if he stretched things. "I don't like talking about that."

With a sympathetic glance, she seemed to take that hint. She passed him the enchiladas, urging him to take another. "You young people don't eat enough."

He focused on the empty milk glass. "I'm not a baby, ma'am. Don't you have a pair of twins to worry about?"

"Yes, but there's always room for more." She glanced at the ceiling. "We savor our meals here when we can. Please," she added, "eat up, Cory. And call me Clara. By the time I'm done with you, you'll need jeans in a bigger size."

"She's not kidding," Hadley muttered. He shoved away from the table. "Another fine dinner, Clara. Thank you for the trouble."

"No trouble at all," she said.

He walked toward the hall. "I'll check on Luke and Gracie."

"I'll keep your pie warm, dear. You, Cory? Ready for ice cream, too?"

Hadley laughed but kept going to the stairs. "Don't even try to refuse." Cory cleaned his plate, carried it with the others to the sink, then sank back onto his chair while Clara McMann sliced the best-looking pie he'd ever seen into generous servings. Then she spooned huge dollops of vanilla ice cream onto the dessert dishes. Despite the four enchiladas he'd eaten and three chunks of corn bread, his stomach begged for more. He hadn't always been able to afford to eat when he was on the road. Maybe this would work out.

Clara set his pie in front of him. "We won't wait for Hadley. He likes to stand a while and watch his babies sleep. I suspect you haven't been eating well—or often," she said.

Cory didn't attempt to correct her. He took Hadley's advice. And ate.

This gig—as long as it lasted—might be

all right if he stayed as careful as he would on some bucking horse.

He just had to keep his head down and stick to himself.

# CHAPTER SIX

HADLEY'S TRIP TO the auction in Wichita had
worked out even better than he'd hoped. From
the last of their combined money, mostly
Clara's, they were the proud new owners
of half a dozen head of sleek Black Angus,
which would command the best price on the
market. As soon as he put in a crop of hay
and, by magic, somehow unearthed more
cash, he'd buy another six cows. Building the
new herd as their shaky finances allowed.
Cory Jennings was hard at work this morning, and for once the twins had only wakened
a couple of times during the night. Hadley
was in an unusually fine mood, which should
have warned him. He spotted Jenna's car rolling up the drive.

And remembered his latest idea.

Naturally, she'd brought gifts for the twins
but didn't mention their encounter in Barney's
office. Jenna had obviously decided not to

bring up the money issue, which left that to Hadley. He seized the opportunity, though, to put off what he had to say, which she probably wouldn't take well.

"You'll go bankrupt spoiling Luke and Gracie," he told her mildly. "The day I saw you at Sherry's, I bought ridiculously tiny socks, more sleepers, some onesies and a couple of stuffed lambs that play sounds little kids are supposed to like. I'd buy anything that puts them to sleep."

She held up another Baby Things bag. "I thought you'd ask if I bought these with Amy's money." So she hadn't forgotten their meeting in the bank.

"Did you?"

"No, of course not. These are simply presents. From me." She looked pointedly at him as if she expected his objection.

"The way they're growing, I can use all the clothes they can get." His good mood overwhelming his common sense, he walked with her to the house. If it wasn't for the guardianship issue and that bank account, he might like Jenna. But it troubled him that he hadn't found the missing application among Amy's papers. "You'll need another loan soon from Barney."

She didn't respond to his teasing tone. "I'm waiting to hear about the one I applied for after you left the bank all fired up about Amy's account."

Hadley laid a hand on her arm to stop her before they reached the back steps. "About that," he began, "I have an idea. Hear me out. What if I use some of that money Amy left to reestablish the ranch?" He surveyed the land around them, the new cattle grazing in a far field. "Without that, Clara and I don't have enough between us to make a real difference in the place. What we did have went into one horse and six cows. Truly building up the herd and getting the ranch on its feet again would benefit the twins."

Jenna pulled away. "How so, when you're not the owner of this ranch?"

"They live here," he insisted.

"Until you decide to move on again."

Hadley briefly pressed his lips tight. "So you don't see the benefit?"

"For Clara, yes. She's a favorite of mine, but I've already decided what to do with the *twins'* money. Which, I should remind you, is for their sole benefit."

"And what's that?"

"I'm going to set up a trust. For their education."

"Ah," he said, "I see. Then after I take off for parts unknown, Luke won't have to become a ranch hand someday instead of going to college. And Gracie won't have to wait tables to make ends meet."

"I didn't say that, Hadley."

He started walking again. "Yeah, you did. You've been more than clear that you don't trust me. I guess that's your call."

They went into the kitchen where Clara was trying to give the twins their bottles. Which they seemed to think was funny. Their eyes looked merry.

Jenna stepped away from Hadley as if she'd been waiting for the opportunity to create distance from him. "Oh, my," she murmured, a laugh in her voice.

Clara said, "I've been spit on, peed on by one cheeky little boy and had my hair pulled by a naughty little girl—and it's not ten o'clock yet." She was all smiles, though.

"Here. Take Grace. She's a bit easier, if not much."

Hadley grabbed a refill of coffee from the pot on the counter. He looked over Jenna's head at the window. "I think the ground's dry enough to start plowing. Soon as Cory's done feeding Mr. Robert, I'll start him on that today, Clara."

Hadley wanted to escape. He wasn't happy that Jenna hadn't taken to his suggestion about the account money. Why was she being stubborn? If Clara's ranch did well, so would the twins, and Hadley could look forward for a change instead of back.

He'd just taken a first sip of his coffee when he saw a car he didn't recognize pull up beside Jenna's at the porch steps. Two people he did know got out, and Hadley's heart stopped for a second before it began beating so hard he could feel it all through his body. "Company," he said to Clara.

She paused. "Who can it be?"

"Amy's folks." His mouth hardened. Walter and Danielle Pearson. Until this moment they'd never come near the twins. At their daughter's funeral they'd stayed far away from Hadley, barely speaking to him until

Walter Pearson had blasted him about Amy.
Both of them blamed him for her death, and
Hadley continued to have nightmares of the
tongue-lashing he'd taken. "I knew this would
happen one day."

But he wasn't worried about himself.

Without thinking, he edged closer to Jenna
as if she might relieve him of having to face
the Pearsons. After a quick rap at the door,
Amy's dad opened it without being asked in
and, a hand on his wife's back, steered her
inside.

Shoulders squared, well into his fifties,
Walter had dark hair with gray at the tem-
ples, flinty dark eyes and a solid build that
Hadley knew he kept toned at a gym. His
slate-colored suit must have cost more than
what Hadley had been making in a month at
the NLS. Pearson had a natural air of command that would make many other men feel
inferior. He reminded Hadley of several of the
foster parents he'd had, people who'd made
him miserable before they finally threw him
out or he ran off. He disliked Pearson almost
as much as Pearson disliked him.

"Mrs. McMann." Walter gently pushed
Amy's mother toward the table where the

twins, now in their baby seats, were playing with their toys. Pearson turned toward Jenna. "And you are?"

"A friend of the family," she said, emphasizing the word *friend* as if she didn't like them any more than Hadley did. "Actually, we met at Amy's funeral."

He didn't offer a hand. His wife, Danielle, was staring fixedly at Luke and Gracie, her brown gaze darting between them. A slight woman, she had Amy's reddish-gold hair, or rather Amy had inherited hers, and she seemed to Hadley like a woman who was easily cowed by her more aggressive husband.

"About time you showed up," Hadley said, taking the offensive.

Pearson glared at him. "Don't start, Smith. Not after what you did to Amy."

"I don't really care what you think of me." He gestured at Luke and Gracie, their eyes wide. "I care about them. You've never bothered to come see the twins before. Why now? I assume they're why you're here."

Walter ignored him. He touched Danielle's shoulder, and she moved closer to the twins, her eyes lighting up. He had to give Danielle marks for some interest. In those first weeks after Amy's death, she'd showered the babies with presents as Jenna did. Now and then she'd called Clara to see how they were doing, but he suspected she did so behind Walter's back. Her gaze practically begged Hadley not to say anything. "Oh, how sweet they are," she murmured, blinking.

Clara rose from the table. "Let me unbuckle them from their seats. Then you can hold them." The invitation seemed natural, but Hadley tensed. It wasn't as if Clara was betraying him...

Then, before Clara freed Luke from his seat, Jenna said, "I should go," becoming the second traitor. She turned, a troubled expression in her eyes, and his gaze sent her a silent message that said *stay*. In this case he liked the odds of three against two, even when one of them was Jenna and they'd just disagreed about Amy's money for the twins.

When she nodded, he released her arm. Hadley picked up Gracie, who promptly smacked his cheek with wet fingers she'd had in her mouth. "Wouldn't want to ruin your dress," he told Danielle as he wiped Gracie's hand.

Her gaze faltered. "It will wash. I'd really like to hold my granddaughter."

The last word, obvious as it was, rattled Hadley. A part of him empathized with her; she seemed so like Amy, who'd always wanted children—even with him—and had talked endlessly about being a mother all during her pregnancy. If Danielle was similarly maternal, why hadn't she kept in better touch with Amy? She'd rarely seen her daughter after she married Hadley. Why just send money for that account? Was it because of him? He eased Gracie's head onto his shoulder, his hand in her hair. "You just now decided to become an adoring grandmother?"

Jenna put a hand on his forearm. "Hadley."

Not to his surprise, Walter flickered a glance at Gracie, then at Luke, who banged his palm against his plastic toy. "Smith is right. They'll probably spit up on you, Dani."

Hadley flinched. "Sure," he said, "but they're kids. It's kind of their job to be messy."

He guessed this visit hadn't been Walter's idea. Maybe he'd finally given in to his wife's pleas to come see the twins. Walter had never seemed a very affectionate father with Amy, their only child, who'd worshipped him from afar anyway during her marriage. Hadley couldn't imagine he meant to play the twins' doting grandfather now.

Danielle faced Hadley. "May I?"

To his dismay, Gracie, the more sociable of the twins, reached out for the woman. If he refused, he'd make Gracie cry, and the brimming tears in Danielle's eyes said a lot. Their fingers brushing, Hadley's too warm and Amy's mother's ice-cold, he handed his girl over and felt his spirits plummet.

Yawning, Gracie nestled into the crook of Danielle's neck and fell asleep. Another act of treason, he thought.

JENNA TRIED TO avoid confrontations. She'd had those with her father, then enough of them with David in the last days of their marriage. With both men she always seemed to finish on the short end of an argument. She usually found it better to defuse any potential problems before they began. Now the growing anger in Hadley's eyes brought out that peacemaking nature. If she didn't intervene, there was no telling what might happen. and as always, she wanted to protect the children. Hadley had given Grace to Mrs. Pearson, but with Walter…

"This isn't my kitchen," she said, stepping between him and Hadley, who gripped his mug with white-knuckled fingers, "but while you…talk, does anyone else want a cup of coffee?"

Clara's stiff shoulders relaxed. "Thank you, Jenna. I was going to ask the same. At the McMann ranch, we pride ourselves on hospitality." With a chiding glance at Hadley, she bustled to the cupboard and pulled out another pair of mugs with bucking horses on them. "Cream? Sugar?" she asked as if she might sweeten the bitter atmosphere. "I made banana bread yesterday…" Clara trailed off, sending Hadley another look that begged him to help defuse the situation. She set a steaming cup in front of Danielle.

"I don't need cake or coffee," Walter said, his voice a low rumble. "I certainly don't need this man's hostility."

Hadley tore his gaze away from Danielle, her head bent over Grace's, to glare at Walter. "Then why don't you say your piece—before you leave?"

"I have every right to be here. I'm surprised to find *you* still in Barren or on this ranch, much less in the same room with these two."

He motioned at Grace, then Luke. Hadley's baby boy was staring at Walter as if he were some alien yet fascinating being. "Amy told me before she—" Walter's voice thickened "—before her twins were born what kind of father she wanted for them. I never thought that should be you. I haven't changed my mind."

Hadley gazed into his cooling coffee. "I don't suppose you have—and all along you undermined our marriage."

"The one you intended to scrap."

"So you decided to give Amy some insurance." A muscle ticked in Hadley's jaw. "I didn't know until the other day about her account at the local bank. Money to tide her over if I left her? Which I didn't," he finished. Yet the money explained her shopping habit.

"Amy called that her rainy-day fund. Since I couldn't change her opinion of you, I was happy to provide security." He glanced at Danielle, whose head was still bowed over Grace. Jenna wondered if she was crying. She felt sorry for Clara, too. The tense air in the kitchen had affected everyone except Grace, who was asleep, oblivious to the adults' quarrel. But Luke's lower lip had begun to quiver, and his face scrunched up.

Hadley set his mug on the counter with a definite clink of stoneware against granite. "And your daughter left the money in that account to someone else—" he looked at Jenna "—for my kids. Gracie and Luke are mine to take care of—"

Walter's eyes snapped. "I wonder. How well are you doing that?"

Clara gasped. Her heart pounding, Jenna lifted Luke from his seat, rocking him gently in her arms. "Hadley. The twins," she said.

He had the sense to appear ashamed. "Sorry."

Jenna spoke up. "Mr. Pearson, Amy designated me as her beneficiary on that account. I'll be seeing to their welfare. You needn't worry. *Amy* wouldn't have to worry," she went on, patting Luke's back.

Clara chimed in. "And I know Hadley. This visit has been a shock—"

"We should have called first," Danielle agreed. "Walt, please. You and Hadley have your differences, but we all have to find common ground now because of these babies, as Jenna pointed out." She kissed the top of Grace's head. "You wondered why we haven't come here until now. I wanted to, but after the loss we'd suffered, I needed time to accept that my dear Amy, after suffering so much…is really gone."

Jenna wondered about the word she'd used. In Amy's labor and delivery, yes, she must have suffered, but Danielle made it seem as if there'd been some longer-term pain involved. Frowning, Hadley took a step back toward the door to the yard. He must hope Jenna, having told the Pearsons she was in charge of the bank account, wouldn't also mention the standby guardianship. She doubted Amy had mentioned it to them, perhaps not wanting them to have control, or she wouldn't have asked Jenna in the first place. Or named her as beneficiary of the account.

Hadley nodded at Danielle. "Enjoy your visit. I have work to do."

"Oh, dear," Clara murmured.

No one else said anything as he slammed out the door.

IN THE BARN Hadley's hands shook as he re-filled Mr. Robert's water bucket. He couldn't seem to settle down. At the house he'd let his temper get the best of him. Or had that been fear? For a man who'd never imagined becoming anyone's dad, much less trying to do a decent job of it, he'd sure changed his tune the minute he first saw Luke and Gracie. Now, with the Pearsons here, what would happen?

"Hadley?" Jenna's voice echoed down the aisle.

"I'm busy," he said. It wasn't as if she or Clara, even Gracie, had set out to betray him, but he craved solitude.

He set the bucket on the hook inside the stall, then slid the door shut. Cory had ridden the horse to check on some loose fence, an endless chore.

"If Pearson wanted to watch me squirm, you sure helped." Hadley's tone reeked of sarcasm. "Thanks for bringing up the account."

"You're welcome." Jenna's mouth firmed. "You didn't do Luke and Grace any good in there," she said, waving toward the house. "You woke Grace and made her cry. Then Luke took his cue and he's bawling, too."

He sighed. "That's the last thing I want. Maybe I was a jerk, but I know enough about that man to be…" He wouldn't say afraid.

He leaned against the stall door. To Walter Pearson, he'd probably looked the part of the down-on-his-luck cowpoke—dirty jeans, scarred boots and all—the drifter Pearson had always thought he was. Hadley couldn't disagree, and probably neither would Jenna. "Everybody in this town expects me to take off for somewhere else." He couldn't meet her gaze. "Obviously, Amy did, too. I'm glad she saw to Luke and Gracie, not that I'm happy with how she did it. But Walter Pearson is a whole other problem. If a guy needed an enemy, he's from central casting."

"You're being overly dramatic."

"I'm sorry Amy didn't live to see the twins." He shook his head. "But man, I don't miss all of our arguments. She sure knew how to make my head spin. Must have learned that from her dad."

Jenna crossed her arms. "I think you're making more of this than it is. Mr. Pearson was only trying to please his wife," she said. "Maybe, once he lets himself really look at Grace and Luke, even hold them, he'll find he's wrong about you, too."

Hadley gaped at her. "Where'd you get that idea?"

Jenna didn't say. In fact, she seemed embarrassed. Shaking his head, he went into the feed room, telling himself not to let down his guard. Most likely she hadn't altered her view of him one bit and was only trying to smooth things over. People had a habit of lulling him into a false sense of security right before the big guns came out. Like Pearson. And now, Jenna was urging him to be optimistic but holding tight to that money. He wouldn't trust either of them.

"I don't expect Pearson to change," he said, half to himself, "but because of Danielle I doubt this visit will be their last."

# CHAPTER SEVEN

As SHE DROVE through the open gates onto Wilson Cattle, Jenna's stomach was tied in a knot. A thousand thoughts spun through her head, most of them creating more panic. What if this appointment didn't work out? It wouldn't be the first. What if she didn't get this client, either? Liza was Shadow's stepmother-in-law, but that didn't guarantee Jenna the job. If she wasn't behind the wheel, she'd be twining her fingers together as if they were a rope.

Two weeks after the confusing conversation she'd had with Hadley in the barn, Jenna was still pondering her words. Why *had* she thought Walter would change his mind about Hadley? Had *she*? He clearly loved his children and took the best care of them he could, but she hadn't liked witnessing his anger. Ever since, she'd been trying to push that from her mind and focus instead on beating the bushes for work. She needed any assignment she could get.

"Talk to Liza," her sister had urged her again. "She's such a dear. The contractors have cleared out of the new house, and she and Everett are ready to move in. I know she could use your expertise with their interior. Confidence," Shadow reminded her. "You are who you say you are—a talented interior designer."

Yet Jenna's troubled childhood and then her disastrous marriage had destroyed her self-esteem. Amazingly, Hadley seemed to be the one person she could stand up to. Frankly, whenever she held her ground with him, Jenna felt as if she were watching someone else. But the mistrust in his eyes that day in the barn had been clear. She couldn't escape the feeling that they would tangle again soon regarding Amy's account.

Not that Amy's money would help Jenna right now. It was for the twins. She had to find clients in order to make her own ends meet.

Hopefully, in that regard, today would turn out better than yesterday when Jenna had run into Barney Caldwell's mother in front of the bank. "I'd like your input on some new furniture for my living room," Bernice had begun.

Then after a brief discussion of style and a suggestion from Jenna that they meet to discuss some choices, Bernice had launched into the real issue—a campaign on her son's behalf. Jenna wasn't interested in coffee with Barney or an afternoon at the spring garden show with him, but apparently Bernice was a matchmaker. Jenna had managed to resist, but she'd probably lost another potential client.

Her meeting with Liza today had to go better. With a quick toot of her horn, she drove past the front porch of the main house, then kept going by the Wilson Cattle barns. At the corral Jenna stopped to watch a mare nuzzle her foal before she continued past the bunkhouse and onto the newer part of the drive that led to Liza and Everett's new home.

*Amazing*, she thought as the structure belonging to Shadow's in-laws came into view. Massive logs, a huge expanse of windows, a prow like that of a ship jutting out as if to take command of the entire ranch. Even surrounded still by construction debris, and without any landscaping yet in place, the effect was stunning. Very different, too, from most others in the area, including the large-frame main house where Shadow lived.

At the door, slender, dark-haired Liza folded Jenna into a warm hug, then led her inside. In her midthirties, Liza was Everett's second wife and his junior by twenty years or so. "Feels cool without the heat on here, but I'm glad this place is done at last." She steered Jenna into the great room. "Thank you for coming." She gestured at the large space. "What do you think?"

"Gorgeous," Jenna said after realizing Liza genuinely wanted her opinion. David had never valued her input, although he had left the interior design of their home in Shawnee Mission to her because he was busy with his law practice. "Real work," he called it. "I understand you'd like to blend your style with Everett's?" Jenna said.

"My husband will give advice," Liza said with a smile, "and I'll indulge his whims—unless they threaten to alter my vision too much—but the aim is to make us both happy here. I want this house to be luxurious Western. What would you suggest? I used a designer for my condo in Dallas, but that was a different life in a big city. Until I met Everett—and he robbed the cradle," she said with a laugh, "I never realized my soul belonged here."

This was Jenna's cue to sell herself. She studied the vast room dominated by a walk-in fireplace faced in rugged stone all the way to the vaulted ceiling. "There's your focal point. I see a big—really big—set of andirons. Rugged. This room can take a lot of scale. And were you thinking of adding a mantel? Heavy wood, chunky and distressed, from a tree on the property might be appropriate."

Liza clapped her hands. "I like that idea. Everett claims I'm too sentimental, but I'd love that kind of mantel to display family photos, starting with our granddaughter, Ava."

"Why not a collection? Ava as a baby, a toddler, a little girl…"

"Oh, yes!"

"And of course the rest of the family."

Liza named some other relatives. "Everett's son Grey and your sister Shadow, his daughter Olivia and her Sawyer, little Zach…all my steps," she said.

Jenna glanced up at the ceiling. "Are you thinking of a chandelier?"

"Not one of those antler things," Liza said with a shudder. "You can't take the city en-

tirely out of this girl. I've told Everett there
will be no stuffed animal heads on our walls."

Jenna laughed with her. She turned in a
circle, surveying the room again. "I'd suggest buttery leather chairs, deeply cushioned
suede sofas—combining the Western theme
with luxury fabrics—lots of pillows... Tex-
ture," she added.

"Pops of color."

"Natural tones. Earthy. Rust, yellow, burnt
orange..."

Liza said, "And no draperies, please."

"To cover these windows—or that view—
would be a crime. And you don't have neighbors to block out." Through the expanse of
glass, the landscape appeared limitless, spring
grass rolling to meet the far sky like green
velvet. When Liza asked if Jenna wanted to
see the rest of the house, she said, "I'd love
to," hoping she'd made the first cut.

Twenty minutes later they descended the
broad sweep of stairs from the second floor
to the two-storied entryway. At the double
doors, Jenna gazed upward again. "Crystal,"
she said. "A modern chandelier dripping with
light. Edgy, surprising. I know a glass artist

in Kansas City who does amazing work. She created sconces for my house there."

"I love it." Liza grasped her hand. "Consider yourself hired, Jenna."

"I've got the job?" After so long without even a nibble, excluding Bernice's approach as a lure for Barney, Jenna couldn't quite believe it. But she was excited, too. Already she could envision each finished room of this splendid home. "Thank you."

"Don't thank me yet. But word of mouth is a powerful thing, and I have friends. I'm getting ahead of myself, though I believe before you know it, you should have more clients than you can handle." Liza grinned. "Just don't start with them before you finish here. How long will it take?"

"Several months, four at the most. First, I'll do a detailed plan, then we'll discuss it and you can make changes as you wish. Once we decide on specific items—furniture, case pieces, accessories—we'll have to wait a bit for the things we order. But is speed important?"

"I want to do things right rather than fast, but there is another factor…"

Jenna had seen that look before, and she

knew Liza, who wanted a family of her own, had already suffered one miscarriage. Now her cheeks flamed, her gaze grew moist, and Jenna didn't need to hear the words to feel the familiar sense of wrenching loss deep inside.

"I didn't plan to make this announcement too soon, but Everett and I are expecting a baby. October. Let's do something wonderful with the nursery."

"THE BABIES ARE obviously the big draw," Hadley stated to Jenna.

She'd come again today to see Luke and Gracie, and after half an hour of keeping busy in the barn, Hadley had given in and joined her in the living room. He told himself it was to help with the twins. Clara was out running errands, and he'd noticed her new habit of making herself scarce when he and Jenna were both here.

He hadn't been wrong when he'd predicted Amy's parents would be back. Their first visit was soon followed by another, then a third until, by late April, they seemed to be at the McMann ranch more than they were at home in Wichita.

"Babies always are," Jenna said with a

wistful expression that made him regret
bringing up the subject. She'd already mentioned Liza and Everett's pregnancy. Jenna
had tried to sound enthusiastic about their
news, but Hadley had picked up on her halting tone. Because there were few secrets in a
small town, he knew she was childless. One
reason she'd agreed to monitor the twins—
and Hadley?

Still. He had to admit that, since that day in
the barn when Jenna had called Hadley on his
anger, he liked having her around more than
he had before. Her initial awkwardness with
his babies had gradually become more natural. She had bought an activity quilt similar
to the one her sister had purchased, and the
gentle look in her eyes as she watched Luke
and Gracie play on it now brought a smile to
Hadley. Until she said, "There's nothing to
stop the Pearsons from seeing their grandchildren, is there?"

"Under Kansas law they have the right,
which Pearson pointed out. I googled that
after they left," he said. "They may have legal
justification, but Walter Pearson doesn't have
a soft spot in his body for my babies. Don't
let him fool you."

"I like his wife," Jenna said.

"I could, too. But I'm telling you, he has another agenda. I doubt there's a simple explanation for his interest in Luke and Gracie. I've met people like him before at the foster homes I stayed in. People who are only in it for themselves." In addition, Hadley had quickly become an expert at reading other people's faces, knowing when to duck for cover before a fist connected or one of those temporary "parents" cuffed the back of his head. More than once, he'd intervened to save Dallas from similar treatment and gotten worse than that himself.

"I guess neither of us had the greatest role models. That's why I wanted something different for my—" Jenna stammered "—for the twins."

Seated on the sofa, he clasped his hands between his spread thighs, then cleared his throat. "I don't mean to pry, but...you and your husband never had kids, I know. Maybe I shouldn't ask, but was that by choice? You don't have to answer if you don't want to."

"I'd have loved as many children as possible, but I...can't. I'm...infertile," she said, her eyes still on Luke and Gracie. Her fond smile dipped. "David and I had all the tests. It was my fault." She shrugged, an unhappy pull to her mouth. "When Amy asked me to serve as standby guardian, I was hesitant. And when she passed, I almost left the hospital. But after I saw the twins, I didn't need any judge to appoint me. I wanted to be in their lives. At first I thought that was only for Amy's sake…"

"Yet you can't keep from coming," he finished for her.

Her smile bloomed. "Because they're so darn cute."

"I'm willing to share," Hadley said, his teasing tone a surprise to himself. "You change their messy diapers. I'll watch 'em sleep."

Jenna glanced at the babies rolling around on the blanket, one of their newer skills. Luke reached out, trying to grab a squeaky toy, but missed. Gracie bumped against him.

Hadley thought he spotted a tear or two well in Jenna's eyes, despite the smile, and his heart went out to her. As resistant as he'd once been to the idea of fatherhood, he couldn't imagine not being a dad now, even if he wasn't the best one the twins might have.

What must it be like for Jenna to know she'd never cherish those babies she'd wanted? To learn her own body prevented that?

He felt sorry for her when she probably wouldn't want him to, and his smile quickly faded along with his attempt to tease her.

"Shouldn't have brought up your troubles, Jenna. Must be a sensitive subject."

"It's the truth," she said. "I need to accept it."

Which she obviously hadn't.

"You could adopt," he suggested.

"I've considered that—but I decided it wouldn't be the same for me."

He thought she'd be missing out on a lot, but that decision was Jenna's to make, not his. He already had the twins. Hadley knew he shouldn't push any further and returned to the previous topic. "The Pearsons were here again a few days ago. Danielle's always willing to deal with diapers or any other nastiness, but Walter never cracks—maybe because he gets distracted finding fault with me."

"Such as?"

Hadley would bet Jenna had a list of his failings, too. The first thing she usually did was to glance into the bed of his pickup as if she expected to find luggage piled there. One day she'd be right. "You remember how he was the first time they came. The second day he found me trying to wrestle Luke into clean pants and I wasn't doing a good job. I must have looked all thumbs, and Pearson was quick to pick up on my clumsiness—as if I'd never changed a diaper before. Not one of my favorite activities, but Luke's getting stronger every day."

"Did you lose your temper again?" Clearly she hadn't forgiven him for his display in the kitchen.

"Not quite. I did snap at Luke to please stop fighting me. Then the next time Clara had just disappeared when Amy's folks turned up. Both babies were yowling. I couldn't heat their bottles fast enough. Luke was so mad he came halfway out of his seat and almost fell on the floor. Gracie got upset and threw up her milk. The kitchen smelled…" He trailed off. No need to explain. "Would Pearson prefer me out of his and the twins' life? Yeah," he said, imagining Jenna might feel the same way.

She didn't avoid him as she had before, but then he was always here when she came to see the twins now, so avoidance would be hard—as it was for Hadley until he'd finally stopped trying. He wouldn't forget, though, that she was here now to also check up on him. It wasn't as if he and Jenna were friends or anything. Especially the "anything."

Jenna wasn't even his type—not that he had one these days. Being young and single was behind him, even when at times he wished things could be different. He wasn't about to get caught up with anyone, put his life in a twist again as he had with Amy. And with this woman who was obviously man-shy after her divorce? Hadley's marriage had been less than good; before that, and foster care, he'd watched his father destroy his mother. He had no time or inclination for another relationship, especially something he was bad at and that Jenna probably wouldn't want.

It wouldn't be wise, either, for her to get close to him. And why would she want to? Being with the twins any more than she already was would be a constant reminder that she couldn't have children of her own.

But didn't the four of them make a pretty picture right now? He and Jenna on the sofa, Luke and Gracie lying on their tummies and kicking their legs for all they were worth. Soon they'd be able to inch around that quilted play thing and onto the rug. And before he blinked twice they'd be crawling.

Walking right out of his life, eventually. But before that day, he'd hold on to them any way he could. And fight off anyone else who might try to take them. Including the Pearsons. And Jenna.

# *CHAPTER EIGHT*

INCREASINGLY WORRIED ABOUT losing his kids,
Hadley reexamined the contents of one of the
bins from the attic at the kitchen table. In
his occasional spare time as summer settled
in, he'd looked everywhere for the application that would have led to the court hearing
appointing Jenna as standby guardian. "Has
to be here. The application wasn't in a safe-
deposit box at the bank," he told Clara.

At the stove she tipped a bowl of carrots into
a bubbling pot of rich beef stew, a too-hearty
meal since the weather had gotten hotter, yet
she'd been given fresh beef from the Circle
H and was determined to use it tonight for
his belated dinner. Outside the windows, full
darkness had fallen while he'd completed his
chores.

Amy's account, which Jenna now con-
trolled, had certainly come as a surprise. But
so far he hadn't found evidence of any safe-

deposit box. The Cattlemen's Bank was the only one in town. Unless Amy had driven to Farrier or beyond to get a box…it didn't exist.

Hadley sighed. If only Jenna would let loose part of the money in that account for the ranch. But he'd had no luck convincing her that the funds would truly benefit the twins. And now he'd come to another dead end.

Meanwhile the ranch was progressing, but not enough yet to make decent money. Cory Jennings, despite the sketchy details of his past, was doing a good job for Clara's ranch. Hadley, too, loved the work, and the fencing already looked better. The stalls had never been cleaner, and daily Cory turned over the bedding in each one even when Mr. Robert was the only horse stabled there. Hadley made a mental note to look for another—if he could find the cash somewhere. Not from Jenna, it seemed. But without his pay from the NLS, things were tight, and he didn't want to ask Clara again for more, which she probably couldn't spare, either. They weren't making enough headway all around.

"Jenna must have a copy, dear," she murmured.

"I won't call her attention to that application," he said. "If I ever find it." Scanning an old grocery list Amy had left in her baby book, he tried to block out a stubborn vision of Jenna. They now often played with the babies together, which he enjoyed. Though he had to admit, part of his enjoyment came from watching Jenna, her auburn hair gleaming in the light. Now and then they'd had a real conversation, like the one about her not having children. Being infertile must be a painful thing for a person, but he knew she cared for Luke and Gracie a lot. Why wouldn't she let him use a small portion of Amy's money to redevelop the ranch? "I'm worried if Jenna learns I'm looking for the application, she'll alert the Pearsons."

"Make trouble for you?" Clara set their places at the table, her hand trembling as she laid a fork beside a plate. "About the babies? Jenna would never do that."

"Considering her attitude about Amy's bank account, the less she knows, the better." And the fewer unwanted visions of her in another context might slide through his mind.

Clara sent him a look he couldn't interpret. "We can handle the Pearsons."

"You think? I'm less optimistic. I have

to admit, there are times when leaving here seems like the best idea I could have. But not before this ranch succeeds again—I promised you, Clara—and not until the twins are older." So, for now he was staying. Clara shouldn't worry.

The Pearsons were another issue. They hadn't said when they would come again, but Danielle was here more frequently. Moving in on his little family of sorts while Walter, whenever he showed up, looked for any chance to prove Hadley unfit.

A serving spoon in hand, Clara said, "Hadley, not everyone in this world is out to get you. Amy's parents included."

His head came up. "Wait a minute. What are you not saying?"

Clara swept back to the stove and stirred the pot of stew again. Then she hustled to the rear door to ring the dinner bell as if Cory couldn't turn up fast enough to suit her.

"Clara," he said. He knew she wouldn't lie.

When she faced him, her eyes didn't meet his. "I may have talked to Danielle this afternoon."

"*May* have?"

"She asked if I could recommend the best

hotel in Barren. The trip back and forth to Wichita in one day is tiring. She'd like to start staying overnight."

"There is no hotel in Barren."

"Yes, I told her so. Then she asked if there were any motels on the road near town… again, no. There used to be a rooming house, remember, on Cutting Horse Road—"

"Went out of business the year I left town." Hadley had a very bad feeling about the direction of this conversation. He was sure she'd struck some deal with Danielle Pearson. Clara's tender heart would allow nothing less than to help in some way. He loved her for it. She'd saved him more than once, including that first time she'd snatched him from a house in Farrier and brought him to the ranch, crying tears she didn't want him to see for the bruises he had.

His childhood memories came flooding back. Packing his bag in the middle of the night, lighting out down the road alone. Getting caught by the cops a few times, then returned to some place of hell. Losing Dallas.

Sometimes, usually after he thought he'd seen his brother on the street somewhere, Hadley searched the internet without ever finding the slightest clue to Dallas's whereabouts. He wished Clara had been Dallas's foster parent, too. But what had she done now?

"You didn't," he went on. "You did not offer those people a room. Where, Clara?"

"The cabin."

Hadley had nearly forgotten about that. Cory was staying in the old foreman's house now. They'd fixed it up, though it remained little more than a shack. But the original homestead on the ranch was still standing, too. Kind of. "That cabin is not habitable. What were you thinking?"

"We won't get in each other's way, and where else could they go?"

"They can stay home in that fancy house of theirs. That's where."

Trying to control his anger, he focused on the scraps in the bin. He dropped loose bits of paper into the wastebasket beside his chair. The bin had been half-full of such pieces of now-useless memories, such as Amy's shopping lists and to-do notes to herself and… He caught the next one that had fallen out of the baby name book Jenna had mentioned at the hospital.

Hadley straightened. He was holding the

list of names Jenna had also talked about. Someday the twins would get a kick out of reading the choices Amy hadn't made. They'd see their own names in her handwriting starred and get a little glimpse of their mother. The better memories he could share.

He placed it on the table, though something about it niggled at his brain.

Hadley sighed. "Do you have any idea how the Pearsons live? I've never been to their house, but Amy described it to me. They've got six bathrooms, eight bedrooms...two kitchens and living rooms. Place must be ten thousand square feet if it's an inch—and you think Danielle Pearson will bed down in an old *cabin*?"

"Danielle is *not* staying at her house," Clara insisted. "The twins are the grandchildren I'll never have. I couldn't deprive anyone else of that pleasure. And don't worry about Walter. He has upcoming meetings in Denver, San Francisco, I forget which other cities." Pearson was in finance and on the boards of several organizations. "Danielle wants to see the babies more often, stay longer each time." Her chin hitched. Obviously, her mind was made up. "I've hired Jenna to help with the homestead. She needs work, and I hear she's doing a lovely job for Liza Wilson. She can give the cabin an updated look."

"With whose money?" What they did have was already stretched to the limit. There was no furniture left in the cabin, but at least the toilet was there and what he hoped was a working, if antiquated, stove. Still, it would require more than a "fresh look" to be livable.

Clara's gaze shifted. "Danielle has offered to pay for any improvements."

Hadley took a breath. His objections had been overruled, but he didn't say another word. Clara was too decent for her own good, a contrast to him. The ranch was hers to do with as she wished. Still, he felt that fresh sense of betrayal. He'd already lost this battle. He moved Amy's green sweater aside in the bin—and heard something crinkle within its folds. A second later he pulled out the paperwork he'd been searching for. Had Amy hidden it there? If so, why?

Without telling Clara he'd found it, he set the application aside to study later. Hadley needed time first to process all the legalese regarding Jenna, too.

For reasons of his own, he didn't favor having her here more often than she already was, either. That would only cause more impossible thoughts of her that he didn't need or want. And what if the application empowered her as he'd suspected?

# *CHAPTER NINE*

"DANIELLE, LET ME DO THAT." Jenna took the broom from Amy's mother, unwilling to let the elegant woman do manual labor. "Why don't you get a feel for this place—" Jenna tried not to notice there wasn't much room to roam "—while Cory and I finish up here?"

Not that long ago, fresh from the ruins of her broken marriage and damaged to her core, Jenna would have gladly slept on a cot in a place like this to have her own space to lick her wounds. But that wouldn't do for Danielle. Jenna had suggested rustic furniture and decor to match the cabin, but she guessed Danielle would expect comfort, too. Jenna ticked over some possibilities. While working for Olivia at her antiques shop, she'd kept her eye on a rough-hewn turn-of-the-century bureau, which had come from one of the original ranch houses in the area. That would fit perfectly in the cabin's bedroom, assuming the piece was still available. She'd deal with that in a few days when she saw Olivia.

Danielle drifted into the other room, and Jenna heard her talking to Cory, their voices low. Then she heard the throaty growl of a truck outside. The pickup pulled close to the scrap of porch in front. A door slammed.

"Where's Cory?" Hadley's voice had preceded him inside, where he filled the small space like a bull about to charge through a china shop. "Cory!" he called.

"Good morning," Jenna said, but he didn't look at her or reply. She'd been expecting this reaction, if not so soon.

Every line of his body appearing clenched, Hadley strode into the other room. "I don't care that you're doing a good deed," she heard him yell at Cory. "I'm paying you to move cattle. Now."

Danielle tried to intervene but failed. A moment later the young cowboy emerged, head hung low as he shuffled to the main door. "Sorry for the dustup, Miss Jenna. I'll come get the trash bags later."

Hadley followed him onto the porch. "The hell you will."

A second later Jenna was out the door. She

grasped Hadley's upper arm, which was a hard knot of bunched biceps muscle. "There's no reason to take out your bad mood—whatever it's about now—on someone who's dependent on that salary you pay him."

"*This* is my reason." Hadley waved a hand, shrugging off Jenna's grip on his arm. "These people are already taking over."

She lowered her voice not to be overheard. Cory was close enough as he ambled toward the barn, and Danielle might be in the next room. "They won't be able to move in for a while yet. Besides, I realize Walter has his less-than-admirable side, but what harm is there in letting them stay while they get to know the twins better?"

His blue eyes turned to flint. "Am I the only person here who doesn't think this is a great idea? Now you're working for the Pearsons—on land that doesn't belong to them. They have no right to—"

"Calm down, Hadley." She knew how he felt about the Pearsons, but was he angrier with Amy's parents, Clara or with her now? Had Amy been right about him? Yet months ago, after he'd moved into Amy's apartment across the hall from Jenna, he'd never left his wife. He'd acted like any other father-to-be, taking Amy to some of her doctors' appointments with Sawyer McCord, carrying groceries up the stairs for her, putting together the crib they'd bought. One night, Hadley had asked Jenna if she had a screwdriver he could borrow; there were plenty of tools at the ranch where he worked, but he'd needed one right then. When Amy went into labor that early morning in November, Jenna had watched him lift and carry her to his truck, Amy's arms tight around his neck. Jenna had glimpsed Hadley talking to her as if to reassure Amy.

Then he'd come home alone.

And much more recently, as Jenna and Hadley had watched the twins play on the floor that first time, she'd seen a different, even tender side of him, though she still regretted telling him about her infertility. Afterward, she'd gone home in a fresh haze of misery. The reminder always made her lose her bearings.

"Amy could find reason to criticize me without half trying," he continued. "Her father is the same. Before you know it, I'll be out on my a—backside and the twins will be in Wichita."

Jenna winced. She remembered how horrible it was to be suddenly turned out of your comfortable home, and from the little she knew of Hadley's past, he must expect that all the time. The thought made her sad.

"Wichita?" She softened her tone. "Hadley, what makes you think that would happen?"

His hand flashed through the air again, encompassing the ranch. "All of this. A rundown spread with half a dozen cows, one horse and a pickup that belongs more to the dealer's financing arm than it does to me. It's sure not what they could provide. Clara's house," he went on, "is hardly a palace—"

"Take a breath. You're jumping to conclusions."

He plowed a hand through his hair. "From what I read online, if I don't let them even have visitation, the Pearsons could go to court. They'd need to prove an established relationship there with Luke and Gracie. They don't have that—unless they're here to make one. See what I mean?"

"We must have visited the same websites. They would also have to demonstrate that visitation is in the best interest of the children. How could they prove that?"

"By gathering evidence that I'm not a good dad." Hadley stared at the far horizon across the flat expanse of the McMann ranch. "They've seen me lose my temper. Fumble that diaper change for Luke and try to deal—unsuccessfully—with him and Gracie in fits of frustration. There've been more incidents since. Frankly, I don't look that good. Now, even with just Danielle around, I'll have to watch everything I do or say 24/7." Just as he must feel he did with Jenna?

"Don't borrow trouble," she finally said. His blowup with Cory had unsettled her, like his display of anger the first time he'd faced Walter. His mercurial temper couldn't help but remind Jenna of her father. She wasn't sure how to feel about Hadley's dilemma, about him. She was sure of how she felt about the twins, though. Their home, as long as he stayed, was here. With Hadley. Like the Pearsons, she, too, had to keep watch.

SATURDAY HAD TO BE Cory's favorite night of the week. Rowdy's Bar would be his usual place to go, but he hadn't been there, for obvious reasons, since his return to Barren months ago. Instead, still smarting after Hadley laid into him yesterday, Cory headed for a barn dance on the far side of Farrier, leaving Rowdy's and the McMann ranch miles behind.

Cory wasn't a two-stepper by any means, yet the barn dance drew him for another reason. So far he'd had no luck spotting her, yet every few weeks he came, looked around the dance, then left. Tonight, as he climbed out of his truck, he straightened his hat and stomped both feet deeper into his boots. A man with a mission, he wandered through the open double doors into the barn where a local band was playing a lively tune Cory didn't recognize. He glanced around, hoping he wouldn't run into anyone he knew—except the one person he was searching for.

He hadn't taken stock of the large room before he felt a solid tap on his shoulder. Tempted to ignore it, he turned around—and saw a ghost. "Cal," he said, not quite meeting the other man's gaze. Cory's pulse pumped blood harder through his veins. This wasn't good. "Thought you were…"

"In prison?" With a laugh, Calvin Stern shook his head. "Not me. Spent time in the county jail—thanks to Finn Donovan—before they let me out, but that was all. Grey Wilson refused to file charges. The guy must have been out of his mind after—"

Cory cut him off. "So. What're you doing now?"

Calvin smoothed the cowlick in his dark hair. He still had the same pale look Cory remembered, as if he'd done more time than he claimed. "Working for my uncle. He 'forgets' to pay me more often than not, but the job buys my beers and a night out." He studied Cory. "Wouldn't expect to run into you here."

The unspoken question hung in the air.

"I got homesick," Cory said at last. "The Kansas plains suit me way more than back east. I had enough of Pennsylvania, Ohio, West Virginia..." There was more to that story, but Calvin wouldn't hear it. Cory had already said too much. He scanned the dance floor, looking for one particular face. "Nice seeing you again. Think I'll kick up my boot heels."

As he walked away, Cory's shoulder blades itched. This was the trouble with small towns, rural areas with sparse populations and people who thought everybody else's business must be theirs, too. He shouldn't have come tonight, Calvin Stern being a prime example of why not. Would he tell another cowboy, or some girl he danced with that he'd spotted Cory? Raise a bunch of questions he didn't want to answer? He'd already jeopardized his job with Hadley by cleaning out the homestead for Mrs. Pearson.

Pulling his hat low, Cory plowed into the crowd toward the bar, which meant going straight through all the dancers who were now do-si-do-ing in every direction. Needing a drink, he barely noticed anyone else until he bumped into a softer, slighter form and inhaled the scent of lemon blossoms. His heart stopped for a second before it began beating again in double time. "Hey, darlin'." It was her, all right.

Cory touched her arm, urging her away from the square dancers, not even hearing the loud music now, his eyes only for her. An angel wearing a gauzy green dress with sparkly boots, her blond hair long and fine, her eyes a cornflower blue.

"How did you know I'd be here tonight?" Willow Bodine asked, her surprised gaze taking him in as if she'd been drowning and Cory had saved her.

"Just got lucky, I guess." He drew her to the far side of the room into the shadows. He wanted to ask if he could get her a drink—he needed one even more now—but wouldn't take the chance of losing her right after he'd found her again.

Alone with him in the darkened corner, she swatted his arm. "Where have you been? You promised we'd be together. Then one day I learned you'd disappeared. When was that?" she demanded although surely she knew as well as he did. "Way more than a year ago, *cowboy*. I hope you don't think I've been waiting all this time for you."

"Have you?"

She grinned, showing soft-looking lips and even, white teeth. "I tried to find you, called around," she said. "Foolish of me, I realize, but there's something about you..." She moved closer, then closer still and raised her face to his. Cory caught another whiff of lemon, the floral perfume that was so uniquely hers.

Cory pushed his hat back on his head. "I swear, I thought of you every day. You know that, don't you?"

Her eyes looked suddenly wet. "I did until

I lost hope that I'd ever see you again. Why didn't you send word you were back in town?"

"I couldn't call or set foot on your father's spread. He's prob'ly had his shotgun loaded since that spring. You've met me right here. Let's walk the edge of all this foot stomping and get ourselves something to drink. Then we'll…talk. We have a lot of catching up to do."

But she stopped him. "First," she said, a hand on the nape of his neck, "let's see if we still work."

Cory lost himself in their kiss, heart racing, hands dry and damp at the same time. She was everything he remembered, had dreamed about every night in all those other places that could never hold him in the end, even when they made him feel safe for a while. He'd been crazy to come home, crazy to stay—Calvin Stern being the unwanted reminder—and he'd be all-out crazier to keep on staying.

A rich rancher's daughter shouldn't wipe her feet on a plain cowhand—and worse— a cowhand like him. The blue-eyed, blond-haired angel of his dreams. "I half expected to find you married to some man your father would approve of, maybe having that man's baby by now..."

"Yet here I am."

In Cory's arms, Willow answered his next kiss with all the sweetness, the give, he'd never forgotten. If he had a scrap of sense left, he should be anywhere else on the planet, not in the deep shadows of this barn, but he shared a moment with her like no other, the two of them wrapped up once more in their own little world. In his loneliest moments, he'd never given up hope she might still want him.

She was the reason he'd come back.

No matter how dangerous that was.

TWO DAYS LATER Jenna sat back in the chair across from Olivia's desk, unable to contain a grin. The turn-of-the-century bureau could be hers—or rather, Danielle Pearson's, if she wanted it. "Thanks for cutting us a deal. Are you sure you'll make a profit on this sale?"

"Are you offering more money than I quoted?" Olivia's voice seemed to soothe her son, who was on her lap, and the few grumbles he'd been making stopped. Sweet baby James, she called him, and Jenna felt an all-too-familiar ripple of joy, then sorrow, deep inside.

Babies were everywhere. First, there'd been Blossom and Logan's little Daisy. Then Olivia and Sawyer's son last May, and more recently Shadow and Grey's baby, Zach, her new nephew born in December. She supposed that, having married last Christmas, Annabelle and Finn would be next. In her way, like Hadley, Jenna was definitely the outsider in Barren. No man in her life, no spouse, no kids…except for Luke and Gracie, she silently added. If only life was different…

"Danielle could afford more but I appreciate what you're doing."

"I figure if she likes the bureau, the discount this time won't hurt. I'll be compensated when she tells all her friends."

"Few of whom live here," Jenna pointed out.

That didn't bother Olivia. Nothing seemed to these days, and as with Shadow, Jenna had never seen her look more satisfied with her life. When she said so, Olivia flicked her blond ponytail off her shoulder and laughed. "Between us, you and I will make plenty of profit. Good for you, with Liza too as a client."

"Her house is finally ready for what's called 'the reveal.'"

"And from what I've seen, it's gorgeous." Olivia sobered. "Now you're working at Clara's. How do you deal with Hadley Smith? There's not a female in this town who can't see him for the fine male specimen he is, and those blue eyes are killer, but he makes your ex seem laid back. The man is as spring-wound as that." She gestured at the big grand-father clock across the room. "You said he wasn't happy about Amy's parents coming to the ranch, but that must be just the tip of an iceberg."

Jenna ignored the part about Hadley's ap-peal as she had Shadow's comment months ago. He was attractive, and she fought her re-action to him every time she saw him, even a few days ago when he'd practically been snorting fire like some dragon. "I can man-age running into Hadley," she said.

Olivia tilted her head to catch Jenna's eye. "You sure? I know you need to establish your business. Believe me, I understand how tough growing a business like mine or Fantastic De-signs can be. And Danielle's a plum client. But to see Hadley every day?"

"Not every day."

"Clara sure put you on the hot seat out there." Olivia's gaze focused on James. "If you ask me—which no one did—I'd have expected Hadley to bolt by now. The question is, would he take the twins, or decide the easier course is to let Amy's parents raise them?"

"He certainly doesn't want that. Hadley always says he doesn't know how to be a father, yet no one sent the twins that memo. They adore him—and the feeling's mutual. Hadley hasn't succeeded at much in his life, but he's trying hard for his children and Clara," she admitted. "I haven't trusted him, in part based on what Amy said, but what if she was wrong about him?"

Olivia agreed. "I don't like to call Amy a whiner when she's not here to defend herself, but she could be at times—and she *was* used to a fancier lifestyle." Olivia patted James's back. "Maybe you'll be the person to tame that bad boy."

Jenna's pulse sped. "You're projecting just because you managed to bring Sawyer home after so many years. All I need *personally* is to do my job for Clara and Danielle. Hadley isn't the one paying me to turn that cabin into a livable space." In spite of her more charitable thoughts of him the other day, she was still bothered by his displays of temper, particularly when they were aimed at her.

Olivia said in a singsong voice, "Why do I suspect that's not all you care about?"

"Olivia, stop." Jenna would never take a chance on a man so like her father. "Hadley Smith isn't on my dance card."

# CHAPTER TEN

"I'M SORRY. I WAS WRONG."

Hadley rehearsed what to say as he searched for Cory. He'd rarely apologized in thirty-two years, but he'd been unfair to his one cowhand at the cabin the other day. He'd let the Pearsons get under his skin, then taken it out on Cory. But now the young hand was nowhere to be found.

In fact, for the last few days he'd obviously been keeping out of Hadley's way. Had Cory quit? Packed his gear and left? That would put a big hole in Hadley's plans for the day and a whole lot more.

Finally, he heard a low voice from behind the barn. Hadley found Cory on his cell phone, his back against the sun-warmed rear wall, his hat low on his head. "Sure, baby... I understand. No, I'm not disappointed." Pause. "Well, yeah, I am, but there's nothing to be done, is there?"

Hadley rapped his knuckles on the corner of the barn and Cory's gaze shot up. He turned away as if to shield the caller, but after a few more words he hung up.

"Sorry to interrupt," Hadley said.

Cory straightened. "On my way to fetch that cow back for the vet to check later. Looks to me like she has milk fever. Just had to take that call first."

"No need to explain." The practiced words threatened to stick in Hadley's throat. "I was out of line before. If you want to help Mrs. Pearson this afternoon, she'll be here after lunch."

Cory eyed him warily. "You okay with that, boss?"

Another flash of guilt ran through him, right along with the pleasure he felt at being called *boss* even though this was Clara's ranch. Hadley kept reminding himself of that. At least he owned—half owned—six cows and Mr. Robert, if not the showy quarter horse he'd fancied. "Guess I have to be," he said at last. "She and Clara have made up their minds."

Cory hesitated. "I don't like the notion of Mr. Pearson being around."

"Neither do I," Hadley admitted, "but in the short term he won't be." Jenna would, though. Since finding the application, he'd taken a hard look at it. He'd found no indication she had any claim now—Amy had died before making the guardianship legal—no loopholes after all, but that wasn't the only point. Even reading about the circumstances under which a person might seek a standby guardian for minor children hadn't reassured him. There'd been nothing wrong with Amy that he knew of, so why did she think she might need a guardian? Hadley thought he could guess. The application itself was proof of her intent. She'd feared he might abandon their babies, and in the event Amy herself couldn't care for them, the children would then need someone else's protection. Meaning Jenna's. And because she knew that, Jenna still had power. What if she tipped off Walter Pearson?

Cory smiled. "Can't picture old Walt spending his days in this barn around cattle, horses and manure."

"Me, either. That's the good part, I guess." Hadley stuck out a hand. "Appreciate your hard work. I didn't mean to blast you—a bad habit of mine with other people, too." Including Jenna. "I'm sorry, Cory."

With the apology said after all, he nodded at the cell phone in Cory's grip. "If there's something you need to tend to, you can take a few hours off."

"Not help Mrs. Pearson? And Jenna?" His smile became a grin. "I don't mind. Sprucing up that cabin isn't half as hard or dirty as digging postholes."

"Point taken," Hadley said, "but I don't want you to feel like some kind of indentured servant. The holes can wait, and Mr. Robert's stall is the only one that needs attention."

Cory glanced toward the nearby pasture where the sorrel nibbled at some grass, yellowing in the heat of summer, his lips flapping. "Robert's a nice horse now that he's settled some."

"Yeah, and I've been thinking we should get another like him. Heard Sawyer McCord might have a good gelding ready over at the Circle H. He and his wife, Olivia, have done a mighty fine job of training her big black there." Hadley couldn't imagine how they both handled everything. Sawyer's medical career here and in his clinic abroad, Olivia's two antiques shops plus some kind of women's group she'd started in far-off Kedar. Two children. Horse training. Made his routine look half-easy. And their marriage didn't have the same volatility he'd had with Amy.

Cory's eyes lit up. "Let me know if you want me to buck out that gelding. My best event when I was on the circuit."

"I doubt there's any bucking to be done, but thanks. I'll drive over tomorrow or the next day to check him out." With things between them straight again, Hadley took a few steps on the dusty, beaten-down path to the front of the barn before Cory's tentative voice stopped him.

"Boss, you any good with women?"

He turned around. "That what your call was about?" From the one-sided conversation, he'd guessed as much.

Cory kicked a dirt clod out of his way. "Met up with her at a dance last weekend and everything seemed fine as it ever was… Thought we were doing okay, but now my head is on backward and I don't know where I stand."

Hadley must have used the right words in his apology because Cory seemed to trust him, but his unexpected confidence reminded Hadley of his shortcomings with women. First with Amy, and now he had an even more complicated relationship with Jenna.

"None of us do," he said. Cory had a girlfriend. Of course he did. He was young, good-looking, with a way about him that would charm any woman. Hadley didn't have that talent. "We're all clueless. If you're asking my advice, I'd let her mull over whatever the issue might be, give it some time." Though that tack hadn't worked so well for him with Jenna after their quarrel at the homestead. The last time he saw her, those blue eyes had snapped at him. Still. He owed her an apology, too—one that would be even more difficult to make than with Cory.

Cory brightened. "Let her come to me 'stead of trying to talk her out of being mad?"

"Maybe you should." Hadley touched the brim of his hat, careful not to let his smile show as he walked with Cory around the barn. The kid's dilemma was kind of tenderhearted, really, yet as he'd noted, Cory rarely talked about his private life, and he never mentioned his past except for those few sometimes boastful references to his rodeo career.

Hadley wasn't really in a position to give advice. With a jolt he thought again of Jenna, when he didn't want to think of her at all. It had been a long time since he fell in love, or believed he had, with Amy, and although he wasn't getting any younger, romance wasn't in his plans.

JENNA SWIPED A HAND across her sweating forehead. She'd stopped the next morning at Liza's to finalize some details in the new house, then met Danielle at Olivia's shop to inspect the bureau. The older woman had loved the piece, and they'd arranged for delivery. A few hours later, Jenna had come to the McMann ranch to scour the two-burner stove in the homestead cabin.

As she gave the range a final inspection, her glance caught movement passing the window. A second later, a knock sounded at the door. *Oh, no.* There'd been no mistaking his tall, powerful frame—not that she wanted to notice—or the way Hadley carried his broad shoulders with an almost military bearing. She wondered if he'd ever been in the army. He'd have made a great drill sergeant.

He poked his head inside, hat in his hand. "Jenna?"

She took her time to respond. "What have I done now?"

Hadley flushed. "Nothing. It's what I did."

Determined not to look into his incredible blue eyes, she blew a strand of hair off her forehead. "Where do we start?"

He cleared his throat. "I take full responsibility for the other day."

Jenna leaned against the kitchen counter, arms folded. "You were harsh with Cory. Rude, considering Danielle was nearby and could hear all the shouting going on. She said nothing to me, but I know she overheard at least part of what was said. That didn't help your case with the Pearsons." She added, "You were pretty tough on me, too."

"I'm a tough guy." He tried a half smile. "I'd have talked to you sooner, but I came by yesterday and you weren't here."

Jenna didn't answer his smile.

He said, "I'm not one for apologies, but this is my second today. I already spoke to Cory."

"Acts of contrition? Why, Hadley?"

He slapped his hat against his jeans-clad thigh. "What do you mean, why? I'm trying to say I'm sorry. This is hard enough. Don't make it harder."

"So just because you feel guilty—" She broke off. "Ah. I see why you're sorry—if you are. You're worried I'll make you look worse with the Pearsons. Cory might, too."

He stared at his boots. "Sometimes you sound like Amy."

"Sometimes you deserve it."

"I'm apologizing because I *should*. But I didn't have loving parents, sure not the way she did. There was no mother like Danielle or Clara to point me in the right direction, no father to make me toe the line."

Although that wasn't strictly true, because Clara and her husband had helped to raise him, Jenna could empathize. She certainly didn't ask her mother for advice these days, and Wanda didn't take hers. About Jenna's father, the less said or thought, the better. As for Hadley… "That's no excuse," she said. "You're not a boy, you're a grown man, and you own the decisions you make. I'm not the one who threw his weight around, yelled this cabin down. I'm not sure I'm ready to forgive you."

He clamped the hat on his head. "I could

never guess what direction Amy was going to take. Sure don't with you, either. What I said to Cory was right," he added.

"What does he have to do with this?"

"He asked me about women. I told him I had no clue. You just proved it."

Jenna pressed her lips tight because she was tempted to laugh. His remorse was kind of cute, really. She'd never seen him so off-balance, and certainly her father had never come to her, hat in hand. Neither had her ex. Before Hadley opened the door to leave, she lightly touched his arm. She hadn't been gracious about his apology, and what did she expect of him? "Hadley. I *don't* know if you're worried about me making you look bad to the Pearsons. I shouldn't have said that."

He almost smiled. "You apologizing now?"

"Yes." She went past him to the door, then walked out onto the porch where her mind filled with possibilities: a small garden with flowers, bright reds and yellows, a stone pathway for better curb appeal. Chairs and a table. She sat on the top step—there were only two—and waited until Hadley sat beside her. She wanted to understand. "Tell me more about your life *before* Amy."

"You already know I'm a foster kid." Did he still think of himself that way? "When I was six, my folks got into trouble with the law—again—and the state took over. Wasn't the first time, but at least it was the last. My father and mother didn't even try to fight for us. They were both hard-core addicts. He'd been convicted on a bunch of charges, possession, intent to sell meth, heroin, you name it. He was a dealer. Neither of them really took care of us, even the few times when they were trying to go straight."

"Us, you said?"

"Me and my brother. Two years younger than me. We stayed together for a while, and I felt guilty for not being a good enough big brother. The system eventually separated us. I haven't seen him since."

"That's awful," Jenna said. "Haven't you looked for him?"

"As an adult, yeah, but without any luck. Sometimes when I'm out somewhere or when I stop in some new town, I think I see him alone or in a crowd, but it's never really him." Hadley shrugged, but Jenna doubted he felt that casual or indifferent.

She briefly touched his arm. "Now *I'm*

sorry, Hadley. Weren't there any good people you stayed with?"

"Sure, one couple on the road to Farrier..."

"They might have information on where your brother is now."

"I've tried," he said. "Both of those people have passed. Of course, Clara and Cliff were the best. I owe her more now than making her ranch profitable. Know what she told me? That when I left there, just shy of turning eighteen when the state would have cut me loose anyway, she kept my room—she called it mine—just as it was."

"Clara's a wonderful woman. It's too bad you and your brother weren't with her all along. She's so good with your twins."

"She and Cliff were childless," he said with a glance at Jenna, "but she's the closest I came to having someone I could lo—like." He didn't go on for a minute, and Jenna didn't want to pry. His voice had sounded hoarse. "That's my sad tale. What's yours? Or were you like Amy and grew up with folks who doted on you, spoiled you?" But surely he'd heard rumors of the opposite.

Jenna wrapped her arms around her knees. "There was no spoiling. My dad was what people often called a wastrel. He hated to work, although he played at it now and then as a hand for ranchers in the area. When he was home, which was most of the time, he called himself a farmer. He preferred staying in his recliner all day, surfing channels… lashing out for no reason. I was never good at defending myself."

"How many other kids? I know there's Shadow."

"Six. Two boys, four girls," she said, her chin beginning to quiver. "My oldest brother, Jared, was killed—an accident—so now there are five."

"I remember that. People thought Grey Wilson was responsible."

"Fortunately, for him and Shadow, and their children now, he wasn't." She looked toward the road that led to Wilson Cattle, where the shooting had occurred. They still weren't sure who was really responsible for his death. She hoped that her younger brother, Derek, wasn't the actual killer. He had worshipped Jared. "Daddy wasn't a solid citizen. If he was short on cash, which he most often was, he occasionally stole from other people, including the Wilsons even when Grey's dad hired him, fired him, then rehired him. Over and over."

"Everett's a forgiving sort," Hadley said with a half smile. He moved on the top step as if to say *enough of this*, and Jenna didn't try to continue. "You ready to forgive me now? After I tugged at your heartstrings? Looking for sympathy?"

He must feel embarrassed, and Jenna could see the shell that seemed to cover him harden again. Yet the atmosphere between them had changed, and she wasn't about to let that go. Because of his babies and her job to redo the cabin, they would both have to deal with the Pearsons. "Apology accepted."

Hadley tipped his hat. "Thanks for listening."

She shrugged. "People are a lot more complex than they seem—us, too."

"Yeah, well, I need to take my complexity to the barn. Clara deserves a full day's work from me, and I aim to see she gets it."

Had she really said *us*? She laid a hand on his arm again, the warmth radiating from his skin through his sleeve to her fingers. "Hadley, I realize we've had our disagreements, but for the twins, let's try better to get along.

Then maybe Amy's parents won't trouble us about Luke and Grace."

To her surprise he grinned at her. "I was hoping you'd say that."

## CHAPTER ELEVEN

"DON'T GET YOUR HOPES UP." Sawyer McCord
flashed a smile. "Today horse handling isn't
my best skill." The next morning Hadley
had driven over to examine the gelding at
the Circle H. Sawyer, on his day off from the
medical clinic in town, was in full rancher
mode, wearing jeans and a checkered shirt
with pearl buttons. It was before 10:00 a.m.
but his clothes were already streaked with
grime. "Took a hoof in the gut before dawn.
Olivia's horse Blue has a few more kinks to
work out."

"Other people have good things to say
about him, but I also heard you've trained
a nice gelding that could make a good cow
pony for Clara's place." Squinting into the
sun, Hadley took in the neat barn and corral, the pastureland farther off. "Can't say her
ranch is near as successful as this one, even
with you all running bison, not cows here."

"I leave those devils to my grandfather and Logan now." Sawyer explained that he'd begun to buy Angus instead and had a good-sized herd already.

Hadley envied him, but he wasn't here to make himself feel bad. "The McMann ranch amounts to a start-up business at this point. Our hay's growing well and I've got a decent sorrel, but I need another horse for the cow-hand I hired."

"Who's that?"

"Cory Jennings. Little more than a kid but a fair hand. Ex-rodeo."

Sawyer scratched his forehead. "Name's not familiar, but I don't know as many people in Farrier or in the county as I do in Barren. Is he from around here?"

"Texas, he says. Cory's not much of a talker, at least about himself."

"So what are you looking for?" Sawyer walked toward the nearby corral where half a dozen horses were dozing on their feet. "The gelding you heard about is sound, sure-footed, but has some moodiness." He pointed at a large dun-colored horse. "Prefers to take his time and do things his way. Can make the ride interesting. You might consider instead the mare we picked up near KC on a tip from Nell Ransom's father, who runs a string of tack shops over there."

"What's she like?"

Sawyer grinned. "Settled down some since she married Cooper."

"I meant the mare," Hadley said with a groan for the too-obvious joke. Nell had been a tough cowgirl and fiercely independent before her husband, and love, helped mellow her a bit.

"Couldn't resist. The mare's smaller than the gelding. Good conformation. Pretty nice bloodlines, and her gaits are like sitting in a rocking chair. Got some Tennessee walker in her."

"Let's check out the two of them."

The bay mare was a sweetie. Covering ground on her back would be a pleasure, but by the time he dismounted at the barn after a twenty-minute ride on each horse, Hadley knew which one he wanted to buy.

"You're kidding," Sawyer said, taking the reins from Hadley. "This mare's a bargain. Olivia wanted to charge more."

"If Cory doesn't take to the gelding, I'll ride him myself. Maybe one stubborn cuss should fight with another." He gazed at the corral where the horse was now rolling in the dirt, legs flailing in the dusty air. "Clean him up and trailer him to Clara's for me, will you? I assume delivery's part of the deal." They walked to Hadley's truck, Sawyer still shaking his head.

"I offer you a bombproof beauty and you pick the bad guy of this barn—other than Blue at times."

"He's the one I want. I got a feeling." Hadley would connect with another bad boy. As he opened his door, he paused. "Given another year or so on the Circle H, you'll be taking down your shingle at the clinic to just train horses."

"Not me. I like balance," Sawyer said. "Being home part of the time instead of working long hours at Farrier General or at the clinic lets me play with James, too."

Hadley couldn't argue with that. He wished he had more hours for the twins, but for now he didn't, and there was no use saying so. He gazed at Sawyer with what he hoped was a bland expression that Sawyer didn't seem to notice.

"James can wear us out," he went on, "but my brother and I ran our mother ragged."

Logan was his identical twin although Sawyer had changed his last name from Hunter to McCord after a fallout with their grandfather. "We lost Mom when we were young, but if we hadn't I hate to think how much we would have aged her by the time we grew up." A lingering sorrow showed in his eyes. "So I know twins firsthand."

The only thing Hadley would change for Luke and Gracie was the Pearsons' meddling in their lives. He tried to feel grateful that only Danielle had come to stay again, but he didn't much like the fact that she'd established a kind of beachhead right on the dry-as-dust McMann ranch at the height of summer.

"Your twins are in a similar situation," Sawyer pointed out. "I wish we could have saved Amy, and once they're older they'll miss her. You have a lot to handle now, and I imagine some regrets. I heard things weren't going well between you and Amy last fall."

"We'll be okay—the three of us."

"Hadley." Sawyer shifted his weight from one foot to the other. "I, uh, couldn't tell you this when Amy was still…with us. Federal privacy laws, you understand. She hadn't given permission for me to discuss her condition with you. That was only between her and her physician. Me," he finished.

"Condition?"

Sawyer looked uneasy. "I hate to tell you this now, but I believe it's important for you to know. Amy was born with a congenital heart defect, a pretty bad one. There was no effective treatment. I won't go into the medical lingo, but her life expectancy wasn't that long."

Hadley felt as if he'd been hit with a hammer. "God, was that why she leaned on me that hard? Why she was so unhinged when we split for a while? Why didn't she say something?"

"I asked her, and she explained that she didn't want to worry you. She wanted to be treated like any normal, healthy woman. Her parents had tried to keep her wrapped in cotton, smothered her at times."

"They knew," Hadley said bitterly. "And yet they blame me for her death."

"Not anyone's fault. But when I saw Amy's first sonogram, I knew we had a real game changer. I saw her more often after that, of course, and recommended bed rest for the duration of her pregnancy, but Amy wouldn't listen. Having twins stressed her body far more than a single birth would have."

"And she still didn't want me to know."

"Amy chose to handle her condition as she saw fit. Hadley, she knew she wasn't well, and nothing would have changed her prognosis, but I'm certain she didn't expect to die just then." Although that certainly explained the guardianship. She'd wanted Jenna's help not only because he might leave, but because Amy had been so ill.

"What about Luke and Gracie? This heart thing?"

"It's likely not an inherited condition. Something probably went awry with Amy's development in the early days of her mother's pregnancy that damaged her heart. I doubt your twins are at risk."

"You're not sure?"

"As sure as I can be. The twins were given a full workup before they left the hospital. They're healthy, but if you still have concerns, bring them in and we'll take a second look."

Nothing to worry about. That was welcome news, but the rest… Had he and Amy been so far apart she couldn't tell him the truth? "What else did she hide from me?" he wondered aloud. Was this yet another layer to the wife he couldn't love enough? "It's as if I didn't know her at all," he said. "At the hospital, I guess you thought I'd hit the road as soon as Amy was gone." And to be honest, with Danielle at the ranch and seeing Jenna all the time, Hadley did feel twitchy.

Sawyer rested one hand on the car's open door frame. "I've got no problem with you, Hadley. Doesn't matter to me what other people say or think. As long as you keep doing fine with your twins, we're good."

Hadley merely nodded. He wasn't used to anyone's approval.

"Besides," Sawyer said, "with you turning Clara's ranch around, I figure you intend to stay a while. Maybe by the time you decide to move on, you won't want to." He hesitated. "Jenna Moran's a nice woman. Pretty, too."

Hadley slipped inside his truck. "She likes the twins. Period. I'm just hoping Amy's parents lose interest in their shiny new toys pretty quick. All that should take is Luke spitting his green beans on their fancy clothes, or Gracie pulling their hair, before they hightail it back to Wichita." At least that's what he'd decided to believe so he wouldn't develop an ulcer. Being under constant surveillance made him sweat. As for Jenna…he still feared she'd reveal the guardianship to the Pearsons. It hung over his head like a sword. Could she and Hadley really go through with the truce they'd made? That was all he'd let himself think about where she was concerned. At least he'd try.

Sawyer stepped away from the pickup. "Jenna's life hasn't been the happiest, similar to yours, I understand. Something in common there. Could be the basis—"

"For what?" Fixing his mind on their bargain, Hadley suppressed a vision of Jenna on the cabin porch yesterday, her soft blue eyes and pretty sun-gilded hair. "I don't have time—or the inclination—to start anything. You can tell the whole town that if you like." He put the truck in gear. "We have enough trouble being civil to each other."

He left Sawyer with his skeptical expression and barreled off down the drive, rapping one hand against the dash as if it were wood for luck, so God wouldn't strike him dead for the lie he'd even told himself.

A BARE SPACE to Jenna was always like a clean slate or a blank page in a book. The kind of new start she'd wanted for her life. Despite her first attack of nerves at Liza's new house, she'd done a great job—Liza's words—and looked forward to doing the same here at Clara's. But Danielle Pearson, she'd discovered, was even more hands-on with the design process than Liza had been.

"Clara," Danielle began, "I know you like the gray you picked out, but maybe taupe would better suit this cabin. Jenna?" The three women consulted the paint swatches Jenna had gotten at the local hardware store, but Clara and Danielle had disagreed on most of their choices. Danielle seemed stronger, more forceful, when her husband wasn't around.

Jenna hated being caught in the middle between two clients. "What's Mr. Pearson's favorite color?"

Danielle thought a moment. "Blue," she said with a laugh. "The man has half a dozen pin-striped suits the same shade of navy. Custom shirts, too—white, for contrast."

"The bolder color would make the room look…contemporary. But remember, this is an old homestead and you wanted a rustic aesthetic, which I agree would be appropriate."

Clara hadn't said another word.

"What if we did one accent wall in a slate blue? The bed can go against that wall and the brass frame will just glow." Jenna showed Clara the color. "A comfortable armchair, down-filled cushions, yellow in a lumbar pillow and some flowers on the bureau…"

"A single wall?" Clara asked.

"I see a lot of that now, and it can be very effective."

"We could use a splash of gray," Danielle put in, obviously trying to get Clara on board with the plan.

"In the bed cover," Clara conceded, "blue and white and gray," giving Danielle a point. If only Hadley could compromise like this with the Pearsons.

"Then let's tie in the rustic theme some more by leaving another wall of unfinished boards." The situation was delicate in more ways than one. It couldn't be easy for Clara to open her home to people she barely knew, yet she'd been willing to do so for the twins. And now she, Danielle and Jenna had reached an agreement. Jenna's rigid shoulders began to relax.

She gathered the paint and fabric swatches. Clara said a few words, then disappeared into the other room, but Danielle stayed behind. Clearly, she had something else to discuss. "I think Walter will like what we're doing. I'm not as sure about Clara." Danielle paused. "I realize this isn't my territory. It's kind of her to 'take us in,' but it won't be easy. Hadley Smith won't let it be, either."

Probably true. Hadley wasn't an easy person, as Amy had said, but his concerns were real. As long as he kept his blue eyes anywhere but on Jenna, and his strong frame at a distance for her peace of mind, they might manage. "He's promised to try," she assured Danielle. The story he'd told her of his foster care years, the loss of his only brother, had made her heart ache. "I realize this is a touchy subject, but he and Amy had some difficult times in their relationship—"

"And he failed to protect her!"

"It wasn't Hadley's fault she didn't survive the twins' births, Danielle. How do you think it makes him feel to be blamed for something he wasn't responsible for?"

"He *was* responsible. He was her *husband*. She should never have gotten pregnant in the first place, though I'm happy to have the twins. But if he'd taken better care of Amy all along, gotten her to that little hospital sooner, she'd still be alive."

Jenna's brow furrowed. She recalled Danielle's comment about Amy's suffering. Could she mean more than pains during labor? Jenna had heard those could be severe.

"Maybe you should talk to Sawyer McCord," she said. "He knows far more than I do about what happened. And why." Jenna didn't realize she'd spoken so sharply, but Danielle's gaze fell and Jenna gentled her tone. "I won't take sides. Losing your only child must have been devastating. When I learned I can never have children, I felt I'd lost a huge part of myself. My own marriage was already falling apart then, and I'm afraid I did some rather unwise things that hurt my family, my sister. I still can't accept my own loss, but please, don't misplace your grief by blaming Hadley."

"I'm surprised you're defending him, a man who can't keep a job, who never provided real support for my daughter. I'm with Walter on that. Do you truly believe Hadley's the most stable person for the twins to be with?"

Danielle had made several good points,

all of which Jenna had considered before. But Hadley wasn't here to defend himself. "There are things you may not know about him." Jenna couldn't be sure she knew everything, either, but it wasn't her place to betray his confidence about what he had revealed. She'd hoped they might all find some meeting ground, but Danielle didn't take well to her comment.

Her mouth worked; her voice trembled. "I know all I need to know about Hadley Smith." Which had been Jenna's opinion once, too, but even now Danielle hadn't finished. She waved a hand at the room. "Is this your only interest here, Jenna? This cabin?"

"If you mean am I interested in Hadley, no," she said, feeling warmth rise in her face. "I'm here to refresh this cabin and for the twins' sakes. I promised Amy I would look out for them, and I will."

At the mention of her daughter's name, Danielle's gaze softened, but her next words hit hard. "Why did Amy need your promise?"

ALONE IN THE living room that night, Hadley took out his wallet. Clara had gone to bed, but he could hear low voices from the TV upstairs. Nothing from the twins yet.

In Barren to buy wire that afternoon, he'd glimpsed someone on the street, and for one instant he'd imagined again it was Dallas. Yet would Hadley even recognize him? Dallas was a man, not the boy he'd known. Hadley rummaged through credit cards, his driver's license and his medical card until his fingers closed on the creased picture he always carried.

He stared at it, feeling his pulse throb through his fingers, remembering. Had there been a time long ago when they'd all been together, their family intact and at least partly functional? When the four of them had lived in the same apartment or rented house or, for that one winter, a drafty trailer in the woods? Far enough from town that his parents could conduct their deals with less fear of being caught by the police. A time when he and his kid brother had a warm bed, clean clothes, enough to eat.

Before the twins were born, still wrapped up in his troubles with Amy, he hadn't given the reality of having children of his own much thought. Yet from that first moment in Farrier General, they'd become the center of his world. No matter how tight the budget got, or where he had to take them, he would always see to their needs. Love them, because he surely did when he'd never loved anyone to such a degree, except Dallas. No matter what he had to do, Luke and Gracie would never want for anything.

Then there was Jenna. He would ignore Sawyer's advice. Sure, he felt attracted to her—time to admit that—but they were both damaged people, and he had his babies to consider. Despite their recent agreement, he hadn't forgotten Jenna's promise at the hospital to make sure he did right by Luke and Gracie—or else. He still didn't trust her, certainly not when he was being watched so closely by the Pearsons. All she'd have to do was say a few words about the guardianship.

He studied the photo again, which had almost worn through from being handled. His brother beamed at the camera. How old, then? Dallas looked about four, so Hadley would have been six. The oversize T-shirt Dallas wore must have been a hand-me-down. It hung to Dallas's bony knees, the shoulder seams partway down his skinny arms, one of which was slung around Hadley's waist. Who had taken the picture? Their mother, probably—that last day? Until the end, she'd been the more caring parent, on her good days, at least, present in their lives sometimes when their dad often was not. Sometimes he wondered what had happened to her.

He couldn't understand their neglect, just as he hadn't yet been able to make sense of Amy's silence about her heart condition.

If he and Dallas could have lived here on the ranch with Clara and Cliff, how different would their lives have been? What if he could find him now?

But then what? He didn't know his brother any longer. How had he changed over the years they'd been apart? If his life had been just as difficult as Hadley's, what effect might those hardships have had on Dallas? If he ever met up with him again, he might as easily make things more difficult for Hadley as plug the hole in Hadley's heart.

And still, he wanted to know.

# CHAPTER TWELVE

JENNA WAS DRIVING past Clara's house when the older woman stepped onto the porch and flagged her down. Jenna was there to await delivery of the bureau. The other furniture she and Danielle had picked out with Clara's approval wouldn't arrive until next week, and the new coat of paint on the cabin walls was still tacky in spots. Except for seeing the twins today, she didn't have much else to do but wait for the truck to arrive.

"Jenna?" With her phone in hand, Clara came down the steps. "Do you have a few hours to spare? I have to go into town. Blossom Hunter offered to babysit, but her Daisy has come down with a cold. I don't want to expose the twins."

"I'm free. I can watch for the delivery truck from your house," she said, swallowing. Playing with Luke and Grace on the living room carpet was always fun. "But I've never been alone with the twins."

"You'll do fine." With a look of relief, Clara turned toward the house. Jenna shut off her engine, then followed her, Clara talking all the way. "They're still napping but as soon as you hear Luke, pluck him right out of his crib. They're no longer sharing, but he makes sure Grace doesn't get another wink of sleep." She paused. "Oh, and she's teething, too. I'm sorry, but they may be grouchy."

"I'll do my best." In the house Jenna mentally crossed her fingers. She asked Clara for further instructions about what to serve for lunch, but before she'd fully absorbed the information, Clara left. Trying not to panic, Jenna heard her car start in the drive, the sound not quite covered by the bleating of the few cattle from the pasture or the answering bellow of a bull Hadley had purchased a few days ago.

After checking on the twins, she tiptoed from their room, then down the stairs. She hadn't reached the bottom before Luke cried out. This was followed by a loud, rhythmic banging, and as soon as Jenna rushed back up the steps into the babies' nursery, she saw his hand slam against the crib rail. "Shh, Luke, your sister's still asleep."

At nine months now, he was sitting up, and tears ran down his face. Jenna saw the lump of a soggy diaper in the rear seat of his onesie. Suddenly, she seemed to be an enemy rather than a friend.

"Da-da," Luke said, turning away from Jenna.

"Don't be scared. You know me. Let's get some clean pants for you."

Luke reached for the big teddy bear he slept with, then buried his face in its brown fur. The tip of the red bow around its neck poked him in the eye, and Luke cried harder. "Oh, dear," Jenna murmured, as Clara might say.

Afraid to pick him up and make things worse, she glanced toward Grace, who was stirring. Another second, and she'd be bawling, too. How many times had Jenna prayed for a baby like either one of these two? Holding and feeding the twins once in a while didn't seem to count for much all of a sudden. She'd always had Hadley or Clara to soothe any tears. Now what? The phrase *Be careful what you wish for* flashed in Jenna's brain. How could she handle two babies at once?

She should have begged off, citing another appointment for Fantastic Designs or, heaven forbid, returned one of Bernice Caldwell's increasingly persistent phone calls, which were all ruses to get Jenna to see Barney. For childcare experience, Jenna's niece didn't count. When Ava was a baby, she and Shadow had lived in Kansas City, not far from Jenna. But Ava was now practically a preteen, her babyhood a distant memory. Jenna hadn't spent that much time with Ava's brother Zach since he was born. So now she was left with no recent experience to draw on while the twins' cries grew louder.

Jenna attempted a no-nonsense tone. "Come on now, kids." With their screams curdling her nerves, she snatched fresh diapers from the shelf on their changing table, then tried to wrestle Luke into his. As with Hadley, Luke stretched and writhed, legs flailing, arms lashing out. One small fist hit Jenna in the stomach; the next blow connected with her chin. "Ouch. Stop, Luke. This won't take a minute if you cooperate."

Obviously he didn't understand the word. Neither of the twins seemed to be at the point when language worked to reason with them.

Grace sat in her crib, thumb in her mouth, the other hand twirling a strand of hair.

"There," Jenna said, panting. The first diaper was on—somehow—and she'd discovered that laying a forearm across Luke's torso kept him still enough to tug on a pair of lightweight summer pants. She popped him back in his crib, which created a fresh spate of tears. Jenna ignored Luke and lifted Grace. "Your turn, sweetheart."

By the time Jenna managed to re-clothe both twins, perspiration dripped down her face, and their crying hadn't eased off one bit. Carrying them downstairs together wouldn't work. What if she dropped Luke? Or Grace? Or both at once? What if Jenna fell down the stairs into a heap on the entry floor and squashed one of the babies? Or broke her arm and, alone in the house, no one else heard her call for help? The twins could be traumatized for life. And she'd been concerned about Hadley as a father?

Despite their continued crying, she settled for toting them down one at a time. But was Luke really safe in his chair while she went back upstairs for Grace? Had she fastened the security strap properly? Much of their high-tech equipment, so much more futuristic than when Ava was small, defied Jenna's comprehension. As she descended the steps, Luke banged on his tray, and Jenna raced back into the kitchen with Grace on her hip. The little girl had a bad case of hiccups from all that weeping. Her breath came in sobs and hitches. "Poor baby," Jenna murmured, near tears herself.

"Da!" Luke kept yelling.

When Hadley appeared at the back door, Jenna sagged in relief.

"Trouble?"

"More than I was prepared for," she said. "I didn't realize you were here."

"Just got back from town. Saw your car."

Hadley came inside, and Luke reached up to him, chanting, "Da-da!" Hadley lifted him from the chair, touched noses with him, then grinned at Jenna. "Need help?"

"Please!"

"What's it worth to you?" He smoothed a hand over Luke's damp hair.

"At this moment?" She rolled her eyes. "Everything I have."

Hadley took over now as if he'd been a father all his life. Barren's last choice for dad of the year, the town's bad boy, had become a pro, which made Jenna feel even worse for her feeble efforts. Grateful, though. Beyond measure. Perhaps she'd been presumptuous, stepping in to check on Hadley, using Amy as her excuse.

"What's on Clara's menu for lunch?" Hadley asked.

"Um, carrots, pureed beef, and she said they like applesauce."

"Luke prefers pieces of apple to munch on. Gracie looks like she needs a teething biscuit. Sweetie pie, those gums hurt, don't they? Let me see." He examined her mouth. "Red as beets. I'll get her some medicine. You get their food." Their screams had faded away with Hadley's presence, but Grace was still dry-sobbing, her breath catching on each hiccup, and Luke's mouth quivered. "Next time bring earplugs," Hadley suggested. "These two are capable of breaking the sound barrier."

Holding Grace, she rummaged in the refrigerator for the baby food until Hadley told her it was in the pantry. An unfamiliar kitchen wasn't helping her appear more competent. "How can you joke?"

"I decided humor should be part of our new plan to deal with the Pearsons."

"If you say so," she said, as if she and Hadley would take care of the twins together all the time. Jenna entertained a brief fantasy, but the feeling of shared intimacy in Clara's kitchen could never become anything more than these brief moments of being bonded by a lunchtime ritual. Hadley must have noticed the unwanted color in her face, because he laughed. He dried Grace's tears, settled her and Luke in their high chairs—securing them without missing a beat—and watched Jenna heat the jars of food all with a smile on his face. Enjoying his obvious superiority as a caregiver?

When lunch was finally ready, Jenna put the dishes on each twin's tray. Luke promptly shoved his bowl onto the floor, and Hadley laughed again. He'd been through that before, too, and he was a sucker for his twins. Why wouldn't he be? Then Grace spewed carrots down the front of Jenna's shirt. By then, she had more food on the outside than the babies did inside. "Don't get so close when you feed them," he advised. "Their aim is deadly."

Jenna's spirits dropped even lower. After

years of pining for a baby of her own, maybe fate had a positive side after all, and she wasn't cut out for this. Even on a temporary basis.

Maybe she ought to consider not coming here again. Hadley clearly had things more under control than she ever would.

AFTER LUNCH, HADLEY went back to the barn. He hadn't had such a good time in quite a while. Watching Jenna struggle with the very chores he'd had to learn on the fly nine months ago had been too much to resist. Now he felt bad for laughing, but darn she'd looked cute, and she'd tried so hard. He supposed he owed her another apology. She'd done all right.

As soon as he reached the barn, his cell rang. Barney Caldwell. With a sinking feeling, Hadley listened as Barney explained the reason for his call, then Hadley said, "Well, that's bad news." After weeks of waiting and supplying more financial documents that hadn't helped after all, the bank had denied him and Clara their loan. Barney had been sitting on it for way too long in spite of Hadley's regular calls to prod him for a decision.

"Sorry to disappoint you."

"Since we're out of luck, I should tell you the last check I wrote is probably going to bounce." The ranch's balance was low, and Hadley had asked the new bull's former owner to hold it for a few days, which he'd agreed to do, "because I like Clara McMann," but apparently extra time wouldn't matter now. He shouldn't have taken such a gamble to get even the bare minimum breeding stock they would need. Clara shouldn't have believed in him.

Barney cleared his throat. "After her husband died, Clara took several loans, hoping to keep that ranch, but her payments were often in arrears. If it were only my decision, I'd try to work with you now, but when I sent the loan application to the higher-ups they gave me a flat no."

Hadley wondered how hard Barney had tried to change his bosses' minds. "I'd leave Clara out of it, apply myself if my own rating was better. It's not." In part because of Amy's outstanding hospital debt, for which he was responsible.

Barney said, "Nothing more I can do."

Hadley hung up, then leaned against the

closed door of an empty stall. He shouldn't have bought the new gelding, either, which he and Cory had named Trouble, because he was. At least the horse was fully paid for, though that purchase had lowered the ranch's account balance to near zero. It wouldn't matter much longer how neat the barn looked, how well the first crop of hay had grown, which he and Cory had mowed and baled this summer, or that the fences were sound again. They were out of money. What were he and Clara going to do now?

Cory ambled out of the tack room and saw Hadley's drawn expression. "Something wrong, boss?"

"Loan was denied." He rubbed his neck. "Don't know how we'll manage another month."

"My pay," Cory said, stroking a hand down Mr. Robert's nose. The horse had stuck his head out of his stall for a scratch, and Hadley imagined the kid was a breath away from quitting his job. If that's what he had meant.

"There's enough left in the till for Friday. Can't say about next week."

"I mean, you can hold my pay if that'll help…"

"Thanks, Cory, but…" He gazed down at the floor. "You better load that bull on the trailer—and be careful. He doesn't like the ramp, or anything else, for that matter. Should give us some strong calves, or he would if I could keep him."

"You're returning the bull?"

"No choice." Just when he'd thought he and Clara were beginning to get on their feet again… He considered asking Jenna a second time for some of Amy's money, then rejected the idea. She'd been clear about her answer.

If things kept going this way, he'd have to sell the cows, because they were cash on the hoof. And anyway, how would he feed them? The little herd he'd been building, and so proud of, would get trucked through the ranch gate to the road one by one until there was nothing left. Then, having let Clara down after all, and by extension his babies, too, he'd have to hit the road. He wouldn't be able to stay—and see the defeat in Clara's eyes every day, her utter loss of hope. Her ranch would go on the market after all.

"Anyway." Hadley straightened from the stall door. Across the aisle, he heard Trouble snuffle through the straw, and one hoof hit the wall. Cory appeared glum, and Hadley couldn't afford to lose him yet. "Enough about my mess. How are things with your girl?"

Cory tugged at Mr. Robert's forelock. "She still keeps standing me up. I'm supposed to see her later. If she shows."

When Cory didn't elaborate, Hadley left him to his confusion over the female of the species as the kid headed off to catch the bull. "Good luck."

"Thanks, boss."

NOT MUCH LATER, Jenna left the house, then stopped. The twins were down for their afternoon naps; Clara had come home and was sewing something in her crafts room across the hall from Luke and Grace. On her way to the cabin, Jenna had heard Hadley's new bull bellow as if he were being murdered. She'd decided to make a quick detour toward the barn in case someone human had been hurt.

She didn't see the animal, but she found Hadley leaning against a stall, staring at the floor, his arms crossed. "What's happened?"

"Nothing good." He told her about Barney's call, then looked toward the near pasture.

"Cory's out there now, running after the bull."
A quick upward glance at Jenna. "Would have
made us some nice Angus babies but we have
to take it back."

"What are you going to do?"

"I wish I could promise Cory and Clara
that I'll think of something, but I'm fresh out
of ideas."

Jenna hesitated. For a long moment she
watched Hadley's face, strong and rugged, a
muscle ticking in his jaw. She saw the bleak-
ness in his blue eyes. And took a deep breath.
"You asked me for part of Amy's money—
the twins' money now." Her fingers twined
around each other at her waist. "I haven't set
up the trust yet for Luke and Grace. There's
plenty of time before they'll need the money
for college. I'm willing to advance you some
of the money so you can do whatever you
have to for Clara's ranch." And because she
couldn't bear the beaten look on his face.
They'd survived lunch with the twins. Maybe
this could work, too. "I was wrong before,
Hadley. I've seen what you and Cory have
already done this spring and summer. If you
succeed, there *is* a benefit to the twins in
being able to keep their lives stable."

"That's a real turnaround on your part. What's the catch?"

"None," she said. "We do this as a loan. Unlike Barney, I don't need approval from any superiors. Do you want it or not?"

His gaze went back to the pasture, the bull. "What's the interest rate?"

"None. Interest-free."

She could almost guess his thoughts before he spoke. "So say I keep the bull. Borrow enough from you to buy more cows. Pay Cory. Fulfill my promise to help Clara—and keep my babies in diapers and teething biscuits a while longer. What if I default on this loan?"

"You won't," she said, a tentative show of trust that surprised her.

"Jenna, I have no collateral to offer."

"You *are* the collateral," she explained. "You don't leave here before I get the money back for the twins." That sounded crass, and Jenna tried to explain. "I believe you can make Clara's ranch profitable. I've seen how hard you work. I'm sure you'll repay every penny." She had to bend to see his downcast face, then smiled into his eyes. "Do we have a deal?"

"What do you think?" Hadley laughed a

little, erasing his dark expression. "That's the sweetest deal I've been offered all day—from the prettiest banker, too."

HADLEY HAD TOLD him to forget trailering the bull to its former owner, and Cory prayed his worries about Willow would soon be over, too. She was sitting beside him now on the front seat of his pickup. But Willow looked like she was about to cry, and Cory was no good with tears. Every time Hadley's twins puckered up, he wanted to do the same. "We can work this out," he said, reaching for Willow's hand.

"My father will never change his mind about you—I haven't even told him you're here." Which was good news. "I'm afraid to."

"That why you stood me up last time? And the one before that?"

Her voice trembled. "You said you weren't disappointed."

"I lied. Willow, you're right. Coming back to Barren wasn't the smartest thing I've done, but I couldn't stay away from you. Ever since we met—"

She pressed one hand to his lips. "Don't. You're making this harder."

Cory leaned away from her touch. He shot a look at her, those cornflower-blue eyes brimming, her blond hair shining halfway down her back. She stared out the window at the creek running through the little park where one kid was playing on the jungle gym even though it was close to dusk. "So this is it? You're breaking up with me?"

And here he'd thought she'd given in and this was a date she would keep. Later that afternoon, when he'd talked to Hadley again and left the bull in his pasture, Cory had scraped together the cash to buy her dinner tonight at the Bon Appetit with candles on the white-clothed tables. Romance. Things had been looking up for the ranch and for him. Not anymore. "I'm wearing my best jeans and boots and before I picked you up, I even had my hair cut. Respectable-like. Which wouldn't be enough for your father. But how about you, Willow?"

"You know how he is, or you did before you left Barren. I'm his baby girl. He doesn't have another, and my brothers feel the same. Besides…" For a long moment she didn't go on. "He never thought you were a good influence on me."

"I got a job now, I work hard… I treat you right, don't I?"

She paused again. "I know, but I don't like what happened before."

"That still your daddy talking?"

To Cory's dismay she didn't disagree. "You've made some poor choices. When you left town, I figured we were done. You *shouldn't* have come back," she said, "and not only because of me."

Cory could guess what would come next. "What happened before was not my fault."

"You took part, though. You did."

He gave her his best wide-eyed look. "Yeah, I admit I was in some bad company then, but I don't see those guys anymore." Which was a slight exaggeration. "I'm done sowing my wild oats, you might say…not with some girl, just doing reckless things in general," he quickly added. That hadn't been a smart expression to use. "Willow, I'm crazy about you. I thought you really liked me, too."

"I do. What I don't like is all this… subterfuge." He didn't recognize the word, but after a second or two he figured out its meaning. Sneaking around. Then she laid a hand on his and her eyes filled all over again and he didn't care about some word.

Cory's chest puffed out. "I could be foreman someday at the McMann ranch." One reason he'd tried to be helpful earlier with Hadley, the other being that he liked his boss. "Hadley won't stay forever. By then I'll be ready for the job. I'll make you proud, convince your father I'm good enough for you." Which, of course, also meant seeing the man again and talking his way out of the trouble he'd gotten himself into before. But not yet, and not when "the trouble" was still an issue.

"Oh, Co—"

Before she could object, he cut her off. "Don't say I can't. You got to believe me. When I'm no longer on your daddy's bad side, I'll buy you a ring—a big, shiny thing that will knock out everyone's eyes when you show it around. We'll get married." Cory sat there, dumbfounded. He'd actually proposed! Half unable to believe he'd asked, he wouldn't take it back. Those words sat just right.

Willow shook her head. "I won't hold you to it."

"But you'll remember? You won't break off with me now?"

"I should," she whispered.

And Cory was right back where he'd started. He would try again to persuade her that they belonged together. In his heart he already knew they did. Yeah, he'd made mistakes, but…who didn't?

*Women,* he thought, at the same instant he drew her into his arms. "I'll make you sure about us. I will."

## *CHAPTER THIRTEEN*

HADLEY BELIEVED IN keeping his distance from people, because most of the time he was already planning to be somewhere else. No use making friends he would have to lose—or couldn't get in the first place. No sense falling for someone as he had, too fast, for Amy, and living to regret that.

He wasn't one to pry into other people's lives. But the next time he was alone with Jenna, he couldn't help but ask for more details about her life. The words popped out before he could stop them. "So, what happened?" he asked. "I know about your father, the farm that Finn now owns, your growing up without much…" In that last they were the same.

After taking that loan of the twins' money, he didn't like feeling obligated to her, but the offer had proved too tempting to ignore. Had she manipulated him? How much did she really trust him? He guessed instead of charging interest she had new power over him instead. Jenna would be watching him even more closely, making sure he didn't take off some night and default on the loan.

Yet ever since they'd first talked about their backgrounds, he'd been wondering about Jenna's early life. She'd already heard about his.

"You mean after I grew up and didn't have to stay on that farm?"

They were seated on the top step of the stairs in Clara's house, their voices softly echoing in the space above the front entryway. Jenna had eaten dinner with them tonight, making conversation with everyone at the table, including Cory, who'd shown up at the exact moment Clara served the meal. He never missed one now.

After Clara's peach cobbler, Cory had gone back to the foreman's bungalow, and Clara had decided to visit a friend down the road for the evening, leaving Hadley with Jenna.

"I know your father could be harsh, but what about your husband?"

"Out of the frying pan into the fire," she admitted. "David was far better educated

than Daddy or me, and way more successful. I didn't even have a job until recently—
he said I didn't need one, which put him in
full control. I always figured I'd 'married up,'
as they say."

"I doubt that."

Jenna twisted her fingers together. "He's
living in Salt Lake City now, and I'm in
Barren, where I intend to stay. Try to make
something of myself."

"Stop," he said. Hadley had endured
enough foster homes where bitter words and
hurtful actions had eaten away at his own
sense of himself. "Don't put yourself down."
Jenna's shoulder rested against his, though
she didn't seem to notice the contact. "I've
had my share of trouble. Still do, but I learned
this way back. Don't let anyone else define
you."

"But you do, Hadley. You buy into that 'bad
boy' image. You shouldn't care what other
people think."

He blinked. "Maybe so," he said, "but I
*don't* care what your ex thought his reasons
were for locking you in a cage—"

"A beautiful cage," she said with a faint
smile. "I loved that house."

"Still, if you couldn't do as you pleased, be your own person…" He glanced at her, their shoulders brushing. "You can be now. You already are," he said.

"Yet there are still moments when I almost call David to solve some problem. I couldn't work out how to carry both twins at once down these stairs to lunch. What if something had happened to Luke or Grace while I was with the other one? I must have been crazy to think I would have been a good mother. At times I'm not sure my design skills are up to par, either."

Hadley wasn't used to being anyone's counselor, but Jenna's confidence needed shoring up tonight, and he owed her that for giving him the loan. She'd believed in him. "Look what you've done at Liza's house, and here for Danielle, although I still can't understand why Clara would allow her to move in on the twins." Years ago, he'd wondered why people took him in, then mistreated him. All they'd wanted, he eventually learned, was the money they earned from the state. Clara wasn't like that.

*Not everyone in this world is out to get you,* she'd said.

"Clara's getting a free update for the cabin," Jenna went on. "Maybe she can rent it after the Pearsons are gone. They're paying her now. Clara meant well."

"Anyway, you're nearly done there, aren't you?" Hadley cocked his head. Was that Luke stirring in his crib down the hall? He'd finally dropped off, fighting sleep all the way, minutes ago—Hadley glanced at his watch—or no, a whole hour? He and Jenna had been sitting here that long. Huh. Hadley sure did like the warmth of her shoulder against his, the scent of her hair, the way their bodies seemed to have synced until they breathed in rhythm. But he didn't care for her control of him through the loan any more than he did for the Pearsons' intrusiveness.

"Yes," she said, "and I'm happy with the design. But, different issue, obviously I'm not over my divorce." She glanced at Hadley. "Ever since then, I've kept to myself. I guess feeling good, even about my work, will take a while." She raised an eyebrow. "But apparently Bernice Caldwell has other plans. She wouldn't hire me to redo her living room. Instead, she keeps pressing me to consider

Barney as, I don't know what, a boyfriend?" Jenna wrinkled her nose.

"Pay no attention to that woman. She's infamous in this town. Barney should have left home long ago."

Her voice dropped lower. "Just up and leave like you always do?"

"What? You mean leave Clara's now? And have you chase after me for that money?" He couldn't tell whether, underneath, she admired him for his freewheeling independence, born of necessity for survival, or expected him to jump up off this step, haul his babies out of bed and hightail it down the road. "Do you see me going anywhere?" he asked, then felt as if he'd hemmed himself in. "Maybe after the twins are at least a year old…"

He was fine talking Jenna down from her miserable past, her bad marriage, but he'd rather not get into his own life any further than he had before.

"I left before because I had to," was all he said. "Right now I'd rather focus on this ranch, on helping Clara. Which you've given me the means to do." Hadley leaned back against the next upper step. "I'll be buying cattle this week, thanks to you."

"Thanks to Luke and Grace," she said. "But you're the one doing the work. Whose confidence is lacking now? You're a better man than people say, Hadley. You didn't have to take on the McMann ranch or save Clara from needing to leave her home."

"Yes, I did," he insisted. She really thought he was a good guy?

Jenna paused. "I wonder if part of the reason is because you *had* to leave so many places as a kid."

Hadley tensed. Jenna didn't know him that well. He wasn't the altruistic type or inclined to be touchy-feely; he wasn't trying to overcome what had happened to him so many years ago. He wasn't.

"I quit a lot of jobs," he said, "moved around before I met Amy. She tried to settle me down, but I wish I hadn't given her such a hard time." He looked at his hands. "Did you know how sick she was? When Amy asked you to be her standby guardian?"

"Sick?" Jenna repeated. Hadley replayed his talk with Sawyer. Appearing shocked, she said, "No. Is that why Danielle told me she'd suffered so much?"

"Maybe. She never mentioned her condition to me, either. The day I bought the gelding, Sawyer said he couldn't tell me before, something about a federal privacy law. Amy didn't want me to know." Hadley swallowed. "From birth she had that heart condition, a bad one. Luckily, Sawyer believes the defect is not genetic."

Jenna looked pale. "Dear Amy. I wish she had told one of us at least." Her gaze sharpened. "So *that's* why she asked me to be a standby guardian. She feared she might not survive the twins' birth."

"That," he agreed, "and because she believed Barren was just another place for me to leave. And to be frank, look what I did to our relationship."

The fact that he managed to care for Luke and Gracie continued to amaze him. He wouldn't repeat his mistakes with someone else. But what if he *could* trust Jenna? Even considering the loan and the power that gave her over him? The standby guardianship Amy had wanted? What if he could tell Jenna his deepest, darkest secrets? And they believed in each other?

Hadley didn't want to think about taking that step, yet the shadows of the upper hallway hid them from view, and no one else was around. For a long moment he gazed at her. Jenna's face was turned away after what she'd said, her hands still twined together, the soft glow of the night-light he kept on for the babies creating an aura above the sheen of her hair like a halo. He wasn't the man she thought he was, or that Amy had wished for. But Jenna *was* a good woman. He'd seen that tonight, and in the barn when she'd offered him the twins' money. And Hadley couldn't resist trying to prove that to her without the need for words he couldn't come up with anyway.

When she angled her body slightly toward him, he edged closer, untangling her fingers, then covering them with his. She didn't resist, and holding hands, he inched nearer still until, finally, he leaned in—and pressed his mouth to hers. He could tell the kiss surprised her, but to his relief, she didn't pull away. After another testing moment while he kept the kiss light, Hadley deepened their contact, his mouth moving on hers. Jenna let out a sigh before she pulled back, her eyes looking blurry, her pulse beating fast under his touch.

At the same instant, shattering the mood,

he heard Luke cry out. Hadley was on his feet before the next wail sounded, but so was Jenna. "Coming, pal," he called, and together they hurried down the hall, still close enough to touch each other.

He had his hand on the doorknob to the twins' room when she stopped him.

"That wasn't good for our business deal," she said.

Hadley should agree. But did he really want to? "I won't stay in Barren forever," he warned her anyway, and the brief intimacy between them ended with a thud. He glimpsed that in Jenna's face. And Hadley made a decision. He'd step back again, too, repay the loan faster than he'd hoped. To make that happen, he'd have to find a second job. By now the Circle H, Wilson Cattle or even the NLS might be able to use him. He almost didn't hear what Jenna said next.

"I didn't think you would."

"I MUST HAVE been crazy, kissing Hadley," Jenna said, nudging a sticky bun around on her plate. Her coffee sat, untasted, at the table opposite her sister. Before she drove out to Clara's, she'd settled on a quick breakfast at the café with Shadow to discuss their mother's bridal shower. Shadow had been asking to meet for a while, but Jenna had been putting her off.

Shadow gazed at her with a knowing smile. "Good for you. Good for Hadley. I'm not sure he's the right replacement for David, but moving on is a great idea."

Jenna's head hurt. Last night's "moment" on the stairs with Hadley had shaken her. At her apartment this morning, she'd considered phoning Clara to say she couldn't work on the cabin today. She didn't want to see Hadley before she'd made sense of last night. And then there was that kiss, times two.

Luke's cry had saved her from doing something more she would regret.

*Do you see me going anywhere?* Hadley had asked, yet she'd been waiting for him to do just that since the twins were born. Though she now assumed he'd take them with him; she could no longer picture him leaving them behind. *Had* she been crazy to consider allowing her fledgling relationship with Hadley to reach another, more personal level? Because then he'd said, *I won't stay in Barren forever.* And he still had traits that reminded her of her father. Amy had tried to manage that, and in part because of her health, with the standby guardianship. Add Jenna's worst memories of David, and she was better off without Hadley.

"Maybe Hadley only felt sorry for me last night," she added.

Shadow snorted, spraying coffee over the table. "Sure, any man's first impulse is to comfort the woman who just talked about her ex. Though your confidence really is a problem." She paused. "Is he a good kisser?"

Jenna buried her nose in her mug. "Shadow."

"You had better get yourself to the next meeting of the Girls' Night Out group. I have to say, I'm fine with him trying to guide you onto a better path away from David, but you need a good talking-to. We'll all set you straight."

"Believe me, I can wait for that," she said, but smiled a little. "All right, so I'm making a big deal out of a few kisses."

Shadow hooted. "Ooh, more than one, then."

Jenna pushed her plate aside. She hadn't wanted that sticky bun in the first place. "I'm not saying another word. You can just keep wondering about Hadley's technique." Awesome as it had been. The man could kiss, which had surprised her, too. His normally gruff manner hid an unexpected romantic side. "Let's get this shower planned instead."

"I'm thinking we should have it right after Thanksgiving."

Jenna couldn't keep quiet. "Mom's actually going through with this?"

"Despite your best effort to talk her out of it, yes. Deal with it, Jen. We can call the event part of your recovery program from David."

Jenna couldn't argue. "I know I have a tendency to dwell on our marriage…"

"That's part of it," Shadow said.

Painful, but true. "Still, for the first time since David announced he wanted a divorce, and I spent days hiding in our house hoping his move to Salt Lake City without me was a temporary glitch, I wanted another man to kiss me. I didn't try to stop Hadley." Far from it—she'd enjoyed the sensation of his mouth on hers when she'd never expected to be drawn to someone else. "You might acknowledge that I've made some progress."

"I can." Shadow took another sip of her coffee, then set it aside. "I'd also like to see you take interest in your own future. Has it occurred to you that you're spending more time at the ranch, and with Hadley? There must be some reason why, and I don't mean redoing that cabin for Danielle Pearson. Gee, Jenna. He actually might be attracted to you, and from the look on your face this morning, you must feel the same about him. Stop trying to deflect a new happiness that could be yours. And after all, he has that adorable set of twins."

Shadow let the words hang there while Jenna's pulse banged against her ribs. "They are adorable," she said, "but don't start planning another bridal shower or a wedding for me. My 'recovery' after David is going to take more time. I sure don't need a ready-made family—one I would probably mess up like I did my marriage."

"You didn't ruin that marriage, David did." Shadow drew a sheaf of papers from her bag. "Do what you think best about Hadley Smith. We'd better talk about this shower before we end up killing each other."

"I'M GOING INTO TOWN," Sawyer McCord informed Hadley. "Logan's in the field seeing to a sick calf. Can you get these stalls finished by the time we get back?"

"Sure. Should be done by noon." On his first day at the Circle H, Hadley was in a foul mood. Lucky for him he hadn't ended up in a cell at Finn Donovan's office for writing a bum check in the first place. But now with the loan from Jenna, at least he'd been able to pay for the bull. He'd done his calculations the other night, and if he worked hard, he might be able to pay Jenna back by Christmas. Now he was working a second job here, grateful for the extra hours but wishing he could spend his time at Clara's. He'd even taken a third job for Finn Donovan. Finn needed someone with knowledge of the cattle he'd bought, and Hadley was helping to make him into a real rancher. But how would he make a go of the McMann place if he wasn't there? Cory, whom he'd left in charge, was good but not as experienced as Hadley.

"Thanks for the help," Sawyer said, starting back down the aisle.

Hadley watched him go. For years, while still in school, he'd been on the outside looking in at the ranchers' sons he'd wanted to call friends. When he'd first returned to Clara's, not as a foster kid but an adult, he'd hoped friendship might be possible, yet even after he married Amy they hadn't been among the local couples like Sawyer and Olivia who were invited to social events.

He reminded himself that Sawyer was his boss. No friendship would cross the line even when Sawyer had said *I've got no problem with you.* Now Hadley was replacing stall boards under the supervision of the Circle H's cowhands. Tobias and Willy had given him the most menial job for the day. Hadley didn't care for being hazed, but he wasn't staying on this job forever, and wasn't the twins' welfare enough for him to worry about?

To make matters worse, the other night he'd given Jenna advice, then let things get out of hand. He'd lost his head and kissed her on the stairs. He already knew she didn't trust him. Last thing on his mind should be a woman who might be as broken as he was. A woman he'd have to leave. At least he'd made that clear.

Hadley's hands twitched on the hammer. He'd like to smash it right into the face of that jerk Jenna had married. On his worst day, Hadley had never treated Amy that bad.

He might not have tried hard enough to love her, but maybe he had tried as much as he was capable of.

"Done with this stall, Smith?" As Sawyer drove off, Willy sauntered through the barn, squinting as his eyes adjusted to the dimness after being outside. Hadley hadn't heard him ride in from wherever he'd been all morning, but he looked like he wanted trouble. "Hurry up. After you finish those stalls, load the rest of the cattle being shipped to the feedlot."

One of Hadley's least favorite chores. The panicked bawling of the steers told him they weren't so dumb; they must know they were taking a one-way ride eventually to the slaughterhouse. This morning he felt like one of them. With two extra jobs, he might be making more money, but he was losing ground at Clara's. And missing sleep every night—not because of the babies these days—while he played catch-up after his long day's absence from the ranch.

"Sure," he told Willy as he had Sawyer. He would do what he had to. "Be with you shortly." He didn't like Willy. Taller than Hadley and with dishwater-blond hair and hands like hams, Willy could be arrogant, even snide. Yet Hadley had no choice but to try to get along...as he should keep doing with Jenna and leave anything else between them off the table.

Leaning against a bale of hay, Willy crossed his arms. "Don't know why Logan and Sawyer hired you. Me and Tobias and the other half-timers we use should be enough. I'd say this is charity on their part."

"That's your opinion." How often as a boy had Hadley heard similar comments from kids at school? There'd definitely been a line drawn between those who belonged and those, like him, who didn't. After a while it had stopped being important to him, but at least now the Circle H owners hadn't taunted him. "They did hire me—whatever their reason."

Willy snorted. "What I hear, you didn't have any option. Clara McMann's spread has been dry dirt for years. Buying a few cows won't fix it. Neither will that one bull you bought." He made another scoffing sound. "You aiming to lose the rest of that ranch for her? Good time, I'd say, to leave town."

Hadley pushed past Willy. "I answer to Sawyer, Logan...even Tobias before I answer to you."

"Unless you don't run those steers up the ramp into the van. Then you will answer to me. Old Sam—" the ranch's owner and Logan and Sawyer's grandfather "—put me in charge." No, he hadn't. Hadley's orders had come from Sawyer.

"You're a hired hand just like me, Willy."

"Get the work done," Willy said as if he'd come up with the idea. "You want to stay here—you *need* the work—play by the rules. Mine included. Do as I tell you."

Hadley's patience, always in short supply, vanished. In the far stall, Olivia's horse Blue danced and snorted. Like the horse, Hadley was ready to stomp someone.

In a heartbeat he had Willy up against the next stall, Hadley's forearm jammed against his throat, cutting Willy's air off. "I understand you. Now you hear me. I dealt with guys like you when I was growing up but I'm not a kid now and I'll say this once." Willy was gasping for breath, his face getting purple now. "Don't mess with me."

For good measure, Hadley pressed harder on Willy's neck.

"Can't…breathe…"

Before he got himself in more trouble,

Hadley eased off. Willy all but sagged to the floor. In his stall, Blue was still doing a quick two-step, puffing like a steam engine. "We clear?" Hadley asked Willy.

"For now." Under his breath, as he labored to refill his lungs, he said a few choice words, then stumbled off down the aisle and out into the sun again.

The hierarchy on the Circle H wasn't working for Hadley any better than those bullies in the schoolyard had years ago.

The notion made him flash back to the picture in his wallet of his missing brother. He'd defended Dallas in a similar way often enough; defending himself felt pretty good, too. Yet thinking of Dallas threatened to derail his better mood. No matter how Hadley tried to see him in some stranger on the street or how many Google searches he did to find him, he had nothing to go on but a name that led nowhere.

Hustling to get his chores done, Hadley hammered the last boards into place before he headed for Blue's stall, hoping he didn't get his brains kicked in his first day on the job.

# CHAPTER FOURTEEN

JENNA WAS GLAD she and her sister hadn't come to blows over her mother's bridal shower. But the plans were underway. The party would be held at Wilson Cattle the week after Thanksgiving, and Shadow was in charge of the invitations, food and decorations. Jenna only had to provide the cake and champagne for a toast, then buy her mother a gift. The light duty on her part wasn't accidental. Because of Jenna's continued uncertainty about her mom's coming marriage to Jack, Shadow had mostly let her off the hook. Jenna couldn't shake her conviction that Wanda was making a serious mistake, but this morning she was back to her usual routine.

And glad of that, too. The work kept her mind off Hadley and his kiss on the stairs.

She gazed around Liza Wilson's new house. Jenna's design suggestions had worked! As she straightened pillows on the sofas that flanked the immense fireplace, she heard the expected sound of a car engine. Liza and Everett, who'd been living with Grey and Shadow, were here.

Everett hadn't seen the interior since the contractors left and his wife had hired Jenna. "You ladies have a good time," he'd told them. "I'd rather work cattle than pick through a bunch of fabrics and pictures of furniture." He'd given Liza full rein to choose the items for their new home, and as promised, Liza had honored his taste.

Heart in her throat, Jenna waited for his reaction.

"My, my, my," Everett exclaimed, one hand on Liza's shoulder as they passed through the entry into the great room, his blue-green eyes twinkling. "When my Texas transplant here decides to make a Kansas house a home, she does it right." He gazed at Jenna and grinned. "My bride and I are very pleased."

Looking quite pregnant now two months before her due date, Liza took Jenna's hand. "Thank you. Everett stewed all the way from the main house, afraid he would hate what we came up with. I told him he abdicated any right to complain when he rode off to see his cattle."

"I'm glad you like what I've done," Jenna said, "with your help, Liza."

Everett, still an impressive-looking man, his brown hair faintly streaked with gray, continued to glance around. "I like this big room, the kitchen—" in all its gleaming stainless-steel and rough-edged-granite glory "—but I really want to see that nursery Liza has talked so much about. We'll need it soon."

Jenna's phone rang. "Why don't you go ahead? I have to take this."

She'd been putting Bernice Caldwell off for months now, and she steeled herself for this conversation.

Bernice didn't waste her breath on pleasantries. "You've been avoiding me. I'm having a dinner party on Saturday. Seven o'clock. Don't be late. Barney and I will expect you."

She didn't give Jenna a chance to refuse. Bernice hung up before she could speak. Barney's mother had obviously given up trying to pair her with Barney on a one-to-one basis and was trying a different tactic. Jenna groaned aloud as Liza leaned over the staircase rail from above. "Everything all right?"

"Not really." Jenna touched her temple, where a headache was brewing. "Barney Caldwell's mother finally reached me. She has some idea he and I would make a perfect match." She mentioned the invitation.

"Bernice has her mind made up and you aren't going to change it." Liza beckoned her. "Come upstairs, Jenna. We'll help you fabricate an excuse. Everett wants to personally smother you in hugs for this whole house. I don't think you'll have a problem finding clients from now on. You won't need to cater to Bernice Caldwell."

That was good news, but how had she attracted Bernice's notice in the first place? Based on that one chance meeting in front of the bank? Or had Barney put her up to it? She wandered through the second-floor rooms behind Liza and Everett, smiling at his obvious satisfaction in spite of her dilemma over the Caldwells. "We're going to be very happy here—even happier than we have been since the day we met. And this wonderful space for the baby..." He turned in the center of the nursery, holding Liza's hand. "The giant stuffed giraffe was inspired. This hammock for his toys..."

"Or *hers*. Everett loves all the color," Liza put in. "Our *daughter* will be thrilled with the dollhouse you and I still need to find for her, Jenna."

"Whenever you like, we can look for one." Liza and Everett had opted not to learn their baby's sex, preferring to be surprised, but it seemed each of them had an opinion. As homework, Jenna mentally thumbed through the various furniture catalogs she kept at home and all over her office.

As they left the nursery, Liza fell into step beside her. "If I were you, I'd go to Bernice's dinner. The evening might be worth the investment of your time."

"And have to spend hours with her and Barney?"

Liza grinned. "Not if you discourage them by taking a date."

After that night on the stairs, Jenna had been avoiding Hadley as much as possible. She didn't want a repeat of the unwise kisses they'd shared. Thank goodness he spent most of his daylight hours at the Circle H or at Finn Donovan's place. Still...

"This is crazy," Hadley muttered. "It's gate-crashing."

As he and Jenna pulled up in his truck at the Caldwell house in Barren, he tugged at his tie. Hadley kept asking himself why he'd agreed to this stunt. After working at the Circle H and more extra hours at Finn's, what he really needed was a bed and twelve hours of uninterrupted sleep.

But Jenna was still trying to sell him on the idea. "You won't have to do much. A few polite words, a meal you'll miss at Clara's tonight, a thank-you to Bernice for a lovely evening, and we'll be on our way home."

*Home.* She must mean her apartment. "Why didn't you just tell that woman you didn't want to come? Say you have serious food allergies—gluten, dairy, you're not a meat eater, whatever—then you could have stayed in tonight. So could I." And with Clara on duty for the twins, he would have slept.

As he spoke, the feeling of dread didn't leave him, but Hadley got out of the pickup, came around and held out a hand to help Jenna from the passenger seat. She'd worn high heels, a V-neck dress with folds that wrapped her figure in an interesting way, and gleaming silver hoops in her ears. He averted his eyes.

Hadley grumbled, "I wasn't invited. You were."

"I invited you. And you said yes." After she'd twisted his arm, he'd told himself he owed her this one night for giving him the loan, but that was half the truth. The uncomfortable thought that he'd endured similar events with Amy's parents and survived didn't help. After all, he wasn't about to take his relationship with Jenna in that direction.

"I appreciate what you're doing." She climbed down without his help, and the memory of their kiss on the stairs at Clara's was suddenly between them again. How was he going to spend the evening with this woman he didn't want to even like when he couldn't seem to convince himself that it was better to keep his distance? "If this goes the way it's supposed to," she said, not sounding as sure now, "I won't have to worry anymore about running into Bernice or Barney."

Hadley gave up. With an inner sigh, he walked Jenna up the path to the door. "Let's hope this works," he muttered.

Maybe it was worth it to see the shocked

look on Bernice Caldwell's face when she opened the door. Years ago she hadn't been kind to him. "Oh. Mr. Smith." She laid a hand over her ample bosom. "I didn't—"

"Invite me, I know." He glanced at the troublesome woman beside him, tried not to notice how pretty she looked tonight. "Jenna didn't like the notion of driving home in the dark alone. I'm her escort."

"I hope you don't mind," Jenna said, not sounding that sincere.

Bernice was speechless, and Barney wore the same expression his mother did, but he seemed to recover more quickly. "Please, come in." His gaze slid away from Hadley's. "There's plenty of food. Would you like a drink before dinner?"

How could he not? Hadley needed a bracer to get through this, but as the designated driver he refused. Jenna chose wine, and with her glass in hand, they all gathered in the living room where Hadley could barely keep from openly staring. The place was a museum. Knickknacks crowded the antique set of dark wood shelves in the corner; the old brick mantel was full of family pictures, mostly of Barney—baby, kid in a baseball uniform, pimply teenager, college grad—and most of them standing by his mother. Crocheted doilies covered every end table. The red velvet-upholstered chair Bernice steered him to had to be from the last century and stuffed with horsehair. Stiff as a board, it crackled when he sat down. Jenna got diverted to the matching sofa where Barney perched next to her.

Hadley preferred the foreman's house at the NLS or definitely Clara's home. He sent Jenna a look that said *you* needed *an escort*. Too bad she was on the other side of the room, the oak floor and furniture between them anchored by a musty Oriental rug.

He was here, he would stay to support Jenna, but there was no way he could make small talk. At dinner he sat across from her, toying with his fork, a heavy silver candelabra with tall ivory tapers blocking his view. Dinner party? They were the only guests. What a setup. No one but Jenna tried to draw him into the stilted conversation, but the very expression of suppressed panic in her eyes kept him in his seat. He decided he was glad he'd come. He imagined Bernice, like some Victorian matron, wanted to ask what his intentions were with Jenna, but he wouldn't give her the satisfaction of getting pulled into that one.

While he might not intend to fall in love with her, Jenna made him want to protect her.

As soon as they finished eating limp salad, dried-out roast chicken, pale vegetables and lumpy mashed potatoes, he wanted to leave. Bernice didn't provide the opportunity. In the living room, she started again to separate Jenna from Hadley, who grasped her hand, then tucked it into the crook of his arm and made haste to the sofa, leaving Barney the chair. Bernice glared at Hadley as she served dessert. Finally, she couldn't keep from saying, "It was good of you to come so you can drive Jenna home. The roads outside of town can be impenetrably dark. I avoid them myself, and I have no issue with an extra guest at my table." Pause. She glanced at Barney, who looked ready to jump out a window. "But you must know why I invited Jenna tonight." *It was not so you could cozy up with her on my sofa*, went unsaid but implied.

Hadley ignored that. "And I came because I like her." Also, because he owed her money. He turned to Barney. "Maybe you think I'm here to make you squirm, but I'm not. You denied Clara McMann and me that loan for her ranch, and I understand. We weren't in a good spot then to take on any debt. Still aren't," he said, and Jenna caught his eye as if to say *stop*. But this whole business made him mad on her behalf. Nor would he mention the loan she'd given him. "Barney, you don't need your mother to find someone for you." He faced Bernice. "Mrs. Caldwell, let your son make his choices. All of them. Maybe while you're doing that, he'll learn to respect a woman's prerogative to make her own decisions, as well." Just like Jenna tonight.

Bernice sniffed the air, obviously put out.

He stood, held out a hand again, and this time Jenna took it. "Let's go."

To her credit, she didn't try to make nice as she always did with the Pearsons. Jenna murmured a quick thank-you, then let him steer her to the door. In minutes they were out of there, leaving poor Barney waving from the doorway, Bernice nowhere to be seen.

Wondering if he'd overstepped his bounds, Hadley waited all the way to Jenna's apartment for her to light into him, but she didn't. With every mile, his gut tightened another notch as if he were wearing a belt three sizes too small.

"I feel kind of guilty," he finally said. "In all the time I spent with Amy's parents—and continue to spend with them—I should have learned to keep my mouth shut."

"No, it's okay. I doubt I'll be invited to dinner again." In the darkness all around them, Jenna settled deeper into the passenger seat. She gazed at him for a long moment, then, to his utter surprise, she said, "My hero."

His hands gripping the wheel, Hadley flushed. He hadn't wanted to go. He hadn't wanted to like her this much, or at all.

Yet he did.

Hadley told himself he had the twins to worry about, not this woman who didn't trust him much, either. So why was he smiling, too?

THE NEXT MORNING Barney came to Jenna's office to apologize.

"There's no need," she reassured him, sorry herself to recognize the humiliation in his brown eyes. It must have taken courage for him to walk down the street from the bank to see her. "Yes, the evening was awkward, but most of all for you, I'm sure."

"My mother can be heavy-handed." He dropped onto a chair in front of her desk, then sighed. "That's my fault. She thinks she has to step in, take over, and I let her. When she said she'd asked you to dinner, I knew that wouldn't work out." He picked up the nameplate on her desk. Barney turned over the brushed nickel in his hands. "I realize I'm not the most eligible bachelor in this town. I once tried to date Olivia Wilson...McCord now. Had my eye, so to speak, on a few other women in Barren from time to time, but I always remembered you from our school days. When you moved back home again..."

"Barney, there are no hard feelings, but..."

He set the nameplate down with a little clunk. "It can be hard to keep striking out."

"Hadley made a good point last night. Maybe if *you* choose someone, someone new," she added, "and ask her out instead of letting your mother make the plans, you might get a different answer. Mine is still the same." Jenna tried to find the right words that wouldn't hurt his feelings more than she already had. "I wish I could say this in a nicer way, but I didn't have a happy marriage, and I'm not over that yet."

"Even for Hadley Smith?"

For a moment she couldn't answer. "For anyone," she said.

Barney studied his shoes.

Jenna waited until he looked up at her. "Never mind Hadley. I have to get myself in order before I even consider another relationship." Certainly taking on someone else's children would be unfair to everyone involved. She tried a faint smile. "Maybe we should both get our lives together, Barney."

He shrugged. "Yes, I suppose that's true. I'm sorry I bothered you."

"You didn't. When your mother told me—she didn't ask—about dinner, I should have simply said I couldn't come. Hadley was only doing me a favor as a…friend, hoping to make your mother see the light. He may have spoken too bluntly, but he was right."

His gaze fell. "So you're in the local camp that says to pack my belongings—as he might do—then head for another town, even another state, to get away from her."

"That sounds drastic," she said, though it was Hadley's usual means of solving a problem. "I probably shouldn't say this, and it's not my place to decide, but your mother is not helping. Isn't it time to make your own way?"

"And lose her if she doesn't approve of what I do?"

Jenna's heart sank. He did love his mother, but… "Oh, Barney. Please. You're the vice president of the bank." Not that he was known to do that good a job, but maybe his mother distracted him and he had more potential than anyone thought. "It may not be necessary to leave Barren. Just stand your ground. I bet there's nothing you could do that would make her love you any less, even when she doesn't show it in a healthy way. I can't believe she approved of *me*," Jenna added.

Yet she'd learned last night she might be wrong, too, about Hadley. For a man who preferred the open road to staying in one place, he'd done a very nice thing for her. At the Caldwell house they'd shared a mission, and with the twins they sometimes had a connection now, too. He hadn't left yet, though he would, as he'd once pointed out, and she doubted he would actually default on the loan she'd given him. He might have some traits she didn't care for, but he was honest. Her attitude toward him had definitely changed for the better, enough for Jenna to have offered the twins' money for Clara's ranch. As for Barney...

"What is it you really want to do with your life?"

"Not grind away at the Cattlemen's Bank, that's for sure."

"There's your answer. Wherever that takes you, including right here. You've already made a start."

He smiled a little. "Maybe I have."

Had she done as much? Jenna was half-willing to explore something new with Hadley, yet she was also half-afraid where he was concerned.

Which half would win out in the end?

# *CHAPTER FIFTEEN*

"HAPPY BIRTHDAY TO LUKE!" The traditional song floated on the air throughout Clara's house, where a small party was in progress for the twins. In November, they had just turned one year old. Then, "Happy birthday to Grace!" rang out, although Hadley, of course, sang his part with "Gracie."

On the dining room table, with help from everyone gathered around, two candles were blown out, but the cakes were already half-demolished. Neither Luke nor Gracie had waited for the ritual they didn't quite understand to be over. With both hands, they had attacked the two cakes.

Hadley exchanged a smile with Jenna. He couldn't believe how fast the time had flown. For a while now, his babies had been crawling, and every day they got closer to independence.

As the song ended, Clara swooped down on Gracie to wipe her face, smeared with yellow frosting. Jenna lent a hand with Luke while Hadley whisked the remains of the cakes out to the kitchen counter. This naturally produced howls of displeasure from the twins.

Hadley's ears hurt from the noise, but Danielle came to the rescue. "Presents," she called out, the perfect distraction, and his pal and sweetie pie were soon sitting on the living room rug, ripping bows and paper off packages containing new clothes and toys. It didn't seem to matter which gift was intended for Gracie or Luke. In minutes the room was littered with trash, and the twins were fighting over a plastic airplane, a toy replica of the real Cessna that Logan Hunter, a pilot as well as a rancher, had bought for his new airstrip at the Circle H.

Jenna leaned against Hadley for a moment. He felt the warmth of her at his shoulder, inhaled the light, fresh scent of her hair. Heady stuff. Perfume or shampoo? It was almost enough to make him forget that she still held too much power over him, that at any moment—even today?—she might let slip something about the guardianship Amy had applied for. Then, a week before that court date, she'd been wheeled into the delivery room. Hard to believe she'd been gone this long.

Danielle was within hearing range. She might pick up on whatever Jenna, who seemed to be in a similarly contemplative mood, said. But it wasn't what Hadley feared. "Don't you wish you could plow into your birthday like that? Total abandon."

"They're sure having fun." Without thinking, he ran a hand over the silky smoothness of Jenna's hair, making Clara's gaze home in on them. He shouldn't worry about anything that overshadowed the twins' first birthday. After the Caldwell dinner, things had improved between him and Jenna. "I never had a birthday like this," he murmured. In fact, the last birthday he remembered was when Dallas was eight, shortly before they were separated, and there'd been no cake or presents at that foster home.

Jenna paused. "Mama tried to give us special days, but Daddy usually created some drama to ruin the celebration. Or he simply forgot."

"Then we should both enjoy this one."

Jenna tilted her head against his shoulder,

and that heady scent rose in the air again. "Yes, we should. Better times."

Did she mean with him? But where could that lead? With Jenna, Clara and Danielle here, and Cory, who was laughing at the twins' antics, he decided not to care, for today at least. The tension inside him began to unravel like an old sweater, and he focused on the other guests. This was Luke and Gracie's day.

After Jenna left his side, Hadley talked with the Wilsons, who'd come from their neighboring ranch, and Clara perched on the sofa to chat with Sawyer. Cory had Luke on his lap and was trying in vain to teach him his ABC's. Luke gazed at him with a puzzled expression. Not to be outdone, Gracie took up the game with Danielle. "Man, these two are something else," Cory said, then laughed. He set Luke on the floor, and Hadley's boy crawled after his new soft ball. Then, to Hadley's amazement, Luke pulled himself up to a standing position, grasping the edge of the sofa.

"Clara!" Hadley said. "He's on his feet!"

Sure enough, Luke was chortling with pride. Clara pressed a hand to her eyes, then grinned. A few people clapped, and several others cheered. Including Danielle.

In the past months his former mother-in-law's visits had become more frequent, and of longer duration, but Hadley avoided her. He wasn't having as much luck with Jenna, who seemed to alternate between comfortable moments with him like today or silence whenever he was around.

That night at Bernice Caldwell's house and on the way to Jenna's apartment, he'd assumed they were in tune somehow, but ever since, she'd done this little dance of advance, then retreat, as if she couldn't make up her mind about Hadley. Maybe the attraction was only on his side, and Jenna didn't have more interest in him than she did in Barney. Not that Hadley saw a future with Jenna. He was getting close to making a profit here at the ranch, and its first haying season had been a good one that would get them through the winter. He was on track to repay the loan by Christmas—roughly six weeks away—and then, with the twins now a year old, he'd be free to think about moving on.

Still lying on her tummy, Gracie stared at

her brother as if he'd suddenly grown two heads. Then she began to cry.

Hadley scooped her into his arms. "Did you see that? Me, too," he said, swiping a finger across her wet cheek. "No tears, sweetie pie. You'll be doing the same thing any day now. And after that happens, Luke should watch out. You'll win every race." Although slower than her brother in some ways, she never liked Luke getting the best of her.

Jenna, who'd been in the kitchen, rushed into the room. "What's wrong?"

She might not always favor Hadley, but she really cared for the babies.

He just pointed at Luke. Jenna stood there as if she couldn't decide how to react.

Danielle blinked rapidly. "Lucas, you big boy." She had also really taken to the twins.

"Pick him up," Hadley said. "He won't bite—not much, anyway."

The babies seemed to be constantly teething these days, and Hadley could barely keep up with their all-around progress. Every day seemed to bring mastery of some new ability they hadn't managed before. Holding up their heads, sitting by themselves, grasping toys. Danielle cradled his boy to her chest. "What a star," she said, glanced at Gracie, then agreed with Hadley. "You, too, princess. Once you're mobile, there'll be no stopping you."

He and Danielle shared a rare smile with Clara, but Jenna still hadn't said a word. In fact, she edged back toward the hallway, then ran up the stairs.

Jenna was usually in good spirits, eager to help. He understood now why Amy had wanted her as standby guardian, though he still wasn't comfortable with the implication if the Pearsons found out. They might well try for custody of the twins. They'd have leverage then, knowing what their daughter had wanted, and along with their relationship to his kids now, to take Luke and Gracie. And Jenna was the one who could give that to them. But that didn't matter now if she was hurting.

On the second floor, Hadley went down the hall to the nursery, where Jenna was weeping softly into her hands. "Hey. What's the matter?"

She shrugged. "Watching Luke stand, the twins' first birthday…but, no, that's not all. I heard from David last night," she said. "We usually talk about money or belongings from our house that he's stored in a unit in Salt Lake. At first he wanted nothing but changed his mind and keeps changing it. Only yesterday, he phoned instead to tell me he's seeing someone. I was shocked, not that he was in a new relationship, because he's free to have one now." Her voice tightened. "But she has three children from her first marriage, and if they marry, he informed me, he'll have an instant family."

Hadley's temper spiked. "He did not remind you that you can't have—"

Another shrug. "Implied but didn't say. I'm still stunned. We're talking about David, who never wanted kids as badly as I do—did, I mean."

"And watching Luke and Gracie smash their birthday cakes, then seeing Luke stand, reminded you of that." Hadley put his arms around her. He tried a lighter tone. "You and Gracie are going to drown if you keep crying." Without stopping to consider the gesture, he planted a kiss on top of her head, her hair silky under his lips, but if his awareness of Jenna was one-sided, he shouldn't dwell on that.

Jenna leaned into him, her softness against his harder, work-honed body.

He had no intention of getting involved again, certainly not with the woman in his arms whose entire being mourned for her failed marriage and a family of her own. The twins were another reminder that she wouldn't have one. And that he wasn't the man she could trust not to hurt her again.

Hadley knew he should pull back, but... "I won't deny the twins came as a surprise. Amy and I had tried for a while, but then our never-all-that-good relationship turned sour, for me at least, and I said we should stop. I sensed we weren't going to make it. We separated, I filed for divorce. Then we slipped up and all at once I was about to become a father." Hadley sighed. "Not the most natural part for me to play."

"You're not playing a part now. Luke and Grace are very real."

He couldn't help a smile. "I like to think they're making a better man of me. Jenna, don't let David get to you. You're one of the finest people I've ever met—"

She sniffed. "High praise from the same person who didn't need my 'involvement' when the twins were born." Jenna eased slightly away to look up into his face. "Yes, as you once said, I've kept coming here, and I've wondered if I should. Am I doing *me* any favors?"

"I know this is pretty hard on you."

"Making myself crazy whenever I drive out here to Clara's? I should stay home, work to make Fantastic Designs successful. It's the only future I can trust in. Maybe I shouldn't have agreed to make the cabin into Danielle's getaway spot from Walter."

His arms were still around her. "You think that's partly why Danielle really comes?"

"I'm not a mind reader, but I went through some bad patches with David, so I recognize the signs. Walter Pearson hasn't been here in weeks," she pointed out. "He even skipped the twins' birthday party."

"Fine by me." Hadley rocked her a little, enjoying their contact. Remembering the kisses they'd shared that night on the stairs outside this door. "I don't know about the Pearsons—Amy always said they were close, devoted to each other—but why did you stay so long with David? A man who didn't give you what you needed?" He didn't mean babies like Luke and Gracie.

Again Jenna drew back a little. "I loved

him then, I suppose, even when things were no longer going well. In that, Amy and I were similar—not that I'm comparing you to him." Hadley thought she was. "I've always had a tendency to stick with a situation—and David offered me a life I'd never had before. Security, that beautiful home in a city I loved…a family eventually, I believed, that would be the opposite from my own childhood."

"You were never inferior to him, Jenna. You know, when I was getting kicked from one foster home to another, I always assumed it was me. My folks didn't want me, so—"

"That's not true. You said yourself they weren't in a position to take care of you, but they did try to see that someone would. I'm sure they hoped another situation would be better for you and your brother."

"They were wrong," he said, "for me, anyway. Don't know what happened to him." Hadley thought of the tattered photo in his wallet, ready for Hadley to torture himself again by looking at it. The way Jenna tormented herself by visiting his babies.

She gazed at him with what he hoped was understanding, not pity. "You told me about that one couple who were good to you other than Clara and her husband. Were there any foster places with people who made you feel included? Part of their family if not your birth one?"

He didn't hesitate. "Clara and Cliff." He gestured at the nursery. "This used to be 'my' room. Had a bunch of rodeo posters on that wall where Clara has hung these photo collages of the babies. My bed was under the window between where the twins' cribs are now."

"Clara made you feel welcome."

"But it's the bad places I remember." And someday, again, he was going to have to take off, to escape. The question was how, with Luke and Gracie to consider now? What harm would he be doing by taking them with him? How could he think to leave them behind? And whether or not she liked his interest in her, there was Jenna.

Nevertheless. He should cut this cord before he got in any deeper with a woman who'd always stuck too long. Like Amy. Or was Jenna about to tell him she wouldn't come to the ranch again? She might feel the twins' birthday was the perfect time to end her visits, but Hadley already felt…abandoned. He didn't appreciate the feeling any more than he had as a kid. There was no sense in prolonging the moment, though. "I appreciate what you've done for Luke and Gracie," he began.

Jenna arched an eyebrow. "I never thought I'd hear you say that."

"If you need to back off now…"

Jenna pulled completely away, and Hadley felt a sudden coolness at her lost warmth against him. Why was he missing her when she hadn't yet left the house?

"I gave up a big part of myself for David," she said. "I'll never stick with something again that doesn't nurture me. Amy and I used to talk about that. She was always so sure that you two could make your marriage work."

"I wonder why we fought about money when Amy had that account at the bank with funds from her parents. Now I realize what her clinginess, the manipulation, even how often she said she loved me really meant. She knew her heart condition might end her life too soon. I think she even found fault with me in order to maintain control, so I'd try harder in our marriage, and at one point

I did promise. Amy must have been desperately afraid that I'd leave her. But I'll never regret that she gave me the twins. She and I worked out fine with them."

"Yes, you did."

For a minute she studied him. "And stepping away might be best for me now, but not for Luke and Grace. I *don't* want to hurt anyone, Hadley, especially not the twins." Jenna's gaze faltered. "But are you telling me to go? If that's what you want..."

He swallowed. "I agree that you'd be hurting them if you left." *Hurting me, too*, yet he couldn't say that. Letting anyone but the babies know he was vulnerable had never worked for Hadley. It had scared him so bad years ago to realize he needed Clara that he'd packed his gear and hit the road. Maybe Jenna didn't have feelings for him now, as he'd thought she might after the Caldwell dinner, but he was used to that. With her, Hadley would keep his emotions to himself.

Then to his surprise, she said, "Luke and Grace have already lost their mother. They don't need more loss. Neither do we. You know how that feels."

Hadley's pulse sent a little blip across his inner radar screen. "Jenna…"

He was halfway to confessing how he felt after all when she turned away, hiding her face. Jenna plucked at the edge of Gracie's quilt that had poked through the crib bars.

"Hadley? Jenna?" Clara's voice rose up the stairs. "Come see Grace!"

He would never know what Jenna might have said, but he could sense that she was torn, too—about the twins, if not him. Yeah, he liked her way too much for his own good.

IN THE LIVING ROOM, Jenna held Grace and pressed her forehead to the little girl's, fighting tears. Grace had stood up, too! Everyone at the party except Clara and Danielle had left while she'd talked with Hadley upstairs, and Jenna was glad. This must be her day for falling apart again, as she'd done right after David moved out. But these at least were happy tears.

"Both standing in the same day," she remarked to Clara and Danielle. Hadley's twins did everything together, as if they were still sharing their mother's womb, so taking their next step together in preparing to walk shouldn't surprise her. The bond they had would last all their lives. But Jenna didn't linger. Hadley had followed her downstairs, and taken his turn to celebrate Grace's milestone, yet he stood back while Jenna said her goodbyes, then left the house.

What had happened between them in the nursery, where Jenna had glimpsed his vulnerability—which he'd tried to hide—and she had exposed her own? What must he think? She didn't love David anymore. Had she used him as a shield to keep Hadley from getting close?

Without saying the exact words, he had asked her to keep coming to visit his babies. And they'd agreed about Luke and Grace, probably a temporary connection, but one she couldn't deny.

Jenna didn't go straight home. By the time she realized where she was headed, she was already in the driveway of her mother's house, or rather the one she shared with Jack. It looked sparkling with new white paint. Even the clean flagstone path to the porch and the wooden sign beside the entry reading Hancock spoke of their relationship. Jenna had her hand poised on the bell when Wanda opened the door. "Didn't expect you today, baby girl. Come on in and see what we've done here."

Jenna followed her blindly through the house, admiring the furniture they'd bought and the warm colors on the walls. It was a stark contrast to the falling-down place where she'd grown up on that five-acre farm, crammed into a home no more welcoming than most of the foster ones Hadley had touched upon in their conversation. Perhaps she was more like him than she'd thought.

"This is beautiful, Mama." She hugged her. "And you look wonderful."

Like Jenna, Wanda had gained a few pounds, and she carried herself straighter than she had years ago. Her hair was always freshly styled now, her clothes in brighter hues than the old-fashioned, drab house-dresses she'd worn.

She searched Jenna's eyes. "Are you ready to accept the fact that Jack and I will be fine together?"

Jenna didn't answer except to kiss her mother's cheek. Her previous warnings had fallen on deaf ears, and part of Jenna was still in the twins' nursery, sharing those moments with Hadley that she didn't understand, either. For a second, she'd thought he might send her packing, in the next that he might kiss her again—and that she'd welcome it.

Wanda must have seen her dilemma. She led Jenna down the steps from the three upstairs bedrooms and into the kitchen, which even in the old house had been the heart of her home. She pulled out a chair for Jenna, opened one cabinet door, then another and laughed. "I reach for everything as if I were still in that house Finn Donovan bought from me." She no longer called it home. Her mother held up two mugs. "Coffee? I'm glad he and Annabelle are fixing up the place. Have you seen his barn? Your father would have been pea green with envy, not that he ever moved to tear down the old one."

Jenna watched her fill the coffee maker, take cream from the fridge and a sugar bowl from another cupboard. "Shadow tells me you two have the bridal shower all set, twice as many people coming as I expected. She and I went shopping for my dress last month—I wish you had joined us—and Jack and I signed the contract for our wedding reception."

Curiosity got the better of Jenna. "Where?"

"That new bed-and-breakfast in Farrier. Have you seen it?"

"No." If Danielle had been able to stay there, Jenna wouldn't have redone the cabin, or spent as much time near Hadley at Clara's ranch.

"A restored Victorian, just beautiful," her mother went on, pouring coffee. "The woman who runs it bought some antiques from Olivia who, as you know, has very good taste. I'd like your input about the dinner menu. The inn needs my final choices. The night of the wedding, Jack and I will stay in their bridal suite. Oh, Jenna, it's all white lace and roses."

She swallowed the lump in her throat that had been there since the twins' birthday party. She couldn't dampen Wanda's enthusiasm when Jenna didn't know which way to go herself. "Sounds lovely, Mama."

As if she'd been given permission, Wanda shot up from her chair, hurried over to a drawer, then took out the menu she'd mentioned. She set it in front of Jenna. "Will you?"

"Of course." She studied the menu, which kept blurring in front of her. "The, um, filet sounds fancy...chicken not as much, and there's pheasant? But the cost..."

"Jack says we're only doing this once. He wants to make the most of it."

The words sank into Jenna's soul. She recalled David's comment about the new woman he was seeing.

She blinked her vision into focus. "I know you feel you're doing the right thing, and I do realize Jack cares about you." She would try to enjoy herself at the bridal shower. "Your wedding sounds perfect." But then, didn't all plans at first? "I just hope you don't—" She couldn't make herself say, *end up as you did with Daddy, or I did with David.* Only it wasn't his face that appeared on the screen of her mind. It was Hadley's.

Certainly she'd never imagined that she'd find someone else, fall in love, make another mistake... But would it be a mistake, as she'd accused her mother of making? Which of them was right?

As always, Wanda seemed to sense what

she was thinking. She squeezed Jenna's hand. "Don't worry. Everything will work out. It always does."

# CHAPTER 2

## CHAPTER SIXTEEN

AFTER JENNA LEFT, Hadley went down to the barn. Exhausted from their first birthday and after inching around the living room sofa, Luke and Gracie were napping. For once, they'd gone to sleep without a fuss. Maybe the more active and independent they became, the easier being a father would become. Ha, wasn't that a nice daydream? Hadley didn't believe in happy endings.

Not that he was still thinking—shouldn't be—of Jenna. After hearing her talk about David again, he knew she was in no shape to follow through on any attraction she might feel to Hadley, who would be a bad bet anyway. The irony wasn't lost on him—he might call himself the ranch foreman here, but he was a temporary guest again at Clara's. He had the twins to take care of; he had nothing to offer Jenna.

"Boss?" Leading Trouble down the aisle,

Cory said, "Finished replacing that latch on Mr. Robert's stall. Figured I'd ride out to check the herd before dark."

"Sure, saddle up." But the gelding, having been in the paddock most of the day, was covered in mud. "Horse needs some heavy grooming before you set off. Seems he had his own fun today rolling around. Celebrating the twins' birthday."

"I envy him his good mood."

Hadley took a closer look at Cory. His hair stuck up at the crown, and his eyes held a defeated expression. Hadley hazarded a guess. "Thought you had a good time at the party yourself, but someone got the best of you today. Girl trouble again?"

"Hard to have any kind of trouble when she won't see me. I'm working on that," he said.

Hadley helped fasten the horse in the crossties opposite Cory. "What's her beef?" He almost welcomed listening to someone else's problems. Why had he felt so downcast watching Jenna drive away?

"Not her, it's her father." Cory ticked off some points. "Doesn't like my looks, my general…lack of ambition. Bottom line, he doesn't like me. Called me shiftless, and she's taken that to heart." Which Hadley guessed was only part of the story.

"Where does he get that impression of you, Cory?" Hadley hadn't seen any of that. The boy came to work on time, put in a full day, never complained. The only negative thing he'd ever heard from Cory was on the subject of his would-be girlfriend.

"He always thought—thinks—I'm a loser. Now she won't even answer my texts." Cory swiped a brush along the gelding's off side. "I like this job, but—no offense—I got bigger ideas for my future. Don't know what I can do to convince Willow of that, though, meaning really her dad. I've even shown her my prize buckles from rodeo... I mean, I was somebody then, a rising star, they said." With a glance at Hadley, who was brushing the horse's near side, he picked up a currycomb. "Maybe I should give up."

"Persistence pays," Hadley said, though with Jenna he should probably quit the field before he even considered trying to create something more with her. He knew better than to believe in that. "Did you say Willow? Willow Bodine?"

Cory drew the comb through some matted hair. "You've heard of her?"

"Sure, and her father can be tough. I worked for him once. Briefly."

For a moment, Cory didn't respond. The color deepened in his face, and Hadley had the impression he wished he hadn't spoken Willow's name. "Makes no never mind," he said at last. "Once a woman decides... I sure wish those two had seen me ride in Vegas that last year, though. I was in my element then, almost got into the top five before the final night, and man, I had me some pretty rides. I did better than Dallas."

Hadley's brush stopped sweeping a path through the caked mud. "Dallas? That's a moniker, all right. Sure suits a cowboy."

"Stage name, maybe, but he was a heck of a rider. Hated competing against him, but I tried not to let that get to me. I lived by the old saying that a rodeo cowboy really competes against himself, not anyone else. Still, we toured a while together, went to the Saturday night dances..." He trailed off. "That was before I met Willow. I'm not a cheating man."

"Was your friend Dallas from Texas? Like you?"

"Naw, from 'everywhere,' he always said. Ol' Dallas didn't talk much about his beginnings or his kin. He stuck to business mostly. But when we roomed together, he'd take out that guitar of his and sit there strumming a tune he made up. Told me once he had some notion of going pro after his rodeo days were over…recording an album. Country, he used to play."

Hadley dropped the brush, hoping his thoughts didn't show on his face. It couldn't be… "He still riding?"

"Not unless he got over his injuries." Above the horse's back, Cory held Hadley's gaze. "Dallas got thrown halfway across the ring in Lubbock one night not too long ago as if he were some kid's stuffed teddy bear, then stomped into the ground. According to reports, they carried him off straight to an ambulance." Cory shook his head. "Last I heard, he was still on the disabled list. I've been meaning to get in touch, check on how he's doing, but his career's a subject I'm not sure how to approach—like Willow now. Plus, the only number I had for him is out of service." He paused. "We didn't exactly part as friends, so I guess my motivation has been low."

Hadley didn't press him. "Too bad," was all he said.

Taking a deep breath, he helped Cory finish grooming, then saddle, the gelding. They worked in silence, each lost in his thoughts. Cory, with whatever regret he might feel about Willow Bodine or his colleague, certainly. The fear of injury, even death, was never far from any cowboy's mind, and he supposed the same would be true of the rodeo crowd. Why not? It was a dangerous business, but Hadley's mind had fixed on what Cory had said. He couldn't seem to shake the feeling. What if, after all these years, it was *him*?

He watched Cory ride out of the barn into the fading light of late afternoon and into the chilly air, wondering if he should join him to cut off imagining something that was more likely than not a coincidence. Instead, he stood in the open barn doorway, one hand on the seat of his jeans pocket, his wallet and that picture.

For the next few weeks, Jenna helped Shadow, who had become a bundle of nerves, put the finishing touches on their mother's bridal shower and tried not to think about

Hadley or even the twins. By the time the big night arrived shortly after Thanksgiving, she hadn't seen Luke and Grace for days. When she didn't visit them, she missed them. Hadley, too. Wrestling a big box containing a sheet cake from the rear seat of her car, she lumbered up the front porch steps at Wilson Cattle.

"Knock, knock," she called, pushing through the door. "Hello, everybody. I didn't have a free hand to ring the bell."

"My favorite sister-in-law." Grey stepped into the hallway from the living room carrying baby Zach. He kissed Jenna's cheek, then indicated the box she held. "Chocolate?"

"Mocha," Jenna told him. "It's Mama's favorite. Cream cheese icing, too."

Grey grinned. "Now I'm sorry Shadow has banished me from the house for the next four hours. Think you can save me a piece?"

Jenna teased him. "One for you, one for Zach." She kissed the top of her now eleven-month-old nephew's head. "But you should eat Zach's share of all that sugar, too."

"Must be my lucky night." Her brother-in-law clearly loved being a dad and a husband

and, as with his trademark black Stetson, he wore his responsibilities well.

With a frazzled expression, Shadow rushed from the kitchen.

"I thought I heard your voice." She clutched Jenna's arm. "Thank heaven you're here! Help. I can manage the agency with one hand behind my back, but tonight I'm so afraid Mama won't be pleased. I still have those tiny quiches in the oven. The ones you used to make in Kansas City? You gave me the recipe. But I've done something wrong. Some of them appear to be almost burnt while the others look raw, and people will be here any second."

"I'll take care of the quiches," Jenna said, patting her shoulder before Shadow hurried back into the kitchen. "Everything else ready?"

"How would I know?" Shadow called after her. "I lost my mind an hour ago."

In her early twenties, fresh off the farm, Jenna had experienced much the same stage fright as Shadow did before this party. But while living with David in the city, she'd had lots of experience playing hostess, mostly for his law firm clients, to make him look good.

Now Jenna was something of a pro in the events department. She liked to think that carried over into Fantastic Designs.

Jenna felt a twinge of guilt. She should have played a bigger role in organizing this bridal shower.

She rotated the quiches and made a mental note to tell Shadow her oven didn't heat evenly. While she monitored the quiches, she rearranged plates, silver, napkins on the dining room table. With a flourish, she straightened a party favor wrapped in white paper and tied with a satin bow, then lit the centerpiece candles, standing back to gauge the effect.

Grey poked his head in. "Zach and I are leaving. Dad's fixing us dinner at his new house—first time in the kitchen there by himself—and the other guys are coming over. We'll have a party of our own." That meant Sam and Logan Hunter would also be there, along with his brother Sawyer with little James, plus Finn Donovan and Cooper Ransom. She wondered if Hadley might be included.

Jenna almost wished she could join them. By the end of the night, her face would feel frozen from smiling too much. This shower seemed to make it official, and her mother's Christmas wedding was getting too close for Jenna's liking. She remembered her mama's words, *everything will work out*, but at the moment it seemed nothing would. Except, she hoped, this party.

Grey had just driven off with Zach when the bell rang, the door opened, and the sound of more female voices filled the entryway. Jenna picked out Liza's laughter. When she went to greet the other guests, she saw Liza holding her new baby daughter bundled in a chic gray snowsuit. There'd been no hint of snow yet this season, even though the weather had turned colder, but Liza was prepared.

She slipped off her daughter's hood. "Jenna, meet our princess. This is Charlotte Wilson."

Her throat threatened to close. "Oh, she's precious."

Unlike the day at the hospital when she'd met Luke and Grace, Jenna didn't hesitate to take Charlotte. "I just washed my hands," she assured Liza. "The baby was certainly worth missing Thanksgiving dinner for."

Charlotte, who had her parents' dark hair and still a newborn's blue eyes, had been born in October, but on the holiday last week the Wilsons had stayed home. "Everett and I were being cautious. Ava had a terrible cold then and so did her buddy Nick." Liza added, "Charlotte's worth the entire world."

"I'm happy for you."

And Jenna was, without the complicated feelings she had about her mother and Jack getting married, or about Hadley and the twins. She didn't let go of Charlotte until she absolutely had to when the rest of the guests arrived. In the meantime she'd savored the feel of the infant's small body against her, the sweet smell of her skin, the way her mouth turned up as if she were smiling, which Clara would be sure she was. For once, Jenna didn't automatically think of her infertility. After her talk with Hadley at the birthday party, could she be coming to terms with the childlessness that had eaten away at her heart?

Once the party got rolling, and Wanda was opening gifts in the living room, Jenna sat with Ava on the sofa. Her niece seemed thrilled with Charlotte, though still not as much with her baby brother, Zach. "She's my aunt," she announced. "The kids at school think that's weird—but I like it. Instead of her helping me grow up, I can help her."

Jenna admired her attitude. Ava wasn't the only one with complex relationships, or doubts, for that matter, but she handled them well. Jenna gazed at her, seeing the newly re-fined features and the hint of pink lip gloss she wore that said she would soon—all too soon—become a teenager.

Ava joined Wanda to help deal with the gift wrappings, and Jenna had to admit the evening seemed to be a success. The guests enjoyed themselves, the quiches were so pop-ular there were none left, including the ones with slightly burnt crusts, and her mother couldn't stop exclaiming over the presents she was being given. "Jack will love this set of cookware!" Wanda held up a saucepan. "He told me yesterday he dreamed of own-ing this brand. Thank you, Liza—and please thank Everett, as well," she murmured. "You all are too good to me."

"Nonsense," Liza said. "How else can you—or Jack—produce amazing meals with-out the proper equipment? I don't mean using these at the Bon Appetit."

"Even at home," Wanda agreed, "I eat like a queen. Now I'll have to cook, too."

While Jenna's mother continued to tear open packages, Liza sat down beside Jenna. Charlotte had fallen asleep in her carriage, and for a short time they talked about everyday things, but after a while Liza clearly had some message to deliver. "I miss working with you, Jenna. But you mustn't be always working. How are *you*?" Her gaze seemed to see right into Jenna's heart. "Heaven knows, growing up on that farm as you and Shadow did, losing your brother, must not have been easy. I didn't have the most loving childhood either, although I never wanted for anything in a material sense. But then, like your mother with Jack, I met Everett. Now I'm truly blessed. What about you, sweetie?"

Jenna's mouth firmed. "I'm okay, but Mama should think twice before she puts herself in another bad position."

"Do you have any reason to believe Jack won't take good care of her? Look at her, Jenna. She's a new woman in part because she found love, as I did."

Jenna twisted her hands together. Like babies, love was all around her. Cooper and Nell, Finn and Annabelle, Sawyer and Olivia,

Grey and Shadow, Logan and Blossom. What should have served as inspiration only reminded Jenna that she had failed before. Why would someone else—Hadley—want her? And even if he did, when he finally made good on his promise to leave, how would she bear losing again?

Liza said, "Making one mistake doesn't mean you'll repeat it. That learning is part of life. Jenna, has it occurred to you that we all have to risk our hearts?"

"I'm not sure I learned…" Jenna didn't go on. Hadley had made mistakes, too. She wondered if their fragile relationship might end before she figured out what *she* wanted from him other than a few kisses that might mean nothing to Hadley. She wondered if one day soon he would stop trying to run Clara's ranch, take the twins and leave Barren without repaying the loan after all.

HADLEY HAD SPENT the evening in Everett's new home with the other men he'd always envied, men who owned ranches he could only dream about. The invitation to join them had come as a pleasant surprise. Did that mean that, because of his attempts to rebuild Clara's ranch, and the work he'd done at the Circle H and Finn Donovan's, he was beginning to be accepted? That these men might even become his friends?

When he returned to Clara's, he didn't go to bed straightaway. He hadn't found time until now to follow up on the Dallas that Cory had mentioned. As the chilly fall weather hinted at the next season rolling in, they'd been occupied from the start of one day to the end of the next with preparations for winter. "Battening down the hatches," Clara's husband, Cliff, used to call it. Winter in Kansas could be brutal, and this one was predicted to be more snow-filled and windy than the last when many people had lost significant heads of cattle to the freezing temperatures. He had two dozen cows and heifers now to feed this coming season, and both horses.

Or had he used winter as an excuse? In any case, he'd hop on Google, see what he could find about Dallas and maybe in the process stop thinking about Jenna.

In the twins' room that day, should he have encouraged her not to come back? Yet the more he learned about her and the more he let her learn about him, the deeper in he got.

He wasn't sure he wanted to climb out of the hole he'd made for himself.

On the computer in Clara's office, he opened a browser. If his brother had become a rodeo cowboy, which seemed unlikely, he should show up on one of the rodeo websites. Hadley might have dismissed the idea of any connection except that Cory had also mentioned a guitar. Even as a kid, his brother had yearned to play, to write songs like the country ballads he'd listened to then. Coincidence? Or at last, the clue Hadley had been hoping to find?

*Dallas Smith.* The unusual first and ordinary last name he typed hunt-and-peck into the search bar made his stomach churn worse than on the black night when he'd watched Dallas get into the van marked Child Protective Services. Because of Hadley's wrongdoing, he'd lost Dallas. What had happened to his brother after that?

There'd been times when Hadley woke up, gasping, certain something terrible had happened to Dallas, even that he was dead. Or he imagined him turning into a criminal with a shady lifestyle, like their parents'. If that was the case, was it a good idea to find him? A no-good brother would only make Hadley's case worse against the Pearsons. Guilt by association.

Hadley visited various rodeo sites, and to his amazement discovered cowboys with the name Dallas on several of them. Not as different then as he'd thought. Whether the names were legal or inventions, none of them led to his brother.

Hadley sat back in the creaking desk chair and ran a hand through his hair.

"Morning will come before you know it, dear." Clara had walked into the office without his hearing her approach. "I thought you'd left night duty to me."

"Luke doing okay?"

"That stubborn tooth appears to have broken the surface of his gums, but he's also running a slight fever. I gave him some baby Tylenol. He went back to sleep. But should I call Sawyer?"

"Luke ran a fever before with another tooth. Let's wait till morning, see how he is, not wake the whole town."

"You're right." Clara peered over his shoulder at the computer screen.

"Just lookin' for someone." Hadley didn't

care to elaborate. He'd come to Clara's long after Dallas disappeared into the system. He still wished she had met him, though.

Clara massaged his neck, which felt as if it were clamped in a vise. Her voice dipped low. "Your brother, dear?"

He tensed under her touch. "I wouldn't be searching for my folks. Shouldn't waste my time on this, either. He'd look right through me now—if he didn't plow a fist in my face. And I wouldn't recognize him." Hadley had inspected each photo he came to, but none of them resembled the Dallas he'd known. One had blond hair and hazel eyes; another had carrot-colored curls, a wide-set brown gaze. Too many years had passed in which Dallas would have turned from that skinny kid into a muscled athlete. Riding a bull? Hadley doubted that.

He remembered the day their father took them to a local fair that had a pony ride. Dad had disappeared—to make another deal?—leaving Hadley to manage his brother's growing hysteria. Dallas had wanted nothing to do with horses.

"A long time ago, then." Clara let her hand

drop from his shoulder. "Hadley. Keep searching. I hope you find him."

He closed the window on the professional rodeo cowboys' site. "I'd better see how Luke's doing instead. I'm wide-awake. Why don't you get some sleep?"

But after he checked on Luke, as if to please Clara he returned to the computer. A lot of the rodeo cowboys had their own websites, some fancy, all with complete statistics and lots of pictures of their rides. He'd read every bio, checked every one of the Dallases when, just as the sun rose over the barn outside the window, Hadley hit pay dirt.

His heart drummed, hard.

This face, he did recognize.

He'd know that shock of dark hair, those blue eyes so like his own, anywhere.

Dallas *Maguire*, the top of the home page read.

His brother—the cowboy—now had a different name.

# CHAPTER SEVENTEEN

AFTER THE BRIDAL SHOWER, Jenna and Shadow helped their mother load her presents in the car to take back to her new house. Wanda loved it there, but she was still worried about Jack's uncle Bertie and asked her daughters' advice. "Jack and I have a spare bedroom but it's upstairs and they're steep. Uncle Bertie can't climb to the second floor."

"Are you sure?" Shadow asked with a jaundiced expression. "I never count Bertie out. When he was in the hospital, people expected him to pass away. Instead, he rallied, and he finally went home."

"Yes, he came home, but to Jack—and then, after I moved in, with me there. Now that we're in our own place, that won't work. Jack's getting exhausted running back and forth to Bertie's house to see to his needs. I know you tried to find an in-place caregiver, yet none of them has suited Bertie."

"Then what's his plan?" Jenna asked.

"We've tried to convince him to sell his house instead, then look at assisted living units in the area, but he still won't."

Shadow scoffed. "I've rarely met a more stubborn individual. You can't imagine how many people I interviewed as in-home caregivers. Any one of them would have taken care of him and allowed him to stay in his own home, but none of them passed muster with Bertie. I'm sorry, Mama. I agree with you, but Bertie knows what he wants."

Wanda's mouth set. "Yes. To live with us— if he can't stay in his house. Even Jack never meant to be there with him forever. You know we want our privacy now, and as much as I do love him, he's not a simple person. What are we going to do? We want only the best for him, but that doesn't mean constantly worrying he'll tumble down our stairs some night in the dark."

Jenna said, "Mama, I understand. Honestly, I think he reminds you of Daddy."

"And your father reminds you that men don't measure up. Like David."

Beginning to feel trapped, she glanced at her sister for help.

"I wouldn't give him another thought," Shadow murmured. "Mama's right."

Jenna said, "I'll be too busy through the end of the year—I have four new clients—to worry about anyone else." That should include Hadley. She looked pointedly at Wanda. "Consider this. Could Jack be urging Bertie to move into assisted living because Jack doesn't plan to stick around?"

"After we bought a house?" Wanda's face paled. "That is unfair. Shame on you, Jenna."

Again, she looked to Shadow, who was studying a colorful picture on the opposite wall. Wanda shot to her feet. "Don't tell me again to reconsider my feelings for Jack. He's my soul mate. If anyone had said that years ago, I'd never have believed it possible. But he is, Jenna." Which reminded her of what Liza had said to her about her relationship with Everett. "If you can't be truly happy for us, then keep that to yourself." She took a breath. "If you won't support me, don't come to my wedding!"

By the time Jenna blinked, her mother was in her coat and out the door, not quite slamming it behind her, leaving Jenna with the new memory of the hurt she'd seen in her eyes. "I've really done it now, haven't I?"

"Don't look at me. I'm with Mama."

"But Shadow—"

"I still believe this is more about you and David than it is about Mama and Jack. Your ex is toxic. You did the sensible thing when you changed your name back to Moran after the divorce and came home, but you still act as if—and probably believe—you're in Shawnee Mission. Or, just as bad, living at the old farm, withdrawing whenever Daddy raised his voice. That is, when he noticed you at all." She paused to soften her tone. "You're *here*, Jen."

The words stung, but Jenna wondered if Shadow was right, and not just about her ex or their father. Or even about Mama and Jack. And yet, while she might be tempted to give in to her feelings for Hadley, he, too, had a temper. What if she did trust in love again, then wound up as she had with David? She'd be alone, starting over once more, not that she couldn't take care of herself now.

Shadow went on, "I'm not saying 'just get over it.' Remember, I made some real blunders with Grey, and I learned how wrong I was then. I'll never jeopardize our relationship again, our marriage or our roles as parents together. You need to decide what you want for yourself—not related to David or our father but just for *you*." Again, she hesitated. "Could that also include Hadley?"

Jenna realized Shadow's advice sounded similar to her own with Barney—until she mentioned Hadley.

"Shadow, why would a man like him take on a woman like me?"

Shadow's tone gentled even more. "You mean a woman who can't have children?"

"Well, I can't," she insisted.

"And he already has two of them. Luke and Grace. Would you turn away from those beautiful babies and him when you could be as happy as Mama is with Jack? Maybe Hadley doesn't want more kids. Did you ever think of that? Maybe he's fine with the twins, and your infertility isn't a factor." She hesitated. "Have you talked to Hadley about your attachment to the twins?"

Jenna couldn't deny that. She did covet Hadley's twins. She loved them. "I long ago stopped hiding my feelings for those babies, but if only they could have been mine, really mine..."

"With Hadley you'd have the twins. You once told me you might adopt on your own."

For a moment the fantasy of having that ready-made family she'd objected to before, to call Luke and Grace her own and...be with Hadley, seemed to fill her soul. It was almost more than she could bear to contemplate or, perhaps, to turn away from?

"I changed my mind."

"But if you *did* want to adopt them, he might agree. No?" Shadow said, an eyebrow arched when Jenna didn't comment. Her voice trembled. "Amy Smith gave her life for those babies, and they don't have her now. They never will. If you want children, there they are. Work this out with Hadley. You can have the kids you've yearned for, just not in the way you planned."

She left the room, left Jenna to think, maybe to dream a little. Did she dare to love Hadley? What if she were able to cherish his babies forever? Trust him as she once had David? And this time things did work out?

"BELIEVE ME, WILLOW. Believe in us." Beginning to sweat, Cory faced her on the front seat of his truck. They were parked in the lot behind Rowdy's Bar on Main Street, which wasn't open yet, happy hour being the time when things started to hum and the night began. Willow's sedan sat beside his pickup, and Cory kept shooting looks down the alley, hoping the sheriff's cruiser didn't roll by. Cory was supposed to be in Farrier this afternoon to pick up a new winch for Hadley's truck in case they needed to pull some cow out of a snow-covered ditch this coming winter, and the wind chill today should have made him hurry. But when Willow had finally called, Cory dropped everything. He'd taken what could be his one chance to meet her again, but in Barren where he had no business showing up.

"I won't sneak around any longer," Willow said, "or keep lying to my father."

"Then you lied to me. Do you…care about *me*, or not? If you don't, say so." His chin jutted out. "I'll put this truck in gear, drive away and never see you again. Never try to. Ever since I came back to Barren—"

"And that's another thing!" The words burst from her. "Why did you?" Cory wasn't about to say, *because of you. Only you.* "Using a phony name," she added, her lip curled in distaste. *"Cory Jennings?"*

His heart thudded. He was steadily losing ground here. If he was honest, his return in the hope of taking his puppy-dog crush on her to another level had been a world-class error. "Who told you that?" but he could already guess.

"Calvin."

That shouldn't surprise him. Since the night of the dance, he'd been waiting for that shoe to drop. Willow knew both of them, worse luck for him.

"No wonder I haven't heard anyone else in town mention you. There's still a warrant for your arrest, but under your real name. If Finn Donovan ever sees you…" She took a shaken breath.

Cory saw red. "Calvin should have kept his mouth shut." If Cory said the wrong thing now, he'd lose her for sure. He'd craved seeing her again so bad even when he knew he shouldn't come within a hundred miles of Barren, Kansas. He'd risked his freedom, and all because he'd fallen for her. Crazy, huh? "You and I are none of Calvin Stern's business—or the sheriff's."

"Is Calvin right, though? Have *you* been lying to me all along?"

He chose his words carefully. "I'm not going to prison, Willow. Sure, I did something bad. But I was a kid."

"You're still a kid," she murmured, but so was she. He'd bet her father didn't know she hung out at Rowdy's, and at the dance in Farrier or—as yet—with him again.

"I've reformed," he insisted. He'd worked his tail off at the McMann ranch, keeping out of more trouble, staying out of sight except to see Willow and the one time he'd bumped into Calvin.

"If my father hears this—"

"Will he?" *From you?* he wanted to ask.

"I hope not. You better hope not, too." She gazed at him with that spark in her eyes that he loved. That fast, her tone had turned coy. "What did you really do? Kill somebody?"

"Nothing like that." Yet she seemed intrigued. He'd suspected Willow had a wild side, and Cory waited, letting her wonder about him as a dangerous character. "Burned down a barn," he finally said, but to his amazement she didn't find that admirable.

Willow's eyes widened. "Grey Wilson's barn? That was you?"

Cory didn't answer. Hoping to steal a kiss, he moved across the bench seat between them, reached out to draw her close—danger enhanced the attraction—and got his face slapped. Willow jumped out of the truck, then ran toward her car.

Feeling miserable, wondering why she'd taken such offense, he raced over to the store in Farrier to get the winch, then rushed back to Clara's place, telling himself he'd wait Willow out again, as Hadley had advised once. He wouldn't give up. She'd be back. He'd been drawing girls' interest from before he first shaved, and Willow was no different—except that he loved her. He was sure of that now. They were practically engaged, and Cory had started saving for that ring. He'd surprised her, that's all, or rather Calvin had. She wouldn't tell a soul. If he thought she might, he'd be gone before dark. *I'm not going to prison* was no joke.

The sun had faded when he finally pulled up at the barn.

And as he got out of the truck, Cory's bad day got worse.

In a flash, woman trouble was the furthest thing from his mind, Willow Bodine included. Hadley stood just inside the barn talking to two men. Cowboys, from the tilt of their hats, the gouges in the worn leather of their boots, and his gut rolled. Even with their backs to him, Cory recognized both of them. Two of the people he'd tried to avoid in this town, in part by using his phony name. For a second, he thought of barreling his pickup down the drive, but there was no use running.

"Where have you been?" Hadley asked, but Cory didn't answer.

The other two turned toward him, and shock widened their eyes. One of the men was Grey Wilson, owner of the barn Cory had torched. Owner of the Angus cattle he had rustled with the help of Calvin Stern. The other man had been their accomplice, the third member of their trio, and now, he'd heard, was Grey's brother-in-law who worked for him. He was the first to speak.

"Well, shoot," Derek Moran muttered, slapping his hat against his jeans-clad thigh. "If it isn't Cody Jones."

# *CHAPTER EIGHTEEN*

"I'M A FOOL." Hadley fought an urge to shove a fist through the back screen door. He'd come up to the house later than usual tonight, missed his supper, but he had little appetite. After Grey and Derek had hauled Cody Jones, aka Cory Jennings, to Grey's truck to take him to the sheriff's office, Hadley had stayed in the barn, his temper steaming like a hot pile of manure. While finishing the chores Cory hadn't done, he hadn't trusted himself to interact with Clara—or, he saw now, Jenna, who was seated at the kitchen table with her. Blinded by his anger and, if he admitted it, disappointment, Hadley hadn't noticed her car outside. He was glad the twins weren't in the room. He didn't want them taking this all in.

A glance at the clock on the stove informed him it was after eight and past their bedtime.

"Why did I not see what I'd gotten myself into?"

The two women stared at him with blank expressions. "What are you talking about, Hadley?" Clara rose from her chair to fix him a plate of dinner, then set it at his place and pointed. "Eat. Whatever has you in a lather can wait until you've gotten some food in your stomach."

Briefly, he outlined the mess named Cory he'd taken on in blind faith. "I should have checked his references—if he'd had any. The only one I'm sure about is Grey Wilson's, and that wouldn't be a raving endorsement. I should have known."

"How could you?" Jenna asked. "He didn't give you his real name."

He dug into the lasagna Clara had made, then tore off a hunk of homemade bread to mop up the sauce, but he couldn't taste anything. "I can't believe I fell for his line of bull—baloney."

"You needed the manpower," Clara said in a soothing tone.

"I need my head examined. Grey refused way back then to press charges against Derek for rustling his cows—"

"Out of regard for Shadow," Jenna put in.

"—but he didn't have the same reservations with Cory, I mean, Cody Jones. The kid torched Grey's barn and was wanted for arson, too. He had no accomplices then."

"Well, now you know," Clara murmured. "The law—Finn Donovan—will take care of the rest. Don't worry, dear. We can put an ad in the local paper, spread the word ourselves, and I'm sure we'll come up with another cowhand."

"Until we find someone, I'll be doing all the work here, plus the hours I spend at the Circle H and Finn's place, but that's not the point," he insisted. "I don't like feeling duped by Cody Jones or anybody else."

Hadley shoveled in the rest of the lasagna and finished off the bread, slathering it with plenty of butter, which Clara also made herself. She preferred knowing what went into the food she served, and ordinarily Hadley could appreciate that. He and the babies ate well, much better than he and Dallas had as kids.

Looking distressed, Clara gathered his empty plate and used cutlery. At the sink she scraped and rinsed them, then loaded the dishwasher.

Hadley stood up, went over to her and wrapped his arms around her. "Sorry, Clara. I didn't mean to upset you."

Jenna got up, too, and touched Clara's shoulder. "Why don't you put your feet up in the living room? *The Bachelor* is on tonight." Clara's favorite show. "Grab a coat, Hadley. Let's go out on the porch. You can vent there however you want." She didn't wait for him to answer.

On the porch he leaned against a post, the night air so cold he could see his breath. A million stars lit the black sky. "Should I apologize again to you, too?"

Jenna's chin rose. "I can take anything you dish out." As if she'd been waiting for him to explode. "Start talking."

Under different circumstances, that would have amused him. When he'd met her, Jenna had avoided anyone's anger. Yet she and their relationship had changed. At first, he hadn't wanted her involvement. Then, somehow, they'd learned to work together for the twins. All he had to do now was trust her not to leak anything about Amy's guardianship to the Pearsons, and maybe they'd be all right. "I said what I had to say."

"No, you didn't. It's not just Cory—Cody— who has you as upset as Clara."

"I'm not upset," he said, his jaw tight. "I'm mad. There's a difference."

"You're not only mad, either." Jenna stood next to him, their shoulders brushing as they had on the stairs that one night. From the barn, he heard the horses whickering to each other in their stalls. Overhead a full moon shone, enough for him to see Jenna's face in the silvery light. The wind had risen earlier but had died down. "What's the other issue, Hadley?"

"I hate it when you're right," he muttered, reaching for her hand. Dallas had been preying on his mind, as if he and Cody Jones were connected. Which, it seemed, they were. "I hopped on the internet a while ago, started looking around for my brother."

Jenna squeezed his fingers. Both their hands were cold. "You found him?"

Hadley nodded. "Turns out, he's been working under an alias, too. Ironic, isn't it, that I got my first clue to his whereabouts from Cody Jones? Cody used to rodeo and mentioned a guy he competed against with the same first name as my brother." He told her about the guitar. The country music. "Still, nothing clicked until I stumbled on Dallas's website—and there he was. Years older yet the same. Goes by the name Dallas Maguire now."

"Did you contact him?"

"No."

"Why not?"

He gazed at the stars, the barn below, the gate to the pasture. "There's a lot of water under our bridge. I'm not sure how he'd feel about meeting up again. He's made a new life for himself, it seems." He didn't go on for a minute. At least Dallas wasn't dead, as Hadley had imagined. "Maybe he doesn't need an older brother, especially the one who let him down."

"I doubt either of those things is true," she said, her hand in his. "Hadley, you two are *brothers*. That doesn't end just because you had some falling-out. Can you imagine Luke and Grace not caring for each other all their lives?"

"They're a year old," he said. "Give 'em time. They're already good at jabbing each other. Wait until one of them really gives the other a reason."

Jenna didn't let that go. "What was your brother's reason?"

He watched a shooting star flash across the sky. He never talked about this part. Ever. In the time he'd known her, he and Jenna had more often been at odds than they were in agreement, unless he was stealing a kiss from her. Why trust that he could spill this dark side of his life now, right here, without making her hate him, too?

"It's getting late," he said, glancing at the moon. "I'd better—"

"Get whatever this is about off your chest." When he would have started for the house, she stopped him. "My sisters and I, my brothers, too, used to scrap like tomcats, but we never got to the point where we didn't care about one another. Obviously, you haven't, either, or you wouldn't have searched for Dallas."

Hadley grunted. "Don't know why I did. There's no way I can make up to him for what happened."

"I assume you mean something in foster care. I know that wasn't a good experience for you. Neither was my childhood with a father who served his own needs rather than ours, and yet if someone asked me, I'd say I loved him anyway. Just for being my father, even when he was never a very good one."

His mouth hardened. "He scarred you, Jenna. He set you up for David. Are you telling me you'd forgive him? Let him back into your life now if you could?" He took a sharp breath. "You did nothing to deserve his neglect—not like I did with Dallas."

With a small sound, Jenna turned, and he found her in his arms without quite knowing when she'd moved or how he'd taken her in. "Tell me," she said.

Hadley gazed over her head at the one light burning in the barn. Still not wanting to explore the painful memories, he shifted. Jenna wasn't going to let him leave this porch, though, unless he did talk. "In the first years after our folks left us to the system, he and I were together. I could take care of him, watch out for him. I was always big for my age, but Dallas was this skinny stick of a kid. The other boys in foster care would bully him, taunt him...and I'd step in to keep him safe." He cleared his throat. "Then, the county sent us to this new place. The couple there had a nice house, plenty of room... Dallas and I had our own space, but they weren't good people.

If we misbehaved, or even when we didn't, the punishment was harsh. One day, Dallas got into trouble at school, and when he got 'home,' they whaled on him."

"That's sad," Jenna murmured, moving deeper in his embrace. "No, it was more than that. It was cruel."

"He went to bed hungry, bruised, not for the first time, and for the next week they didn't see to his wounds and wouldn't let him eat. I tried to smuggle food to him, but they always caught me. I didn't mind a whipping or missing a few meals—my defiance always got me through—but Dallas did, and he lost weight. He cried all the time. Locked up in our room. Whimpering so I could hear him through the door."

"He didn't go to school? Where he could talk to someone?"

"Our foster parents kept him home. Told our principal he had some virus." He paused. "They made me bunk with a couple of the other boys. None of us ever ate that well because these people spent whatever they were paid for us on themselves. She drove a fancy BMW. He'd treated himself to a top-of-the-line Mercedes. They wore the best clothes,

furnished their house…you get the idea. I'm
sure their home looked great to the social
workers who sometimes checked on the situation, but when no one else was around…"

"What happened, Hadley? You must have
done something to help him."

"I tried—which didn't help." He gazed
down at his boots. "I took food from a local
market, sneaked it into the house for him after
school. I was afraid he'd starve to death if I
didn't. So, yeah, I stole."

"And you were caught?"

He drew back to see her face. "When the
store owner turned me in—the way Grey did
Cody today—I wouldn't stop talking. I told
child services, the cops, anybody who would
listen, about those people. A judge agreed
with me. They lost their foster kids, all of
them, their easy living."

"What about you? And Dallas?"

"I don't mean to bad-mouth the whole system, Jenna. It works for some, and it worked
for me here at Clara's. But after that, Dallas
and I were separated and sent to different
homes. Later on, I went back and repaid that
store owner but never Dallas." Hadley fin-

ished, "He was eight years old then. I was ten."

"You don't need to repay Dallas." Jenna briefly closed her eyes. "I don't think the years matter. I spent a lot of them apart from my parents, my father, really. I shortchanged my family, but I realized I had to turn that around." She added, "Listen to me, still at odds with my mom because she's getting married."

"That's different. You didn't commit a crime." He made a scoffing sound directed at himself. "So, say I do see him—after I fed him to the wolves that day—and he only wants to pay *me* back."

Jenna's eyes filled. "For what? Loving him? You didn't let him down, Hadley. You saved him." Her tone was tender. "I think part of you inside is still that boy. Maybe Dallas is, too—and all this time he's been searching for you."

WITH HADLEY MANAGING the ranch on his own, and still working two part-time jobs, Jenna helped Clara with the twins. Hadley didn't have time to eat lunch with them now or to play on the rug, but today the twins were less than their usual charming selves. Luke was grumpy, and from the way she'd started to fuss, Grace soon would be, too.

"Here, baby." Seated with them on the living room floor, Jenna handed her a teething ring, ice-cold from the freezer where Clara kept a supply. Grace clamped down on it, then began to cry. "Too chilly? Aww." Jenna hugged her close, singing softly to her. She'd discovered that music soothed Hadley's little girl, and as they cuddled a warm sensation ran through her. Maternal instinct?

Dangerous waters, she thought, especially since she'd talked with Liza and Shadow. After those moments on the porch with Hadley, she'd realized what a truly good man he really was, though he'd never agree. But how could he not see his love for his brother for what it was? Maybe she shouldn't have interfered, but what about his devotion to the twins? His kindly way with Clara, and even his tenderness with Jenna when she'd told him about her family, her inability to conceive? If she didn't already love him, she was definitely falling in love with him. Like her mama, the question was: Would that be good for her?

Hadley shook the new foundation she'd built for herself. The twins, adorable even when they were screaming, made that a triple threat.

Hearing a car out front, Jenna welcomed the interruption of her brooding and got to her feet, holding Grace. "Let's see who's here," she said. Clara was doing laundry, leaving Jenna alone to watch Luke and Grace. This time, she'd had more luck on her own.

Danielle was coming up the walk, towing her wheeled suitcase behind her. She called out with a wave, "Good morning. Am I too early?"

"Not at all." Jenna ushered her inside.

"I visited a friend overnight, then made the drive here this morning when she left for work." With the cabin finished, this was another unplanned stay that made Jenna wonder about that getaway from her husband. But Danielle disabused Jenna of that. "Walter's meetings have died down, and he'll be here this weekend."

The women soon gathered in the kitchen where they cooed over the still-fussy twins. "They're standing constantly," Clara reported. "I'm betting they walk before Christmas."

"Shouldn't they have walked by now?" Danielle asked.

"There's no set time." Clara laughed. "I'm inclined to enjoy their limited mobility a while longer."

Danielle gazed down at Grace, sheer pleasure in her eyes. "Are you going to let your brother walk first, little girl?"

To everyone's delight, Grace vigorously shook her head. At one, she often understood language even before she could talk except to say "Da-da," like Luke, and "Mum-mum" for Clara.

Jenna laughed, too. "She hasn't let him reach the other side of the living room ahead of her since she started to crawl or stand."

Danielle handed Grace to Jenna and took Luke from Clara so "Mum-mum" could serve coffee. "What do you have to say, little man? Don't be shy. Defend your territory." She nuzzled his nose, making Luke screw up his face with a shiver. "Don't you love these two?" she asked Jenna.

"They are lovable," Jenna said, her throat tight. *You can have the kids you've yearned for, just not in the way you planned.*

Hadley's voice preceded him into the

house. "Who's lovable? Luke and Gracie Smith? Can't be," he said, grinning and in an obviously better frame of mind than the night on the porch. Jenna couldn't blame him. The story of his brother had been horrific.

Hadley went to the sink, washed his hands, then reached for both twins, settling them into the crooks of his strong arms. He kissed the tops of their heads, and the babies cuffed him on the chin. Jenna felt her heart turn to mush again. "Ms. and Mr. Grouch," he said. "Clara can vouch for that. We were up all night."

"It's never a sacrifice," she assured him with another doting look on her face. At the stove she heated the twins' lunch. They ate before noon every day, then took their naps—or they should. Teething, Clara had told her, played havoc with their schedules. On second thought Jenna wasn't sure she would like the all-night part, not that she had to.

When he came in, Hadley had nodded at Danielle but not Jenna, who'd received no greeting. Maybe he'd decided he'd said too much on the porch and wanted to step back a little or, more likely, a lot.

"Everything okay?" she finally asked.

He blinked above the twins' heads. "Why wouldn't it be?"

His eyes had shuttered, as if a metal shop grate had been pulled over them. *Not open for business.* So much for the rush of caring she'd had for him. Clara and Danielle were looking at them now.

"I should go." Jenna grabbed her bag. "I have an appointment this afternoon at the office, then an on-site meeting with one of my new clients. With Danielle here, you won't need me, Clara. It was nice seeing you, Danielle."

Danielle frowned a little. "You as well."

"Don't rush off before we make plans." Clara stood at the stove, the twins' jars of heated peas in hand. "You are coming to help decorate the tree?"

"Oh, I nearly forgot." No, she hadn't, but wasn't sure now whether she should help—or come again at all. She glanced at Hadley, who was making a business of pouring himself a cup of coffee, then carefully cutting a slice of banana bread. His back to her. He handed pieces to the twins that quickly became sticky crumbs falling from their mouths.

"Tomorrow evening," Clara said. "You won't have meetings then."

Because she saw no graceful way out and didn't want to hurt Clara, Jenna agreed. She was halfway down the hall before she realized Hadley was behind her. He reached around to open the door, then followed her outside. On the porch where they'd talked, he lightly caught her arm. "Don't stay away from the tree-decorating party Clara has in the works because of me, okay?"

"I said I'd be here." She slipped from his grasp, then started down the steps, hoping she wouldn't trip. She couldn't seem to see where she was going. The memory of what he'd said, the powerful tug she'd felt not only of attraction—that, at least, she'd become used to where Hadley was concerned—but of something even more tempting yet potentially dire, had rattled her.

"By the way. Thanks," he muttered, "for the other night."

Jenna startled. "I wasn't sure you still felt that way this morning."

"Yeah. I do." He hesitated. "I'm glad you were here for me then."

My, he changed moods rapidly—just like

her father. Jenna didn't know whether to go, to stay or...to believe in Hadley, but the sooner she drove off now, the better.

"Jenna." His voice made her turn. "After we talked, I sent him a message through his website."

She gave him a faint smile as her heart melted again. Jenna was tumbling deeper into a new love she'd never expected to find. She just didn't know where that would lead.

THE NEXT NIGHT Jenna stood beside Danielle while Clara directed Hadley on the top step of a ladder by the Christmas tree.

"Higher, dear." Clara's bell-like voice rang out in the warm living room as if it were part of the chorus in one of the Christmas carols playing on the stereo system. "Loop the lights around up there, then begin winding them down around the tree. Evenly spaced, please."

"Clara, I have zero experience at this," Hadley grumbled, "but I still think we should only decorate the top third of this tree. The babies are like curious kittens. For such little things, they can reach everywhere now. You want broken glass ornaments all over the floor? Shards in their hair? Cuts?"

"One of my boys once ate a Christmas ball," she told him, referring, Jenna supposed, to a foster child she'd cared for. "Would you believe? I called the clinic in a panic. Doc Baxter then—not Sawyer—said the pieces would likely be tiny fragments and would work their way through his system and come out the other…way, eventually. Which they did. With sparkles. Lordy, that was a pretty diaper." She clapped her hands. "I can't wait for Luke and Grace to see this tree tomorrow morning."

Hadley cursed under his breath at the tangled strings of lights, but with Jenna's help and Danielle's, he finally had them on the tree. With a look of satisfaction, he gestured at Jenna to push the plug in the wall socket. "This will either be spectacular—or the whole house will go up in a blaze of fire."

His words made Jenna think of Cody Jones and arson. Jenna guessed the disturbing truth about him must still trouble Hadley. He'd trusted the younger cowboy, but his trust had been misplaced. Cody had been arraigned and was in the county jail where, Finn had said, he seemed remorseful.

Clara gazed up at Hadley. "This house may be old, but the wiring is sound."

Dutifully, Jenna switched off the room lights, plugged the tree in, and all at once the McMann living room became a fairyland. "Oh, how beautiful."

Hadley's electric-blue gaze skimmed Jenna, making her flush as if she'd stuck a finger in the socket instead of the lights. Surely he wasn't thinking about her that way. Or could he have seen her own awareness of him in her eyes?

Clara said, "Put the star on top, Hadley, then come down here."

"Yes, ma'am." He couldn't hide a grin. His complaints, Jenna assumed, had been mostly an act to tweak Clara. It was plain to see he loved her, no matter that he'd told Amy he couldn't love anyone. Still, Jenna needed to remember that he must prefer to keep his distance. "Satisfied?"

Clara hugged him. "I will be once all the ornaments are in place. Thank you, dear." She drew away with a pointed look at Hadley, who groaned, then at Danielle, and finally Jenna. "Remember, no identical color next to another, icicles one by one, not thrown in clumps."

Everyone laughed. But obeyed.

When they finished, the music had started over again and Jenna was about to leave for home, but Clara started toward the kitchen. "Danielle, will you help me? I've mulled some cider, and the twins and I made gingerbread cookies earlier."

"Really?" Hadley said. "That sounds like a stretch."

"They watched from their high chairs—and tried to eat cookie dough."

"Clara has her traditions," Hadley said when he and Jenna were alone to assess the tree. He shifted an ornament from a low branch to a higher one. "I haven't seen her this happy since I got back."

"You don't think there's a connection?"

"Clara's happiest taking care of others."

"And I can tell she loves you and the twins living here." Hadley didn't say anything more, so Jenna decided to go for it and tease out his plans. She wouldn't live in limbo forever. "Not bad, is it, doing work *you* love here?"

He paused. "I'm happy wherever the road takes me."

Jenna's smile faded. "But the twins are almost walking, and before you know it they'll be in school with friends and activities, baseball practice, cheerleading… They won't want to leave."

"I'll cross that bridge when I come to it," he said, avoiding her eyes.

Jenna swallowed. "Don't you want a permanent place? A home?"

"Never had one. Don't…miss it."

In spite of his foster care experience, Jenna thought that must be a lie. Who didn't want a home? A family? Or was she merely projecting? His marriage to Amy hadn't worked out that well. Did he mean he wouldn't want a home with Jenna? "For the twins then, and you do miss your brother. I could see that in your eyes."

He plucked another ornament off the tree, then put it back in the same spot. The lights made Hadley's face appear softer, but his words sounded hard. "Roots can ground you, like Clara, or they can tie you down."

Jenna turned from the tree. Was he trying to tell her he didn't intend to remain much longer? *I won't stay in Barren forever*, he'd said. What about the loan? Better to hear it before her feelings for him got even stronger.

Yet she couldn't help saying, "The babies are your roots now, Hadley."

He made a sound she couldn't interpret. "You know where I stand. What about you?"

She tensed, tempted to back off. Yet this was supposedly the new Jenna who'd pushed Hadley to open up, who held her own, who believed in herself—most of the time—and didn't let anyone else silence her. "David made the mistake of thinking he could run over me, but I'm not who I was then."

He raised an eyebrow. "Once, when we were arguing, Amy said she wasn't the weak woman I thought I'd married."

"Good for her." Jenna's pride stung. "Maybe I shouldn't have started this conversation, but let me correct you, Hadley—*we* aren't married."

"Right and, Jenna, I'm not the guy you should pick."

"You mean a guy who leaves every place he's ever been? Because that's what you do, Hadley. You always leave." So now she'd heard the truth. "Why would I take on a man who probably keeps his bag packed in a closet? I hope this eases your mind, but I'd rather live the rest of my life alone."

LEIGH RIKER 311

"No, you wouldn't. *I* know that much about you. Even after your ex, you're still the marrying type."

"Did you just say 'the marrying type'?"

"You sure that's not what this is about? And children?" He turned her to face him. "Months ago, when I sorted through Amy's things, picking what to keep for the babies, what to send to her folks, I found that baby book you'd mentioned. Something bothered me about that, but I couldn't figure out what. I'm pretty sure I have now." He sought Jenna's gaze. "Tucked inside, just as you said, was the list of names Amy might have chosen. There were quite a few of them starred."

"Yes," Jenna murmured, wishing she hadn't exposed herself to him after all. She had a bad feeling.

"Luke and Grace weren't among them."

She blinked. "They must have been. Amy and I used to talk about her choices, laugh at the silly ones, discuss the serious ones. It frustrated her that you weren't taking part in that decision—"

"Is that all you remember?" His gaze was riveted to hers. "I didn't miss anything, and I can see why."

Her heart bumped against her rib cage. Hadley had somehow discovered the truth that hit her now like a slap from the dimmest recess of memory. *Oh, God.* Even she hadn't guessed this was coming, hadn't quite remembered...

When she spoke, Jenna's tone was barely audible. "Do you need to hear me say it? Luke and Grace were the names *I* chose—not Amy—for the babies I never had. Amy liked them, Hadley. A lot. But I guess she never added them to her list. Maybe there wasn't time." And she began to cry.

"Ah, Jenna." He pulled her close. "I realize what you've been through, how you've fought to overcome that, and I don't want to hurt you. Those roots we talked about are important to you, but for me this ranch is another temporary stopover." He hesitated again. "Obviously, I'm attracted to you, and Clara keeps hoping I'll stay, but—" He broke off, then tried again. "If I were looking for someone, you'd be—"

"A handy option?" She would have pulled away but couldn't seem to move.

"No, what I'm trying to say is if I wasn't the way I am, things would be different. But

I'm not what you need—just like I wasn't right for Amy. Then there's Dallas. You tried to convince me I did what I could for him when I know I didn't, and he hasn't answered my message. Maybe I should let it go at that. This, too." He leaned away, his eyes somber on hers. He tilted her chin up with one finger. "Because all I really have to offer you is this."

With the tears trailing down her cheeks, he lowered his mouth to hers and kissed her. His lips felt firm yet soft, and she wanted to tell him he was wrong. He could care about someone other than his twins and his brother and Clara. He could care about her, and she sensed it in his kiss. But was he telling her goodbye? Was that the best thing for Jenna? She'd always imagined this time would come, that she shouldn't trust that he would stay.

For another brief moment it didn't seem to matter. She cared about him, and even with the words between them that should make her leave now, as he would leave Clara's ranch, she stayed in Hadley's arms. His gentle kiss deepened—nothing wrong with his technique—until she couldn't help but join him in a random meshing of souls that she knew now could never last.

The sound of a throat clearing jerked them apart.

The cold wind rushing in behind him, a man stood in the doorway. Lost in their embrace, neither Jenna nor Hadley had heard the door open. Walter Pearson glared at Hadley. He sent Jenna a dismissive look.

And abruptly, she came to her senses.

As she should have done before now.

# CHAPTER NINETEEN

"YOU'RE A DISGRACE," Walter Pearson said, his mouth a set line. "I stopped by to let you know I'm here before going to the cabin and this is what I find?"

"We were only kissing," Hadley insisted. "It's Christmastime." He reached for Jenna's hand, but she'd put a few feet of space between them that told Hadley she'd thought twice about their brief intimacy.

"A kiss that meant nothing," she said, holding Hadley's gaze.

Pearson turned on him. "How could you defile the memory of my daughter? Because that's what that was. After little more than a year, you've *forgotten* her? Amy *loved* you—God knows why." He jabbed a finger in Hadley's chest. Ordinarily, that would have provoked a response, but for a change Hadley held his temper. "Her mother and I are still heartbroken, while *you*—you're already with this woman who called herself Amy's friend!" His angry gaze raked Jenna. "And I'm supposed to be okay with this? Let me inform you. He's using you as a convenience, Miss Moran."

Hadley winced. Jenna had used a similar term minutes ago, calling herself a handy option. "We're not involved. Your timing's bad, that's all."

Pearson glowered. "Not as bad as yours. What about the twins? You have some glib answer for them? I never thought you'd be any kind of a father—"

Hadley's jaw clenched. "I'm the only father they've got. Maybe you should make peace with that, Pearson, and leave me to raise them. Like Amy wanted."

"Did she? Don't think she didn't complain to us about how you treated her."

Hadley crossed his arms. "Amy had a tendency to embellish. I'd bet most of whatever she told you was fiction."

The increasingly bitter quarrels they'd had during the last months of Amy's life had made him doubt they could survive as a couple, even when he'd said he would try.

Pearson's face was purple. "My daughter

was no liar. I see now how prudent I was to send money for her, the only protection I could provide as long as she stayed with you."

"You didn't trust me to provide for her—and okay, I didn't in the way she was accustomed to living—but after she died, I did grieve for Amy," he told Pearson. "You can believe me or not. But we still weren't right for each other, and if she had lived, we would probably be divorced by now." Amy, the spoiled daughter of wealthy parents, Hadley the abandoned, drifter son of drug dealers. "Is that what you wanted to hear?" Hadley had the sudden feeling he was fighting for his life. "The best thing we did was to create the twins. *My* babies now, without her."

Pearson's gaze bored through him. "I wish I'd followed my instincts when Amy first told us she was pregnant by you."

"And that's another thing. Why wasn't I informed about Amy's heart condition? You and Danielle were aware of it. That's on both of you. If I'd known, I might have taken more care, tried to better protect her health."

For a moment Pearson appeared chastened. Then he said, "Amy begged us not to tell you. She was afraid you'd see her differently, even walk away from her, and we wished you had.

I shouldn't have listened to her. I should have taken her home where she belonged. Instead, you're still in the picture holding my grandbabies hostage."

Hadley held up a hand. "Stop right there. I've made it easy enough for you to visit them, not because I wanted to but because that's your right by law. But we're never going to agree about Amy or anything else."

"Mr. Pearson." Jenna spoke for the second time since Amy's father had found them locked in a kiss that still flowed through Hadley's veins like warm butter, but he wished she'd stayed quiet. "I don't mean to butt in," she said, "but I did promise Amy that if anything happened to her I'd watch over the twins, make sure they were being well cared for...and they are."

Which didn't help at all. Hadley's feeling of dread grew worse.

Pearson's gaze had sharpened. "Danielle mentioned that. We didn't know what to make of it. An overseer?"

"I'd hoped it would never come to that, but yes. Amy asked me to serve as—"

"Jenna, don't," Hadley warned her.

"—what's called a standby guardian, but

the court hearing to officially appoint me never occurred. Amy had the babies a few days before the hearing. But from what I've read and learned since, I doubt the order would have been granted. Even though Amy was ill—which I didn't realize then—and her wishes make sense in retrospect, I wasn't a blood relative, just a friend."

"Then she *was* worried." Pearson glared at Hadley. "You knew about this guardianship?"

"Yes, and I would never have agreed to it. At the time I figured I'd humor Amy, wait until she saw the judge. I thought she was frightened about giving birth—afraid I wouldn't be there for her afterward. But the court would never have gotten my signature on any document." Now he knew that Amy had also been warned she could possibly die in childbirth.

Her eyes wide, Jenna appeared as if she wanted to bite her tongue. "I wouldn't say Amy was *worried.*" By then she must have realized she'd said exactly the wrong thing. In a few words, she'd implicated Hadley as someone who'd needed to be watched, who probably still did. Why on earth had Jenna felt the urge to confirm Pearson's opinion of him? Because she and Hadley had argued earlier? Because he'd admitted he wouldn't stay so she was getting back at him?

Amy's father spun on his heel and headed for the door. "Let me promise *you* something, Smith. You haven't heard the last of this."

HADLEY LOWERED THE GATE on the open-sided stock trailer, but even the bellowing of the new cattle inside couldn't override his regrets about his fight with Pearson. Thanks to his temper, he hadn't handled that well.

But this morning, as it had been for the past three days, his head was full of Jenna. So much for his attempt, then, to cool off his feelings for her.

Hadley pulled down the rear ramp, determined to focus on the ranch. He'd bought a dozen head from Logan Hunter's herd, and Logan himself had come to deliver them with his family.

Logan climbed out of the pickup's cab with a smile Hadley didn't return.

The other man was the spitting image of Sawyer, his twin. "Three pregnant heifers in the lot," he said, a definite bonus for the Mc-Mann ranch.

Logan's wife, Blossom, her russet curls bouncing, unbuckled their daughter from her car seat. But little Daisy had a mind of her own, for as soon as her mother set her down, the toddler charged off in the direction of the house. "She wants to see Luke and Grace," Blossom explained as Logan started after her. Halfway across the yard, he swept Daisy into his arms, then planted a kiss on her neck.

Instead of laughing, Daisy started to yell. Hadley thought of the twins, of Pearson and what had clearly been a threat.

His mind replayed the scene as he and the Hunters exchanged parenting stories of epic temper tantrums, which Daisy had discovered as a means of getting what she wanted. If Luke and Gracie walked by Christmas, then the real fun would begin. Assuming he was here for the holiday. Logan and Blossom were teasing Hadley about being outnumbered when he spied Jenna heading their way from the house.

He tensed. He'd said too much the other night. Worse, so had she. He realized she'd only intended to back him up after all, to reassure Walter the twins were fine with Hadley, but instead she'd affirmed Amy and her parents' fears about him. Hadley was surprised

Jenna had come to the ranch today. The only good part was that after Pearson's tirade, Walter had gone home the same night.

Hadley couldn't read Jenna's expression. She said hello to Logan and Blossom, then wordlessly handed Hadley an envelope. Maybe she was giving up on her promise to Amy and was about to tender a resignation of sorts. Abandon the twins. And him. Never mind that he'd practically told her to. "What's this?"

Her tone was cool. "I don't open other people's mail, but the return address is familiar."

So were the names at the top of the letter inside. Walter and Danielle Pearson, engraved in black on thick, cream-colored stationery. The names seemed to taunt him again. After an exchange of looks, Blossom and Logan had quickly carried Daisy into the barn to visit the horses, so he and Jenna were now alone.

As he scanned the brief message, his stomach tightened.

*Hadley. After our recent discussion, my wife and I—as Amy's parents—have decided our grandchildren belong with us. We intend to sue for permanent custody of Lucas and*

*Grace. We believe we are the better option to raise them, as Amy, our beloved daughter, clearly would have wished.*

While he was trying to digest those few sentences that swam in front of his eyes, Logan and Blossom came out of the barn, Daisy chattering in some unknown language about Mr. Robert, Hadley supposed. The horse nickered after them, wanting more attention. Hadley stood stock-still, sure his face must be blanched dead white. Jenna stood nearby as if she, too, had been turned to stone.

"Bad news?" Blossom asked with a concerned expression.

"The worst." But why was he so shocked? He'd been waiting for this for the past year. With a hard sigh, he said, "The twins' grandparents want custody."

Blossom's brown eyes widened. "Why? No one could possibly accuse you of neglect, of not taking care of them. If you need witnesses to testify—"

"Easy, Blossom." Logan put his arm around her. "Likely it won't come to that. I've been dealing with similar antics from my grandfather for decades. He's always more bark than he is bite. Pearson may be, too. Let me see what we're up against."

Hadley gave him the letter. *We*, Logan had said, as if they were friends instead of rancher and cowhand bound only by a business transaction for Clara's cattle and because Logan had given him a second job. Blossom read over her husband's shoulder. Looking tentative, Jenna stepped closer, too, perhaps remembering Pearson's rant. "Hadley, I'm so sorry. I shouldn't have said anything about Amy's guardianship. I didn't intend to. If I hadn't blurted that out, he'd never have gone this far."

Logan waved the curt message. "If anyone threatened us like this—" He stopped. "Actually, someone did. Blossom's ex-fiancé."

She groaned. "Now, thank goodness, he's completely off our radar. He relinquished any right to Daisy. I'm sure you won't have any trouble, Hadley, proving yourself to the court—winning against the Pearsons—if it ever comes to that."

Hadley wasn't as sure. "My track record's not the best. I have no permanent address. This ranch is Clara's. Even the horse I ride half belongs to her. I'm single, a cowpoke without much money, with little education, or anything else to give the twins..."

"You give them all they need." Blossom patted his arm. "Maybe, like Logan says, Mr. Pearson is all talk and he'll never follow through on this threat."

Hadley's jaw clenched. "I'm betting he will. If the Pearsons do sue for custody, I'll have to move on." Even though he realized leaving wouldn't help his cause, Amy's parents now had Jenna's would-be guardianship as proof of Amy's concerns, including her fear that he would leave her, and he didn't have the money for a court battle. "I won't give up the twins, especially not to him."

"This is all my fault," Jenna said in a mournful tone.

Hadley wanted to reassure her, but actually, even if she had tried to help him, she'd said the wrong words.

"Who writes a stilted letter like this?" he asked, wanting to lash out. "It sounds like some foreign language."

Hadley tried to repress a thousand memories of his foster days, including his betrayal of Dallas. Now his loss would be the twins—if he stuck around and let the Pearsons win.

WHAT IF HADLEY did lose the twins? Because of her? It didn't seem to matter now that he'd rejected Jenna, or that Walter Pearson had assumed she was the new woman in Hadley's life. Without meaning to, she'd made him look again like the loser people used to say he was. She hadn't heard that in a while except from Amy's dad.

Alone in her office above her sister's health care agency, she tried to concentrate on her design plans for one of her new clients. But when the phone rang and she recognized the number, she stopped trying to focus. She was ready for this confrontation today.

"Jenna, you haven't let me know if you want the grandfather clock," her ex began without a greeting. "It's taking up space in my storage unit."

"That clock is from your family, not mine. Do with it as you please." Still, the beautiful walnut piece had stood on the landing of the stairs in their Shawnee Mission house, a memento of kinship, of connection. For years Jenna had thought that meant her, too, David and the children they would have to carry on his line. "And you're about to give me more news," she guessed, tempted to hang up. David never called these days without some other purpose, usually one that ended up hurting her. Last time he'd crowed about the woman he was now seeing and her three children.

*Luke and Grace*, she thought instead, stunned that she'd actually suggested those names for Hadley's twins. Amy had said they were her favorite, too, but they'd been Jenna's choices first, and Hadley had seen right through her. And that wasn't all he'd seen. *I'm not the guy you should pick.*

At her ongoing silence, David sighed. "Big news, yes," he said. "I've asked Sheila to marry me. We're doing a destination wedding in Barbados next spring." She heard a smile in his voice. "On the beach, at sunset…"

Jenna stiffened in her chair. "Why do you do this? We're divorced, David." And he knew she didn't want him back. She'd made that clear some time ago in his office in Kansas City then. "I don't care what your plans are. I don't have to anymore. But by the way, I *will* take that clock. I could use it for a client. You pay the shipping cost. Send it to Olivia McCord Antiques." She rattled off the shop's Main Street address. "Please give your bride-to-be my best wishes. She'll need them. I hope Sheila knows, for her own good, that she's marrying a man to whom family—a wife, for that matter—is not as important as his ego."

At the other end of the line, he sputtered. "I never thought you were vindictive. If you can't be happy for me—"

Those were the same words her mother had used. "I'm very happy." He'd just proved her point by saying "me," not "us." "Be a better husband to her, if you can, than you were to me. A better father to her children than you might have been for ours." When he didn't answer—shocked, she hoped, into silence— Jenna added, "I learned my own worth the hard way. Don't call me again." Then, with a definite feeling of relief, she did hang up. Finally, and for the second time, she'd stood up for herself with David Collins, and he was now totally part of her past.

She spent the rest of the afternoon checking in with her clients. Her latest had come to her via a recommendation from Barney, who'd resigned from the bank. She made appointments for others to see certain pieces they might like at Olivia's, alerted her friend to the clock's arrival and arranged to meet a client at the tile store in Farrier tomorrow to pick out flooring for a new house. Then she hopped online to order herself the pricey cashmere robe she'd had her eye on, simply because she deserved an indulgence. A celebration of sorts about David.

Though she couldn't feel completely satisfied. She wished things had gone differently with Hadley and Walter Pearson. She wished she and Hadley could have made something more of their mutual attraction—he'd admitted that much—but if this was to be her lot now, she would make the most of it, successful in her work if nowhere else.

At five o'clock Jenna heard a door open below, then footsteps on the stairs. A minute later her sister appeared.

"Virtual bottle of wine," Shadow said, empty hand in the air. "Believe me. It took some doing, but I found Bertie a new place after all and he actually loves it! Mama's thrilled. With the wedding a week away, she had enough to worry about. By the time she and Jack leave on their honeymoon to Mexico, I'll have his uncle settled. He's already put his house on the market. Want to help me make his assisted-living apartment into a home for him?"

"I will. Of course." Jenna paused. "Congratulations. As long as we're celebrating, see me lift a glass of your excellent wine here. I told David off this afternoon."

Shadow grinned, ear to ear. "Details, please."

Jenna related her conversation with her ex-husband, mostly her side of it. Indeed, she felt as if she'd closed one door and opened another, even if it wasn't a door that led to the future she'd yearned for.

She also told Shadow that Hadley wasn't interested in a relationship, and how she'd made him look bad with Amy's parents. By the time she finished, she felt drained.

"Then apologize to Hadley. Make this work for you, Jenna, if that's what you want."

"I doubt there's any way to fix it. After Pearson's threats to take the twins, Hadley said he'll leave Clara's before the court ever rules on a custody suit. I don't think that's wise, and certainly not good for the twins to be uprooted so abruptly, but that seems to be what he has in mind." *I'm happy wherever the road takes me.*

"Why wouldn't he win in court?"

"Hadley doesn't believe he would, and I've always known Barren was never the place he meant to stay. He has no more faith in himself than I did when I was living at home with Daddy or married to David. I think in his heart he's still the bad boy of Barren."

"After his upbringing, I can understand how he might feel rootless, but he's not making decisions only for himself now." She gazed at Jenna. "Neither are you. I want to cheer loud enough for Jack to hear me down at the café—or better, David in Salt Lake. Finally, you're done with him, but..." Shadow rounded the desk, pulled Jenna out of her seat and hugged her fiercely. "Sisters don't let each other off the hook. Jen, I can see you love Hadley and those babies, too. Why don't you stop beating yourself up now because you can't have kids? If I were you, I wouldn't let them all slip away."

For a second Jenna envisioned herself living in a house near Clara's with Hadley, caring for the twins every day, sitting up with them all night whenever they were sick, watching them grow, loving and being loved in return. As if she were their mother. And Hadley's wife. A part of her wondered now if she'd thought her only chance to be a parent of sorts might be that guardianship. And that was why she'd insisted on stepping in after the twins were born. Yet she'd heard Hadley say, *If the Pearsons do sue for custody, I'll have to move on. I won't give up the twins.*

"After his marriage to Amy," Jenna said, "he doesn't want another, and my bottom line? The twins *aren't* mine. They're Hadley's."

Shadow rolled her eyes. "You need to talk to Annabelle," she said.

# *CHAPTER TWENTY*

ON CHRISTMAS EVE, Hadley packed his bags
while Luke and Gracie played in the other
room. He tried to ignore the notice he'd received an hour ago from a lawyer. As Hadley
had expected when he'd first read the Pearsons' curt note, they would indeed file suit
to gain custody of the twins.

This morning, for the first time in his life
as a cowboy, Hadley had neglected to feed
the horses. By now they were probably tear-
ing down the barn. No one else was around
to feed them. Cody Jones hadn't made bail
and was living in a cell at the sheriff's office. Hadley hated leaving Clara with the
task, but he had no choice. With jerky mo-
tions he threw shirts, jeans, underwear into a
suitcase, then squashed his spare Stetson on
top. By noon he'd be on his way. Maybe, if
he hurried, he'd find time to feed the horses
before he left.

At a slight noise he pivoted to find Clara standing half in the hallway and half inside his room. She eyed the bags. "I never thought of you as a quitter. What makes you so sure the court will decide in the Pearsons' favor?"

"You know the answer to that."

"Because you've lived in too many places with people who didn't care about you? Changed jobs? Worked for a number of ranchers? Made a few mistakes, including with Amy? None of that makes you a bad person or an unfit father." She came into the room, shutting the door behind her. "Let's not trouble the twins with loud voices, but you need to reconsider. Where will you go with a pair of one-year-olds? The day before Christmas? What will Luke and Grace do tomorrow morning when there are no presents for them?"

"I doubt they're even aware it's Christmas." He'd make it up to them. There was no way all those brightly wrapped packages piled under the tree downstairs would fit in his truck with the luggage, the twins' high chairs, the double stroller and the newest bulk shipment from Amazon of diapers.

Clara plowed on, increasing his sense of

guilt. "Stuck in their car seats, their holiday spent helping you escape?" Her voice quavered. "Who will take the star and lights off our tree after New Year's?"

She made him feel like the worst kind of heel, the same way he had when he'd lowered the boom on Jenna. *If I were looking for someone...* But it wasn't his Christmas tree; he'd only done the decorating at Clara's bidding with Jenna's help, her face aglow in the lights, her hand brushing his as they passed ornaments to each other. One of the rare times he'd been anywhere to observe the holidays. He'd looked forward to that this year. He even had a present for Jenna that he hoped would please her. "Clara, when Pearson caught me kissing Jenna, he made up his mind. I'm sorry as all get-out that I can't stay, but I won't wait around until the county comes to snatch my kids."

"What about this ranch? Your promise to make it better than before?" Clara asked. "And the other jobs you took? You'll be letting the Circle H and Finn down, too. Hadley, you're a wonderful dad. Certainly Walter wouldn't be a replacement. I'm fond of Danielle, but I don't understand why she went along with this—"

"I didn't." White-faced, Danielle walked into the room. "But did I hear correctly?" At Hadley's gesture, she plucked the lawyer's notice off the bed to scan it. Her expression soured. "I can't believe this. I knew he was angry, but Walter called our attorney and started these proceedings without telling me."

"Did you know about the letter he sent me a few days ago in both your names?"

"Letter?" Hadley told her what it had said, and Danielle's face became a mask of fury. "I knew nothing about that, either. I'll be giving him a piece of my mind soon." Hadley glanced behind her and saw her suitcase in the hall. "In person," she added, having followed his gaze. "I adore Luke and Grace and being with them has made…losing Amy a bit easier to bear. I've said as much to Walter. Frankly, I'm as guilty as he is for keeping Amy's condition from you. If only knowing could have helped… But does he really think he's doing this for me? He's wrong."

"Danielle, I admit I didn't want you here," Hadley said, "but I can see how much the twins like you, too. They deserve to have doting grandmothers." Hadley included Clara as he turned to close his last suitcase. "If I could give you your daughter back, I would, but I won't sacrifice *my* babies," he said, his voice breaking. "Tell your husband if he tries to have me arrested for kidnapping my own children, which wouldn't surprise me, I'll find some way to make him sorry. I still have sole custody of Luke and Gracie."

Clara wrung her hands, as Jenna tended to do whenever she felt stressed. "More threats from you won't help." Her mouth puckered like a prune. "Hadley. Running with those babies—you'll be giving the judge reason to find against you. As a fugitive you will be caught, just as Cody Jones was. Has your own life ever gotten better because you left one place for another? No," she answered herself. "You're not seeing things clearly. You already *have* a place here. The twins and I are your family, and if you're as smart a man as I believe you are, Jenna could be part of that, too. Before you drive off this ranch, you should really consider that."

JENNA TOOK HER SISTER'S ADVICE. An hour later she pulled into the driveway of the house where she'd been raised. Annabelle lived there now with Finn, and they'd definitely spruced it up—double-paned windows and insulation to make the house weathertight instead of drafty all winter, new appliances to update the kitchen, a gleaming wooden floor in the living room to replace the worn carpet. The yard didn't seem the same, either, with Finn's new barn, horses in the nearby field and cattle roaming the farther pasture. The falling-down fence had been rebuilt, and next to the house a new garage was under construction. With all the improvements, she hardly recognized the farm. With added acreage it was becoming a real ranch. Jenna shouldn't have to revisit her own worst memories here any longer.

As if Annabelle had been expecting her, she met Jenna at the door, where she'd hung a big wreath. In the small entryway, Jenna kissed her cheek. "Did my sister call you?"

"Shadow? Was she supposed to?"

"No. I guess she did leave me to do this alone then."

In the front corner by the windows a Christmas tree glowed with light, its ornaments sparkling, wrapped presents piled underneath. Jenna tried not to glance at the spot where her father's recliner, its stuffing falling out, used to sit in front of a TV, oblivious, largely to her, as if Jenna didn't exist. Finn and Annabelle had rearranged the room, added a new entertainment center and a play area for their daughter.

On the sofa, Jenna suppressed the urge to tangle her fingers together in her lap. She was about to explain the reason for her visit when Annabelle's daughter, Emmie, raced down the short hall into the living room.

"Mama! I did my alph-bets puzzle! Every letter!" Seeing Jenna, she stopped.

Jenna couldn't help but smile at the blonde, blue-eyed little girl. "Hey, Emmie."

"Santa tonight! He come your house?"

"Use your sentences, sweetie," Annabelle said gently.

"I forget sometimes." Emmie leaned against Jenna, who slipped an arm around her and felt the usual wave of warmth she always did for a child. "I try… I keep trying. Is that better, Mama?" Emmie hugged Jenna, then, without waiting for an answer, rushed off to her room, and Jenna thought, *I may not see Luke and Grace ever again.*

"Emmie's home today from day care," Annabelle was saying. "She loves seeing her friends there, Seth Barnes most of all. So even though I'm no longer strapped with the diner, I send her to her 'school' three days a week."

Jenna decided to let Annabelle set the topic of conversation for the moment. Now that she was here, Jenna wasn't eager to talk about the twins or Hadley. She didn't know how to start.

"Seth? You mean the mayor's little boy."

Ever since the news leaked out that Harry Barnes was Emmie's biological father, the gossip had abounded all over town. "Yes. You know Harry gave up any claim on Emmie, which pleased Finn as much as it did me. We rejected Harry's offer to pay child support. And her adoption has gone through at last, the best Christmas gift any of us could get."

Adoption. Jenna had considered adopting once, but in spite of what Shadow had said, she still yearned for a baby of her own.

Annabelle continued. "Harry's poor wife. Elizabeth tried to make a go of it with him, but they've separated."

"That's too bad. Having his affair with your cousin had to be painful for her. I hope Harry loses his next election."

"I heard he's not going to run."

Jenna's fingers twined in her lap. This was her chance. "Speaking of children, Shadow thought you might be able to help me sort out a few things."

After she explained, Annabelle said, "You've come to love Luke and Grace, haven't you?"

"To be honest, I'm head over heels for those two."

"And the twins do have a hunky dad." Annabelle sent a fond glance toward Emmie's room. "Or am I imagining you with Hadley because I'm glad I have Finn? I want everyone to be this happy. I imagine you've waited a long time, as I did, to find that." *I wouldn't let them all slip away*, Shadow had said.

Jenna told her more about Walter Pearson and how she'd ruined things by tipping off Amy's father to the standby guardianship. "I feel guilty for putting Hadley in such a bad spot. I know he's not interested in, um, a relationship with me…"

Annabelle's smile grew. "Finn used to push me away, but then he fell for Emmie. Now, for the most part, he's put that terrible tragedy in Chicago—the loss of his first wife and son—behind him. Is it possible Hadley hasn't done the same yet? From what I hear, he carries some baggage, not just about Amy." She sobered. "Jenna, together you and Hadley might heal each other. The twins could be part of that."

Jenna couldn't speak. *They're not mine. They're Hadley's.* And why think he'd want her as his children's stand-in mother? When, from the start, he'd objected to Jenna even as a potential guardian?

Annabelle sensed her hesitation. "If you're reluctant, I understand. After my cousin Sierra died, I wasn't eager to take in Emmie. I already had my family's diner on the market. I couldn't wait to sell it, then run off to see the world." She gestured at the house around them. "Now this is the biggest adventure I can think of. When Emmie's a little older, I'll ramp up my career as a tour director, but for now I wouldn't give up Emmie—or Finn—for a minute." Annabelle's tender gaze seemed to see into her very heart. "This could be your chance to have children, even if they're not your own." But Annabelle wasn't finished. "Believe me, I know," she said. "You don't have to give birth, Jenna, to be a mother."

AFTER DANIELLE LEFT THE BEDROOM, Hadley finished packing. Clara had vanished, probably because she didn't want him to see her cry. A ten-foot-high wave of regret made him feel like he was drowning.

Still, he wasn't about to wait at the ranch for some judge to order him to give up his kids. He wouldn't attend any scheduled hearing to prove he was an unfit parent. He was sure Pearson had hired a topflight legal team, which Hadley couldn't afford. So, not a fair fight. There was no way he could let Luke and Gracie go. That hadn't changed since the day they were born. His best option was to leave. Now. He only wished Clara could see things his way.

The house echoed with her words. *The twins and I are your family, and if you're as smart a man as I believe you are, Jenna could be part of that, too.*

Yes, he was attracted to Jenna—more than that, to be honest. But how to believe he could have something special with her when he never had before?

Just like Amy, Jenna wanted something he couldn't supply. Shattered by her divorce from that creep who was now her ex, she'd

come home to make a new life for herself—
and she had. Why should he throw a spanner
in the works when she deserved a man who
could give her the happily-ever-after he didn't
believe in?

If Hadley let himself love Jenna, she would
always fear he'd leave someday, as he had
all those foster homes that had scarred him
inside. Just as Amy had worried about him.
Even now, quitting Clara's ranch, as sorrow-
ful as that would be, was necessary, but it
couldn't compare to losing the twins. And
that was why he had to take them and go.

Hadley made a brief stop in the office,
where he checked over the ranch accounts.
Again, this month Clara was showing a profit,
a small one but a bit larger than in October
and November, and the next promised to
be even better. He was leaving her in good
shape. But who would take over now? With
Cody in jail, she'd have no one. What would
happen then to the stock that relied on him or
Hadley for feed and water? Who would muck
Mr. Robert's and Trouble's stalls? Shovel a
path from the house to the barn when the
first blizzard that was predicted came rushing across the plains?

He was letting Jenna down, too. With his share of the ranch profits and the pay he'd managed to save from his other jobs, he'd have to find another way to at least give back what he owed her. Wire it, maybe, from his bank account to hers. But he'd rather watch her face when he handed her the check. And repaid the loan.

Frowning, Hadley carried his bags to the door. In his haste to pack for the twins, he'd have to leave things behind, ask Clara to send their toys and Christmas gifts once he got settled again. After they woke from their naps, he could be on his way to...where? Hadley hadn't considered that, as he'd never planned in the past. But then, he'd been by himself, as Clara had said, without even Dallas to consider.

At his truck, parked under a leaden gray sky that forecast the first snow of the season, he loaded the bags. Hadley flipped up the collar of his jacket against the wind. As he turned to go back inside, Clara reappeared on the porch steps. Her reddened eyes told him she was in no mood to be nice, which might be a first for Clara. "Grace and Luke are up," she said in a flat tone. "Do you want me to feed them? Or were you planning to stop on the road?"

"They won't be able to wait." Hadley could smell some enticing aroma from the kitchen, and a growing sense of loss ran through him. He knew this house as if it were really his own, the layout of each room, every creak of the wooden floorboards in the night, the scents of Clara's cooking. "I'll get their things while you feed them an early lunch—if that's okay."

When he climbed the steps to her, Clara avoided his touch. "Cliff and I gave you a home when you most needed one. You came to us a broken boy then who'd lost his brother. We would have taken in Dallas, too, you know. If you must go anywhere now, go to him—leave the twins with me until you come back for them. You need to settle things with him, Hadley, and unless you're too afraid to be cast out again, I wish you would with Jenna, too." She added, "Or would you rather lose her?"

"I already have, Clara." Yet her words had struck to the very core of him. He didn't want to hurt her, yet he couldn't make himself stay even when Clara was staring at him with her heart in her eyes.

"This is your home," she went on, her tone thick. "You're my son, Hadley, as surely as if I'd given birth to you. How can you not realize that?" When he didn't answer, she made a gesture of frustration. "I see this isn't getting me anywhere. But before you go, I want to give you your Christmas present." Was she changing the subject? "It's nothing wrapped. And I hate using this to try to keep you here, but the McMann ranch would be yours one day—if you'd stayed. Who else would I leave it to?"

"Clara." His dream of not being simply a cowboy on someone else's land but of riding the open range on a horse that was truly his, owning that land, was suddenly within his grasp.

Clara's voice was as hard as a diamond, and, yes, forever.

"But if you go now, Hadley Smith, don't come back again."

WHILE CLARA FED the twins their lunch, Hadley riffled through their chest of drawers, picking clothes that still fit and would suit the winter weather. Luke needed new sleepers. Gracie had run out of socks without holes in the toes.

Hadley stared at the overstuffed duffel bag. He couldn't get Clara's last words out of his head. How had he really helped her? Sure, the ranch was on its feet again. But were repaired fences, clean stalls in the barn, enough hay in the loft to get the animals through the frigid days and nights until spring, enough? When there was no one to take over the work?

Outside again, he put the twins' belongings in the truck. Was he really going to turn his back on Clara with this winter storm brewing? Drive off into a blizzard? Kansas roads were mostly flat and straight as a stick, yet in the next few hours they might become treacherous. He envisioned the truck sliding, unable to stop it, ending up in a ditch or wrapped around a tree. The twins terrified or hurt. And all because Hadley didn't have the guts to stay. He was leaving the McMann ranch, the one place in his world that had never caused him any harm.

Jenna hadn't, either. Yet he'd all but told her he didn't want her, which wasn't true.

He'd let down Amy, who had died knowing he couldn't love her. He must have, though, at least in the beginning, or he never would have married her. He'd let down Dallas, too, whom he might never see again. He still hadn't answered Hadley's message.

Clara had been wrong. What kind of father was he if he couldn't set a better example for the twins? What kind of man? If he couldn't *stop* and face himself? Or did he want to keep leaving every place he went, as Jenna had once said? Leaving her, this time, behind.

His chest was tight; his eyes seemed to have grit in them as Hadley reached into the truck bed and hauled out the bags. His and the babies' too.

He'd talk to Clara, then to Jenna. Maybe it was too late for them to have a future, but he had to try. Even better would be giving her his heart.

He could only wonder what *she'd* have to say to that.

## CHAPTER TWENTY-ONE

"DA-DA!" In Hadley's embrace, Luke waved the yellow plastic truck he'd opened Christmas morning. "Da!" he cried as if to say, *look*. At dawn, Hadley, the twins and Clara had gathered in front of the tree. The air buzzed with the children's excitement. With his other arm, he cradled Gracie and the soft doll with orange braids she'd gotten from Santa Claus.

Outside, the first real snow of the season was still falling, the dark clouds yesterday having given way to fat white flakes that drifted past the windows and accumulated on the lawn, the driveway, the hood of his truck. In the barn, Mr. Robert and Trouble, wearing their coarse winter coats, were enjoying extra grain, water buckets full, breaths frosting in the cold air. Anticipating the storm, Hadley had delivered flakes of hay to the cattle in the field.

Not quite in the holiday spirit himself, he

gently pushed Luke's arm down before the little boy hit Hadley in the face with the truck. As Luke wailed, Gracie leaned over to wordlessly offer her brother her doll. The twins exchanged their gifts and Hadley sent Clara a look.

"They share everything," she said with a smile.

Clara had been in charge of handing out the presents, this last with Hadley's name on the tag in her handwriting.

"Clara, you shouldn't give me anything more."

It wasn't her offer to pass the ranch to him one day that had changed his mind about staying. Clara had already given him all she had to give, and he remembered her saying, *This is your home. You're my son.* Hadley felt a lingering regret for Jenna, who wasn't here this morning, and for Dallas, the other person still missing from his life. If it wasn't for the twins, or Clara's delight at the goings-on, he would have skipped Christmas after all. He had no idea how he was going to approach Jenna.

"Open it," Clara murmured, handing him a modest-sized box.

With Luke's help, he tore off the shiny red paper, revealing first the corner of a small framed picture showing Hadley's younger face, his dark hair and, finally, the complete picture of him standing beside his four-year-old brother. It was the same image Hadley carried in his wallet. "Where did you get this?"

"I have my ways," she told him, looking far too mysterious. "It's not the best copy, but we can fix that tomorrow, dear, if you're willing to brave the stores in town the day after Christmas when everyone else is exchanging their unwanted gifts."

The small dig at him was to let Hadley know she was pleased that he'd stayed. Nothing could trouble Clara at the moment. "I won't be one of those people," he managed. "Thank you, Clara. This means a lot to me."

So did she, the calm and steady presence he relied on. Clara was a huge part of why he was still here, and he had to let her know how he felt. Yet for long moments he studied the photograph, holding it out of Luke's reach while his boy fussed until, finally, Hadley put him and Gracie in their playpen. Then once more Hadley traced a finger over the glass surface between his and Dallas's faces. Four years later, Dallas had been whisked away from Hadley, the food thief.

The old sorrow flowed along his veins. But it was Luke's face that threatened to crumple— he always guessed Hadley's mood before he knew it himself—and Hadley leaned over the playpen to press a quick kiss to Luke's cheek. "I'm okay, pal."

He couldn't stop staring, though, at that last picture of the other little boy he'd wronged. No wonder Dallas hated him and, since he hadn't answered Hadley's messages, seemed to want no contact with him.

The front bell chimed, but he scarcely heard it except to hope briefly it might be Jenna. Clara jumped up from her chair. "You stay with the twins. I'll get the door."

"What's going on?" he asked.

As the door opened, to Hadley's amazement there stood the man himself, tall and broad, wearing jeans and a sheepskin-lined jacket, stamping his boots to free them of snow and…leaning on a cane. His brother's face, although older, looked much the same with that glint in his eyes, that smile.

"Hey," Dallas said, then made his way

across the living room, propped the cane
against one leg, eyed Gracie, then Luke. And
grinned. "Your favorite uncle is here," he told
them, even when the twins had begun to howl
like banshees. They weren't fond of strangers
these days. Dallas had barely noticed Hadley.

Hadley swallowed, speechless. He'd sent a
follow-up message yesterday to Dallas, who
seemed to have read his mind. "I was up in
Cheyenne, thought I'd take a drive. Man, this
was a long way. Snow coming down hori-
zontal, a near whiteout." He turned to Clara.
"You have any coffee, ma'am? The all-nighter
has me wanting a nap."

To settle himself, and the twins, Hadley
plucked them from the playpen. As soon as
they both stopped crying, he set Gracie on the
rug, too, and she crawled at top speed after
Luke. His boy idly inspected the toys under
the tree, but then Luke suddenly stood up,
using the playpen for support. He did that all
the time, but now, to Hadley's astonishment,
he turned, took one halting step, then another,
and staggered into Hadley's arms. A second
later, not to be outdone, Gracie scrambled to
her feet, then took off and flung herself at
him, too.

"They're walking," he said.

"Better than me." Dallas watched them. "First time?"

Hadley swallowed. "Yeah," and Gracie laughed, being the newest center of attention. Hadley said to Dallas, "Maybe they were waiting for you to show up."

"About time," Dallas agreed. "Let's talk."

His heart pounding, Hadley led him to the kitchen. He poured Dallas a cup of strong coffee, then handed him the mug, which had the twins' faces printed on it. He felt certain he was in for a real tongue-lashing, at best. "For openers, where did Clara get that picture of us?"

"From me." Dallas grinned. "I got your messages. At first, I didn't know what to do, wasn't sure it was you. Then yesterday, when you didn't answer your cell, I called the other number you'd sent, Clara's house phone." Hadley had probably been putting bags in the car when Dallas tried his number. "After we talked, I scanned and sent the image to her. She wanted to surprise you." Dallas reached into his back pocket and drew out his billfold that contained the same photograph. "You gave this to me the last time I saw you. You still have yours?"

"Yeah." Which Clara had never seen, and Hadley shook his head. He couldn't believe Dallas still cared for him. "I threw you to the wolves. Aren't you angry with me?"

"Because you took some beef jerky and a couple of Devil Dogs from the corner market?" He raised his dark eyebrows. "Not that I condone theft, but I admired that more in my case than I can tell you."

"But because of that, because of me, they sent you away—both of us—I never found out where you went."

"And yeah, I was a mad little guy for a while. Not at you," he added. "At those people, the whole system... I know how you fought to keep me with you. If I'd been able to locate you, I would have, but yours is a pretty low profile. Once or twice I thought I'd tracked you down, but you'd already left for somewhere else. You're a hard man to find."

"Not anymore." Hadley spoke around the lump in his throat. "You don't blame me for betraying you? We were the only two people left in what passed for our family. I don't even know what happened to Mom or our dad."

Dallas winced. "Last I heard he was in prison where he belongs." His voice lowered. "Sorry to tell you like this, but I hear Mom died of an overdose years ago. He probably gave the drugs to her." Hadley would have cursed them, yet he still felt a sense of loss. Dallas continued. "They hung on to us as long as they could." Just as Jenna had thought. "They were all messed up, Hadley, but I can't spend the rest of my life hating them for who they were."

Then, like the rodeo rider he was, as if an eight-second bell was about to ring and he had to stay on his bull, Dallas moved fast. His cane dropped to the floor. He stopped less than a foot from Hadley. "Just say you're glad to see me, will you?"

The words choked out. "God, Dallas, you'll never know how glad. I missed you…like someone had torn out my…heart."

Dallas rolled his eyes. "Don't get mushy on me. A woman in tears, like Clara when I phoned last night, is bad enough."

Hadley opened his arms and Dallas limped right into them. Where had his brother been all these years? Did he plan to return to the rodeo circuit? Was that even an option, considering the injury he'd suffered? But those questions could wait.

"Hadley, you're getting my new shirt wet." Dallas drew back a little, his eyes moist, too. "I'm here now," he said, holding Hadley's gaze.

"We're really okay? You and me?"

"We are. Why not? Those bad years are behind us, and I'm grateful you thought— finally, after twenty-two years—to look at my website. Good sleuthing on your part. By the way, the Maguire name is from my adoptive parents. The first home the state sent me to after you and I parted was theirs. Great people, like your Clara." He paused. "What do you say? Can I stay a while?"

"As long as you want." He'd never imagined that he couldn't find Dallas because his brother had taken a new last name. Or that Dallas couldn't find him because Hadley moved so much. And all this time his brother had been just fine. He'd never been hurt again but, in-stead, loved. It was Hadley who'd suffered. His defiance, even temper, had gotten him through those years, protected him, but not completely. Now they were together again. He couldn't seem to take it in, a Christmas miracle to go with the twins walking for the first time. And the fact that, for once, Hadley had stayed on the McMann ranch instead of heading out in a snowstorm for yet another temporary place.

There was still an empty space inside him that belonged to Jenna, but today was for Dallas. "I understand you're a big deal rodeo star, and that you knew Cody Jones—"

Dallas scowled. "That weasel? He owes me five hundred bucks I'll never see."

Hadley filled him in on Cody's current whereabouts and why, but he couldn't bring himself to despise Cody when he'd been the key to finding Dallas. It was too bad the kid was headed for prison, even when he deserved punishment. In a way, Hadley and Cody were alike. In another, they weren't. Cody was an outlaw; whatever else Hadley might be, he was not. Still, they were two bad boys who needed redemption.

"Cody's not all bad," he told Dallas. "After he does his time, I hope to offer him another chance here. The ranch is doing well, and we can always use a good hand." Hadley turned toward the living room where Luke and Gracie were building up to some demand, which they always did in unison. "Let's see what the trouble is in there," he said, taking Dallas's arm so he didn't need to rely on the cane. "I'm warning you, those two are like having a dozen kids."

"Twins," Dallas murmured. "Huh."

Just as Hadley's twins were inseparable, he and Dallas would be close again, too. After all, they were brothers.

LATER THAT AFTERNOON, Jenna took her seat on one of the white-with-gilt chairs in the new bed-and-breakfast near Farrier. Thankfully, as with the bridal shower, she wouldn't have to take part in the ceremony that would join her mother and Jack Hancock in holy matrimony. Jack, waiting at the altar, dressed in a dark suit and paisley tie, was an attractive man, if slighter in build than Hadley, who seemed to have become her standard of measurement. She had to believe Jack loved her mom, but Wanda's warning kept playing in her mind. *If you can't support me, then don't come to my wedding.*

To the strains of a classical piece played by the pianist Jenna and Shadow had hired, their mother stepped from the hallway into the room. There was only one word to describe her: glowing. Jenna blinked back sudden tears.

She had so many memories of Mama in their old house, scurrying to answer Jenna's father's commands, always eager to please yet never getting even a thank-you for her efforts—a reminder for Jenna of David, too. Her mother hadn't deserved so much pain, but then neither had Jenna.

The wedding was relatively small—family and friends. She exchanged a look with Shadow, who sat beside Grey holding baby Zach with Ava between them. On Jenna's other side, their brother Derek fidgeted with his program. And there was Jack's uncle, smiling at Jenna, who had begun to decorate his new assisted-living apartment. She'd taken a shine to Bertie.

After weighing her options, Jenna had come alone. What if she'd asked Hadley to escort her, as he had to dinner at Bernice Caldwell's house? But that wasn't to be, and Jenna tried not to sink into a fresh spiral of despair for what she'd done regarding Walter Pearson right after Hadley nixed her hopes for their relationship. *I'm not the guy you should pick.*

In front of the officiate, Wanda and Jack

said their simple vows while Jenna prayed at last for her mother's happiness. When the short service ended with the exchange of rings and a kiss, she did shed a few tears. She sat alone today when years ago, and far more recently, she'd envisioned a better life with a man she loved, the children she'd always yearned for. Was this what *she* wanted for the rest of her life?

The filet mignon dinner she had helped to plan seemed to last forever. While the champagne toasts went on and on, she couldn't get her mind off Hadley or the twins. Today was their second Christmas, although they'd been only a month old for their first and not aware of what the holiday entailed. Or had Hadley already left? She imagined the three of them driving down some road, the twins fussing in their car seats until Hadley found a decent motel with a restaurant. Christmas dinner in some strange town rather than the close-knit community of Barren. She pictured Clara wandering around her empty house, certain she'd never see the three of them again. Jenna should stop by to check how she was doing. Could Hadley still be there?

As people rose from the tables, Jenna decided to make her excuses, then edge toward the inn's door. She wasn't in the proper frame of mind for a party, especially on Christmas, and in spite of her friends and family, she felt excluded. Tonight, even holding Zach and chatting with Ava hadn't helped assuage her loneliness.

"Jenna?" Her mother followed her into the hall. In her pretty white dress studded with crystals, her hair done in a knot at the nape of her neck, and with the new wedding ring flanking her engagement diamond, she looked beautiful. But more, she seemed at peace within herself. "You aren't leaving yet?"

A rush of remorse weakened her resolve. "Mama, I can't stay, but I hope you'll have the most wonderful honeymoon. I'm sorry for how I've acted. I didn't support you and Jack, and I was wrong."

Earlier, he had taken Jenna aside. He'd assured her she needn't worry about him with her mother. "We're all family now," he'd said. "Your mom and I, you and Bertie, too. You're always welcome in our home, *chérie*."

Wanda's dark eyes softened. "Oh, baby, I understand. I'm glad you came. It's hard, isn't it, to witness someone else's joy when you're hurting inside?"

Jenna thought for a moment. "You're right, Mama. I am hurting. Months ago, after Amy died, I realized that seeing Luke and Grace was a joy but also a sorrow. Maybe I focused too much on the latter."

Wanda took Jenna's hands in hers, the whisper of her silk and satin dress between them. "Honey, I wish your daddy and I had given you a better life growing up. You didn't get the example you needed for a good relationship as an adult. But Shadow told me you've finally dropped David like a hot rock—that's a start. Now you'll have the chance to make that better life with someone else."

"Hadley," Jenna murmured. "But we said things, Mama. I lost him. He may be halfway to Montana by now or anywhere else." Looking for another ranch that needed a good hand for a while.

Wanda gently pushed her away. "You can't be sure of that. Go," she said. "I only want what's best for you, but you're the only one who knows what that is. Just as I do with Jack. I love you, Jenna."

"I love you, too, Mama." Jenna hugged her,

wished her mother all the joy she so richly deserved, said the same to Jack, who had come up to them and couldn't seem to stop smiling. Then Jenna made her goodbyes to everyone else and, with Wanda's blessing, walked out of the inn into the heavy snowfall.

As she picked her way in heels to her car, she thought of Clara's cozy living room, the Christmas lights, the ornaments Jenna and Hadley had hung on the tree. The trunk of her car was stuffed with presents for him and Clara, for Luke and Grace, which she'd bought weeks ago. She might reach the McMann ranch only to learn Hadley and the babies were indeed gone, that he'd left after all without repaying the loan. Running from the Pearsons. But what if he *was* there, at Clara's house, still sharing Christmas? For the twins, at least, he might have stayed.

If she followed her mother's advice, as she had listened to Shadow and Annabelle, would she invite more heartache? Yet as she'd told Hadley, Jenna was not the girl who'd fled her parents' unhappy home only to fly into the wrong man's arms—the arms of a man who'd never really loved her. She wasn't the broken woman who'd returned to Barren to be near her family. But then, Hadley wasn't the same wounded kid he'd once been, or the supposed bad boy he thought he'd become. How wrong he was about that.

If he *was* at the ranch, what could she say to him? Jenna would have to trust him, risk losing again, as she had with David. Getting hurt once more, as her father had hurt her with his neglect, his anger. Yet if she didn't try, if she couldn't convince Hadley to stay, to take that chance on her, on them, this time she'd be losing Luke and Grace, too.

And Jenna remembered what Jack had said earlier. There were different ways to be a family, she realized. Just as Hadley had once told her there could be different ways to have a child. And, of course, she recalled Annabelle's wise words.

*You don't have to give birth to be a mother.*

In her car Jenna called the ranch, but Clara didn't answer. Instead, she talked briefly to a man whose voice she didn't recognize. Hadley was putting the kids to bed, he said. She should call later, or he could have Hadley call her.

Jenna didn't choose either option. He *was* still there.

She hung up, slipped the car into gear and drove away into the blinding snow.

HADLEY CAME DOWNSTAIRS after putting the twins to bed. Their nightly ritual had given him comfort tonight, tucking them in, watching them settle in their cribs and giving kisses. He was grateful to be warm and dry, not risking the twins' safety on the road somewhere as Dallas had risked his last night to get here.

Better to hunker down while the snow kept falling, be here tomorrow morning to clear the driveway and see to the livestock. The horses would need oats and a bran mash as extra fuel to help combat the cold. Without him here, Clara might have been forced eventually to sell the ranch after all. Any other decision would have been the wrong one. His home, she'd said.

At the dining room table, Clara and Dallas were trying to fit pieces into an elaborate jigsaw puzzle. The picture on the box showed a wintry scene from somewhere up north like Montreal with blurred lights along a snowy street flanked by shops. Hadley didn't join them. A part of him wanted to be alone.

He glanced at Clara, surprised to see a worried expression in her eyes. She said, "Your Christmas wasn't everything it could be, was it?" No, even with his brother here, the miracle he'd prayed for. He needed another, too, which didn't seem likely. All day he'd kept thinking of Jenna and how much he'd missed her today.

"I wish Jenna could have come," Clara went on, noting the stack of toys under the tree as if some were absent. "Or at least drop by for a minute to see Luke and Grace."

"I guess that would have been awkward—after the guardianship thing. Pearson," he added. "Besides, today was her mother's wedding."

"Of course. Does Jenna know you're staying?"

"Not yet." Hadley shook his head. "I haven't talked to her."

She paused. "I'm sure she'd like to meet Dallas. And—forgive me if I speak plainly—Jenna is not Amy. That marriage didn't work for you, which doesn't mean you and Jenna wouldn't. I can see you're miserable—and on such a beautiful night. We've had a white Christmas. Why spend it alone?"

"I'm not. You and Dallas are here. The

twins." He drew Clara up from the table and into his arms. Dallas watched them. "Stop poking at me like there's a cattle prod in your hand. I'll talk to her, okay? I already planned to, but she's probably still at her mother's wedding reception. I wouldn't want to intrude." In case she didn't care to hear whatever he had to say.

Clara sent him a look that practically shouted *coward*.

Did he really want to spend his life without Jenna? Again, no, not if she'd consider giving him another shot. He couldn't spend another Christmas day without her sitting on the rug with the twins, helping them open presents, showering them with the gifts she always brought, filling Hadley up inside with the warmth she exuded. Sometimes he craved the feel of her soft mouth under his, her slighter weight in his arms until he ached. Was he the wrong man for Jenna? Why was that his choice to make? She had a mind of her own. If she was willing to put up with him, why not? He'd never expected to make this decision, but there it was. Tomorrow he would try.

But first, there was that something he needed to tell Clara. "If I'm like a son to you, I'd better start living up to that." Then he all but whispered, "Because you're my mother, the best mother I could have, Clara, and I... I love you."

There, that wasn't so hard to say, especially when he meant the words with all his heart. Hadley had just released her, Clara crying happy tears, when he heard the hush of tires on the snowy drive outside. A second later, through the frosted window, he made out the shape of Jenna's car. Was she here, as Clara had said, for the babies? Or for him, too? He was about to find out.

As soon as Jenna reached the top step to the porch, her high heels slipping and sliding in the snow, Hadley opened the front door. "A Christmas wedding would never be my choice," he said.

She stopped just inside the house, drinking him in because she'd feared she might never see him again. The sheen of his dark hair, the look she couldn't decipher in those electric-blue eyes, the breadth of his shoulders. Was he still here only because of the bad weather?

"The wedding was lovely," she said. "But this snow may never end. I thought more than once of turning around, driving back into town, but I have gifts for the twins," she announced, still uncertain of her welcome with Hadley. Luke and Grace were more familiar territory.

"They're asleep—I hope." He drew her into the living room, where Clara greeted her with a Christmas kiss, then introduced a shocked Jenna to Hadley's brother. The two of them quickly went back to their jigsaw puzzle before Jenna could ask how Hadley had found Dallas. She sent Hadley a searching look he didn't respond to.

Instead, he said, "There are things I have to say. In private." He steered her toward the stairs to the second floor, leaving Clara to gaze after them with what appeared to be a satisfied expression. Dallas raised his eyebrows as Hadley and Jenna began to climb the steps. Hadley led her to the nursery but stopped outside, his voice low. "Let's start with Cody, aka Cory." At her puzzled look, he said, "Strange subject, but this is about me, too. When I hired him, I didn't let myself see what he really was. Remember, Grey didn't press charges against Cody's two accomplices—including your brother—for cattle rustling. But then, Derek didn't set Grey's barn on fire. That was all

Cody. Hoping to avoid the law, he ran—sound familiar where *I'm* concerned?—and it was as dangerous for him to come back as it was for me to stay anywhere years ago. That became the pattern of my life, as you pointed out, in which everything has been temporary. Until now." His tone was tentative, as if he were asking her some question.

"You're comparing yourself to a felon?"

"In the way we approached things, I guess I am. I haven't led my life the way I should have. I did try to love Amy the way she wanted me to, but I always had one foot out the door. Sure, we fought too much and of course her folks were always between us, telling Amy I wasn't good enough for her, that I was a loser." He shrugged. "That shouldn't have bothered me. I'd heard the same message from a lot of foster people."

Jenna touched his arm. She couldn't let him believe he was still that bad boy when he wasn't. "You aren't like Cody Jones."

"No," he agreed, "but maybe Cody's not as bad as people believe, either. I'm going to speak to Finn about him. I want to help him turn his life in the right direction."

"Just as you have," Jenna said. "Maybe you

felt you had to run away from those foster homes, but you never left your brother."

"I guess he'd agree with you." As if he couldn't contain himself any longer, Hadley told her about Dallas's homecoming and how his brother had been adopted, not left in some other terrible situation. "Maybe I did him a favor by stealing that food for him. Jenna," he said, then reached for her hand. "While I was packing the truck yesterday, Clara told me if I left here I should never come back. Quite the wake-up call, and I remembered that first time she and Cliff took me in, how they saw the best in me. They didn't just give me a warm bed and the best food I'd ever eaten. Or simply teach me the skills that have supported me as a cowboy. They gave me unconditional love, and what did I do? I left them."

"You came back, though."

"Sure. Years later, after I'd already hurt them. Cliff was gone, and Clara was alone here on a broken-down ranch. I wish I'd come sooner, thanked him before he passed on, but you know what? Yesterday I realized that if I left Clara now, I wouldn't be running from a bad place this time but from a good one." He glanced away. "Maybe all these years I was the one who couldn't let myself belong. I was afraid I'd finally found some place to fit in but was too scared that, having found that, it couldn't last." In the dark hallway he held her gaze. "That place—*my* place—is here. It includes you," he said.

Jenna felt a flash of what could only be hope laced with doubt. "What are you saying, Hadley?" Her voice hitched. "You told me you aren't looking for someone."

"I thought I wasn't, but I'll try really hard to be what you need, Jenna. If I can find the courage to stay, can you trust that I won't leave?"

"I trust you," she said without hesitation. She had to.

Still holding her hand, he eased open the door to the nursery. They went into the room lit only by a night-light and stood between the two cribs, listening to the soft sound of the twins' breathing. "Clara teases me when I check on them every night to make sure they're okay and watch them sleep."

And this man had thought he was a bad person? "That's sweet, Hadley."

She imagined his face coloring. "Jenna, I know they're not your own babies, but does that really matter?" He attempted a smile. "Luke and Gracie are a whole family in themselves." They'd kept their voices low, but the twins stirred. Luke snuffled into his blanket, and Grace rolled from her tummy onto her back, one arm flung above her head. Their rose-gold hair shone in the low light.

"No, it doesn't matter in the least." Jenna squeezed Hadley's hand. She'd once thought she'd put David behind her yet she really hadn't until that day on the phone, and she'd never confronted her own infertility. Until now. "I love them as much as I could ever love my own."

He took a breath. "Good. Because I want much more than a start-up relationship here. This isn't the most romantic spot, and it's probably too soon for me to say this, but I want to marry you."

Her fingers were still laced with his, and Jenna thought *I'm ready now to be happy.* And this nursery was the perfect place to ask his question. Was he serious?

"I don't propose to a woman very often," he said, lifting their joined hands to kiss her knuckles. "But I'm as sure about this—us—

as I've ever been about anything." He looked deeply into her eyes. "I love you, Jenna."

"But you always say you can't lov—"

"I think I have for quite a while." He held Jenna's gaze for a long moment. "For years, I believed I didn't need, or maybe deserve, a good woman, kids. That I couldn't love anybody. Of course the twins changed that, and I never would have married Amy if I didn't love her at all. I think it's possible I've always had a deep-seated wish for a home, a family, that I just refused to recognize."

And her heart melted as the snow would months from now during spring thaw. From downstairs she heard Clara and Dallas talking, laughing a little. In the hallway a floorboard creaked. And at last, remembering what her mother had said, Jenna knew she could put her father's neglect behind her, too. Like him, Hadley also had a temper, but he never unleashed it without warning or reason. In spite of any flaws he had, he would be her protector, her safe place in the world. For her, for Luke and Grace. And Jenna would be his. "You're the best man I've ever met. I love you, too, Hadley."

He smiled in the dark. "Is that you saying yes? We can wait to tie the knot if you want, but—" He broke off. "I don't want to wait very long."

His fingers were warm in hers, and she realized how much she wanted to keep holding his hand for the rest of her life. Although she didn't want to let go for a second, Jenna wrapped her arms around his neck. Standing by the cribs, she drew Hadley's head down to hers, then kissed him. By the time he raised it to look at her, she knew the tenderness in his eyes must be in hers, too, the love. "My answer is yes," she murmured, unafraid. "We'll fight Walter Pearson for the twins. We'll win."

"I bet we would have." He added with a grin, "Won't be necessary, though. Danielle phoned this morning to ask about the twins' Christmas extravaganza. She's convinced Walter to forget the suit. I don't think she's speaking to him."

"He won't try for custody?"

"Nope, and I said they're welcome to see the twins whenever they want, stay however long they like, but the terms will be min—ours." Hadley pulled her closer to the cribs, pointing out Luke's favorite position, up on his knees with his little bottom in the air. In

TWINS UNDER THE TREE

the corner of his bed the orange-haired doll
Grace had gotten for Christmas crowded a
bunch of stuffed animals. Grace had turned
over again and had one arm around Luke's
yellow truck. Outside the windows, the snow
continued to fall in soundless big white
flakes, and Jenna hoped that by morning
they'd all be shut in. She'd be fine here until
New Year's. Or even better, forever.

Hadley followed her gaze. His incredible
blue eyes twinkled. "White Christmas, Clara
said. The best kind, and there'll be more."

"Tomorrow morning," Jenna murmured.
"I have all those gifts in the car."

"You always do," he said. "And by the
way—" Hadley drew something from his
back pocket "—part of your Christmas
present." He handed her a check. "This is
the money to repay the loan you gave me.
With hefty interest," he went on. "I insist, because the twins should get every penny and
then some for their education. We'll need to
set up that trust." Then he turned her, putting her back to his chest. He hadn't left—
he never would, she knew—and of course he
hadn't defaulted on the loan. Jenna tipped her
head against his shoulder for another kiss and

thought, *this is what happiness feels like*. She had everything she needed, and so would he. She gazed down at Luke and Grace.

The twins weren't just his now. They were hers, too.

Wrapped in each other's arms, she and Hadley watched their babies sleep.

\* \* \* \* \*

# Get 4 FREE REWARDS!

### We'll send you 2 FREE Books plus 2 FREE Mystery Gifts.

**Love Inspired®** books feature contemporary inspirational romances with Christian characters facing the challenges of life and love.

**FREE** Value Over **$20**

---

**YES!** Please send me 2 FREE Love Inspired® Romance novels and my 2 FREE mystery gifts (gifts are worth about $10 retail). After receiving them, if I don't wish to receive any more books, I can return the shipping statement marked "cancel." If I don't cancel, I will receive 6 brand-new novels every month and be billed just $5.24 for the regular-print edition or $5.99 each for the larger-print edition in the U.S., or $5.74 each for the regular-print edition or $6.24 each for the larger-print edition in Canada. That's a savings of at least 13% off the cover price. It's quite a bargain! Shipping and handling is just 50¢ per book in the U.S. and $1.25 per book in Canada.* I understand that accepting the 2 free books and gifts places me under no obligation to buy anything. I can always return a shipment and cancel at any time. The free books and gifts are mine to keep no matter what I decide.

Choose one:  ☐ **Love Inspired® Romance Regular-Print** (105/305 IDN GNWC)    ☐ **Love Inspired® Romance Larger-Print** (122/322 IDN GNWC)

Name (please print)

Address                                                                          Apt. #

City                                        State/Province                        Zip/Postal Code

> ### Mail to the Reader Service:
> **IN U.S.A.:** P.O. Box 1341, Buffalo, NY 14240-8531
> **IN CANADA:** P.O. Box 603, Fort Erie, Ontario L2A 5X3

**Want to try 2 free books from another series? Call 1-800-873-8635 or visit www.ReaderService.com.**